"Dr. Georgia Thackery is smart, ..., and determined to be a great single mom to her teenager. Georgia is normal in every respect—except that her best friend happens to be a skeleton named Sid. You'll love the adventures of this unexpected mystery-solving duo."

—Charlaine Harris, #1 *New York Times* bestselling author

"Adjunct English professor Georgia Thackery makes a charming debut in *A Skeleton in the Family*. Georgia is fiercely loyal to her best friend, Sid, an actual skeleton who is somehow still 'alive.' When Sid sees someone he remembers from his past life—who later turns up dead—Georgia finds herself trying to put together the pieces of Sid's past as she works to hunt down a killer. Amateur sleuth Georgia, and her sidekick, Sid, are just plain fun!"

—Sofie Kelly, *New York Times* bestselling author of *Faux Paw*

"No bones about it, Leigh Perry hooked me right from the beginning. An unusual premise, quirky characters and smart, dry humor season this well-told mystery that kept me guessing until the very end. It's too bad Perry's sleuth is fictional—I'd invite Georgia over for dinner in a heartbeat."

—Bailey Cates,
New York Times bestselling author of *Magic and Macaroons*
on *A Skeleton in the Family*

"A delightful cozy with a skeleton who will tickle your funny bone."

—Paige Shelton,
New York Times bestselling author of
If Onions Could Spring Leeks on *A Skeleton in the Family*

"An effortlessly narrated, meticulously crafted cozy mystery."

—*The Big Thrill* on *A Skeleton in the Family*

"I had a grand time reading this fresh, original novel peopled (and skeletoned) with enchanting characters and a warm, engaging story. The undercurrent of the gift of love and loyalty between friends and family members gives this book a burnished glow of strength and peace. I totally loved every page and want to visit with Georgia and Sid again and again."

—*Criminal Element* on *A Skeleton in the Family*

"This newest in the Family Skeleton Mystery series is absolutely terrific. Yet again, Perry has come up with a fantastic concept that has never been done . . . Such a fun read . . . and because Perry has, yet again, come up with a barrel of surprises it's a good bet that there will be more tales of Sid and family in the not too distant future."

—*Suspense Magazine* on *The Skeleton Takes a Bow*

"The book [is] very funny, and Sid is a great character. Not to slight the humans. Georgia, Madison, and Deb are fun, too, but it's Sid who steals the show. If you like a good cozy, this is one to look for."

—*Bill Crider's Pop Culture Magazine*
on *The Skeleton Takes a Bow*

"This fun cozy paranormal mystery provides a unique look at the investigative process when one of the sleuths has been distilled down to bare bones—literally . . . The characters are fun and the wacky situations escalate nicely to the exciting climax."

—*Night Owl Suspense* on *The Skeleton Haunts a House*

"Leigh Perry does a marvelous job utilizing the humorous aspects to full effect as there are more than a few laugh-out-loud moments. However, the sense of family togetherness is what truly makes *The Skeleton Haunts a House* perfect . . . each and every aspect of *The Skeleton Haunts a House* is a true delight."

—*Fresh Fiction*

THE
SKELETON
MAKES A
FRIEND

LEIGH PERRY

DIVERSION
BOOKS

FAMILY SKELETON MYSTERIES
A Skeleton in the Family
The Skeleton Takes a Bow
The Skeleton Haunts a House
The Skeleton Paints a Picture

Diversion Books
A Division of Diversion Publishing Corp.
443 Park Avenue South, Suite 1004
New York, New York 10016
www.DiversionBooks.com

For more information, email info@diversionbooks.com

First Diversion Books edition November 2018.
Paperback ISBN: 978-1-63576-444-4
eBook ISBN: 978-1-63576-443-7

LSIDB/1811

To my amazing trio of sisters-in-law:

D'Arcy Kelner Klappenbach

Kathleen Ward Kelner

Tamsin Kelner Euart

CHAPTER ONE

I sat in the sun on a wrought iron bench on the town green on a lovely summer afternoon that was perfect for relaxing. Unfortunately, I was waiting, not relaxing. I wanted Dobson, the college administration building across the street, to be as empty as possible before I went inside, but I couldn't delay too long because if everybody left, the building would be locked. I checked my watch for the umpteenth time and saw another text from my best friend Sid nagging me to get on with it. Okay, time to make the attempt.

I whispered, "I'm going in," and then sauntered over to the building and up the granite steps. At least I meant it to be a saunter—it might have been more of a scurry.

I pushed the door open, looked around, then stepped into the quiet building. I'd hoped to get past the main office unseen, but I heard a friendly voice from the open door to the left.

"Hi, Georgia. Hope you don't need anything that requires signatures. Everybody but us has gone home for the day." Mo Heedles, whose formal title I didn't know but which should have been something like "She Who Knows Where All the Bodies Are Buried," was leaning against the reception desk with a cup of coffee in one hand. Two other admin people I knew just enough to nod to were examining the contents of a Dunkin' Donuts box.

"Nope, just wanted to use the ladies room, if that's okay."

"Knock yourself out. Just be warned, it's a little smelly in that part of the building. I don't know if somebody made a mess in the men's room or if somebody left some food in their trashcan before going on vacation, but maintenance hasn't cleared it out yet."

"We called them Monday morning," one of the other admins said. "All they did was go into the men's room and say it's not in there."

"They are kind of overwhelmed these days, so we can wait," Mo said. "As long as I don't have to clean up the mess."

"Don't be so sure," the other admin said darkly. "If those lay-offs really happen—"

"Enough with the doom and gloom. It's summer and we have donut holes—one of which better be a jelly-filled. Life is good!"

"Enjoy." I started to head down the hall.

"Oh, Georgia?," Mo said.

I froze.

"Stop by when you're done—you can have a donut."

"Thanks, but no, thanks. I'm heading in the other direction, and I'll let myself out the back door."

"Your loss." Mo took a bite. "So what's with the suitcase?"

I'd been hoping she wouldn't notice, but like all good admin people, she had an eye for details. To be fair, it was pretty notice-able—a hard-sided rolling bag with a wavy striped pattern that the sale tag had identified as antelope, but which always reminded me of bacon. "It's to carry my skeleton."

The other two women goggled, but Mo just nodded. "Of course it is. Have a good one."

"You, too." And this time I did make my escape.

I'd been in Dobson a few times before, so I knew the way. There were half a dozen glass-fronted doors along the tiled hallway. All were closed and dark, which was fine with me. Gorgeous summer evenings were made for skipping out early, especially on college campuses, and it meant I didn't encounter anybody else. On the bad side, it meant that my footsteps echoed, and combined with a couple of burned-out light bulbs overhead, it was a little creepy.

The hall ended at a flight of stairs, with corridors to the right and left. I went to the ladies' room, the first door on the left. The light was off, which I figured was a good indication that nobody was inside, but I checked each stall to be sure. Then, just in case Mo or either of her friends came to use the facilities, I pushed the metal trashcan in front of the bathroom door so it would clatter if anybody opened it. Then I went into the stall at the very back and unzipped the suitcase.

I hadn't been lying. I really did have a skeleton in there.

What I hadn't told Mo was that it was a living skeleton. Or at least a walking, talking one. The living part is a philosophical question my family and I had been debating ever since an ambulatory skeleton named Sid first showed up at our door over twenty years before and moved into our attic. Whatever else Sid is, he's my best friend, and on this outing, he was my partner in crime.

Sid assembled himself quickly and silently in an uncanny process that makes no sense, then looked around. "Why are we in the bathroom?"

"I just wanted to make sure we're on the same page."

"Georgia!" He gave me an aggravated look, which isn't easy with a bare skull. "I know the drill. I go in, I look around the office for obvious clues, and if there's a computer, I root for information. But I don't spend any more time than I have to. You stay in the hall and keep watch. Twenty minutes tops."

"Fifteen."

"Seriously?"

"I don't know when they lock up or when the janitors come by, and I don't have a good excuse for being in that part of the building."

"Fifteen," he agreed. "Now let's get moving!"

He collapsed back into the suitcase, with only his hand staying together to zip it closed, and after flushing the toilet for paranoia's sake and returning the trashcan to where it belonged, I rolled Sid back out into the hall.

There was still nobody in sight, and I didn't hear any footsteps, so I opened yet another glass-fronted door as quietly as I could, closed it just as quietly behind me, and started lugging the suitcase with its cargo of twenty pounds of bone up the stairs. There was an elevator in an out-of-the way corner of the building, but I knew it rattled as much as Sid did when he was irritated, and I didn't want to attract attention.

Mo had been right about the smell, which got worse the further up the stairs I went. I wondered if one of the power outages that had been plaguing the campus all summer had blown out the fuse on an office refrigerator. The stench I was trying to avoid inhaling was awfully rank for a single spoiled lunch.

There was another unlocked door at the head of the stairs and then doors to the right and the left that led to suites of offices. Neither showed signs of life, which was what I'd expected to be the case. According to what I'd gleaned via the campus grapevine, everybody in both the financial aid office and Human Resources was either on vacation, on maternity leave, or working remotely, leaving the floor deserted. I didn't blame the maintenance crew for not wasting their time cleaning when nobody was around, but the smell was definitely coming from up there. Unfortunately, it was worse closer to the Human Resources office, which was our target.

"Can you smell that?" I whispered. Of course, it made no sense that Sid could smell, since he had neither nose nor nerve endings, but he insisted that he could, in fact, smell, so who was I to argue?

"Not from in here." He unzipped the suitcase partway and stuck his nasal cavity close to the resulting gap. "That's nasty. What do you think? Rotten fruit?"

"More like rotten eggs. Are you going to be able to stand it?" I could hold my nose, but Sid didn't have that option.

"Sure. I just won't breathe while I'm in here."

"You're a better man than I am, Gunga Din." Of course, breathing wasn't optional for me the way it was for Sid.

"Is the department door locked?"

I was reaching for the knob to check when Sid said, "No touching!"

"Right, sorry." Now that we were reasonably sure we were alone, Sid would do the honors—he didn't have fingerprints to worry about.

Sid unzipped the rest of the way, pulled himself out of the suitcase and back together, and tried to turn the knob. "It's locked."

"Can you open it?"

"Easy peasy," he said, pulling a set of lock picks from inside the suitcase. My locksmith sister Deborah probably hadn't realized that teaching my daughter Madison how to pick locks was tantamount to teaching Sid. Madison had shared everything she'd learned with him, and he'd promptly ordered his own picks online. "You really should learn to do this, Georgia. It's not that hard."

Despite his assurance, it seemed to take an awful long time to get the door open. Or maybe it just seemed like a long time because I kept looking down the stairs, worried that somebody would hear us and come to see what was going on.

Finally there was a loud click, and Sid said, "Nailed it!" He opened the door, and cold air streamed out.

"Brr!" I said. "Wouldn't you know that a department with everybody on vacation would be the one with overachieving air conditioners?" The window unit in my classroom had gone out twice. "Not to mention the waste of electricity."

"You can complain about it later," Sid said. "Come on."

I followed him into the Human Resources department, pulling the empty suitcase along.

There were four more closed doors: three offices labeled with names and one marked *File Room*.

"Here we go," Sid said, using his picks on one of the office doors. This lock was easier to deal with, which was a relief, but unfortunately, the smell seemed to be coming from that office. "I'm going in."

"Remember what I said. Get in, look around fast, get out."

"Got it." He stepped inside.

Between the cold, the horrid stink, and the fear of being caught, I was hoping that Sid would be swift, but I was surprised when he came out in under two minutes. "That was fast. Did you find something?"

"Don't go in there."

"I wasn't going to—"

Then I looked at him.

He shouldn't have been able to look like anything but bone-colored, but somehow he seemed paler than usual, and his bones were so loose he was nearly falling apart. "What's wrong?"

"He's in there. At least I think it's him."

"Did he see you?" I said stupidly.

He slowly shook his skull, and only then did I realize what it was we'd been smelling.

CHAPTER TWO

FIVE DAYS EARLIER

The cabin I was renting that summer was far from ideal. It was out in the middle of nowhere and could only be reached via a poorly paved track through the woods, which made for a long commute to my current job. Once you arrived, it was to find cramped bedrooms, a kitchen the owner had furnished at a time when turquoise blue appliances had been the fashion, and a noisy generator. Still, the advantages outweighed the disadvantages. The living room was plenty roomy, we each had our own private cramped bedroom, and thanks to a business school with an executive retreat center nearby, the internet access was solid. Best of all, it was next to a small lake that was mostly surrounded by undeveloped forest. There were three other cabins with access to the water, but they were only inhabited on weekends, meaning that from midday Monday to late Friday afternoon, the lake was our private swimming hole.

That Wednesday evening in July, there was a lot of splashing going on as Madison, Sid, and I played in the water. We'd intended to keep at it until the mosquitos came out but were interrupted by Madison's Akita, Byron, who started barking as he ran toward the front of the cabin.

"Dive!" I said to Sid.

"Diving!" He instantly sank down into the water, where he would stay until we gave him the signal that it was safe to come out.

Like the cabin, a skeletal roommate has advantages and disadvantages. On the plus side, since he doesn't breathe, there's no limit to how long he can stay on the bottom of the lake; his meatless physique doesn't appeal to any fish that might swim by looking for a snack; and without skin, he doesn't have to worry about getting pruney. On the minus side, there's that whole don't-let-anybody-see-him thing.

Once we realized it might be possible for Sid to go swimming for the first time in his life, or what passed for a life, we'd had to plan for the occasional unexpected visitor. Hence Sid's immediate retreat into the depths.

A moment later, Byron escorted a girl I didn't recognize from around the front of the cabin. She was wearing a royal blue polo shirt tucked into her khaki shorts, her sneakers were as white as if she'd just bought them on her way to the cabin, her medium-brown hair was tightly braided down her back, and her bangs looked as if they could give straight-line lessons to a ruler. I guessed she was sixteen or seventeen years old, close to Madison's age.

A moment later, a woman followed them into the yard, hurrying a bit to catch up. She had curly hair the same shade as the girl's and was wearing blue jeans that might as well have had MOM embroidered on the back pocket.

I looked at Madison to see if she knew either of the intruders, but she shook her head.

"Hello?" I said. "Can I help you?"

The girl said, "Nobody answered the door, but I saw the dog so I came out here."

"I'm sorry," the woman added. "She kind of got away from me."

I waited a moment for more of an explanation, but when none came, I repeated, "Can I help you?"

"I'm looking for somebody," the younger one said. She glanced at Madison, then back at me. "Are either of you Skalle Beinagrind?"

"No, I don't think I know anybody named . . ." I wasn't about to try repeating what she'd said. "I don't know anybody with that name. You must have the wrong house."

"It's a Scandinavian name. I checked online, but I could be pronouncing it incorrectly."

"Well, I'm Georgia Thackery, and this is my daughter Madison, so we're not even close. The dog is Byron."

"Skalle isn't an IRL name."

"She means 'in real life,'" the woman I assumed was her mother explained. "Jen is talking about the name her friend uses while playing an online game."

"What game?" Madison asked.

"Runes of Legend," Jen said.

"I've heard of it, but I've never played. It's an MMORPG, right?" In case I hadn't caught all the letters, Madison added, "That's a Massively Multiplayer Online Role-Playing Game."

I knew the term, though I was more of a Candy Crush kind of gal. "Are you sure you have the right address?"

"I don't have an address, but I do have a picture." She reached into a blue canvas messenger bag slung on her shoulder and retrieved a photo. "That's the view from where I'm standing." Then she looked at the picture again, and stepped three steps to the left. "Precisely from where I'm standing." She handed it to me.

I looked at the picture, and as far as I could tell, it really had been taken from that spot, but I hadn't taken it. "Madison?"

My daughter took a peek. "It's not mine. I sent a couple of selfies to Samantha and Liam, but I took them from closer to the dock."

I gave the girl back her picture. "I'm sorry, but we didn't take this, and we don't know anybody by that name. We're just renting the place for the summer, so maybe it was taken by the owner or a previous tenant."

She squinted across the lake. "The trees are almost exactly the same height in the picture as they are now, and the leaves are the same color. It couldn't possibly be that exact a match over multiple seasons, could it? Is anybody else living here?"

"Jen!" her mother said in an exasperated tone. "The lady already said your friend Scaley or Scully or whatever-his-name-is isn't here."

"It's Skalle," Jen said, "not Skully."

I tried not to show it, but thanks to Jen's mother's mispronunciation, I had a strong hunch that I knew who Skalle Beinagrind was in real life. Well, in real existence. "I'm afraid . . . Jen, is it?"

"I'm sorry," the woman said. "This is my daughter Jen Cater-Brame, and I'm Judy Cater."

"Pleased to meet you both," I said, "but I'm afraid I don't know what to tell you. Madison and I are the only people living in the cabin this summer." Sid was not, by the strictest definition, alive.

"Have you had any guests?"

"Jen!" her mother said again, but I thought the best way to get rid of them was to answer her questions.

I said, "No one who plays Runes of Legend." My parents had come up for a couple of weekends, and my sister had been up once, but none of them were gamers.

"This doesn't make sense," Jen said. "This is definitely the lake in the picture, and Skalle Beinagrind definitely resides in this region."

I probably shouldn't have, since I wasn't supposed to have any idea who Skalle Beinagrind was, but I had to ask, "Is there some particular reason you need to find him?"

"I need his help."

"His help with what?"

"With a case. You see, in real life, Skalle is a detective."

That's when I decided that as soon as I got Sid out of the lake, I was going to push him right back in.

CHAPTER THREE

"A detective?" I said, trying my darnedest to sound curious instead of furious.

"That's what he says, anyway," Judy said, "but it's like I told Jen, anybody can say anything online."

Jen shot her mother a look, then stared at the lake for another moment before saying, "I'm sorry to have interrupted you. We'll leave now." Then she turned around and did just that, with Byron following her out of sight.

"It was nice to meet you two, despite the circumstances," Judy said. "Maybe we'll run into each other again. Are you on vacation all summer?"

"Actually, we're not on vacation. Well, Madison is, but I've been teaching at Overfeld College's high school enrichment program."

"Oh," Judy said stiffly. "Well." She seemed to be resisting the urge to say something, and apparently her efforts were successful because she smiled a tight little smile before turning back toward the road. A minute later, I heard a car start up and drive off, and Byron returned.

"That was strange," Madison said.

"More than a little." Usually when strange things happened around me, one particular person was involved, and I was pretty sure that was true in this instance, too. "Can you tell Sid he can come back up?"

When we moved into the cabin, we found a bright yellow fishing pole that guests were invited to use. Neither Madison nor I fished, but it was perfect for letting Sid know that the coast was clear. Madison stood on the dock and stuck it into the water near where Sid had gone down, and a few seconds later, his skull surfaced, followed by the rest of his bones.

"About time!" he said. "Who was it?"

"Some kid," Madison said. "Jen something."

"Jen Cater-Brame," I said, watching Sid's face.

"Never heard of her. What did she want?"

"She was looking for Skalle Beinagrind," I said.

Apparently my pronunciation was close enough because Sid froze, his eye sockets widening in an impossible way which gave him away immediately. "Oh coccyx!" he said and sunk back into the water.

"What was that about?" Madison asked.

"Have you got your phone handy?"

"Of course." She pulled it from her pocket.

"Google up the translations of *skalle* and *beinagrind*."

"How am I supposed to spell those?" she grumbled but took a stab at it. "Okay, *skalle* translates as conk, cranium, crumpet . . . skull." She looked at me. "Oh."

"What about *beinagrind*?"

"Um . . . Skeleton." She looked at where Sid still hadn't reappeared. "Does that mean—?"

"Given the way Sid is hiding under the water, I'm going to say it probably does."

We waited a full fifteen minutes before he finally rose up again.

"Ah, you're still there," he said.

I nodded.

"I can explain."

"I look forward to hearing that."

"Maybe we should go inside first."

Since it was getting dark and the mosquitos were starting to come out, I said, "Let's do that."

Madison and I gathered up our books and leftover snacks, Sid toweled himself dry, and we went into the cabin. I took a seat on the beat-up green vinyl couch, but after one look at my face, Madison said, "I think I need some alone time in my room." She exited swiftly, calling for Byron to follow.

"So . . . Where do I start?" Sid said. It was easy to see how nervous he was—his bones were hanging more loosely than usual. As far as I have been able to figure out, Sid only stays together by sheer force of will. Anxiety makes his will weaker, and the connections between his bones mirror that.

I said, "Maybe with how that girl knew where to find you."

"I swear, Georgia, I don't know. What did she say?"

"That she was looking for Skalle Beinagrind."

"Then she must be somebody from Runes of Legend. That's the only place I use that name. Did she tell you her in-game name?"

"It didn't occur to me to ask since I couldn't very well admit I that I know who Skalle is."

"Right. She's got to be a member of my party. You remember? I told you I play with a regular group."

"Okay, I did know that." I hadn't known which game he was playing, but that wasn't the issue. "But you didn't tell me you were giving out our address."

"I didn't! I never tell anybody online where I live! I mean, clearly I told them more than I should have, but I never thought anybody would be able to track me down."

"What exactly did you tell them?"

"I said that I live in New England, and of course they'd know I'd been in roughly this part of New Hampshire at some point."

"How would they know that?"

"Because of the server."

"What server? You didn't play at a restaurant, did you?" Sid gave me a look, and I knew that only the fact that he didn't have eyes was keeping him from rolling them at me. "Okay, not that kind of server. What are you talking about?"

"A network server," he said. "When you create an account on Runes of Legend, you're automatically assigned to a network server—that's where your profile and game information are stored. Runes of Legend has servers for every region, and since there are a lot of players in New England, there are several New England servers. So Jen would know that I'd registered in this region, but that covers a lot of ground!"

"Why are you registered in this region?" Even though I was working in Overfeld, New Hampshire, for the summer, our home base was in Pennycross, Massachusetts, and I'd spent most of the last winter and spring teaching in Falstone, Mass. Such was the life of an adjunct professor—no tenure meant no job security, and as a result, I moved around a lot.

"Because I first heard about Runes of Legend that day we came up here for you to interview for the job at Overfeld, and I created my account that night when you were asleep." Since Sid doesn't sleep, he has plenty of time for online gaming.

"But you never mentioned the town of Overfeld to your party?"

"I might have, but only in passing, and I know I mentioned other towns, too. I definitely never said what town I live in, let alone gave an address. How did she find me?"

"She said you sent her a photo of our lake."

"Our lake? I mean, yeah, I posted a picture I took a couple of weeks ago, but I was careful. Hang on! I'll show you." He scooted into his bedroom and brought out his laptop, flipped through applications with enviable speed, opened up a file, and enlarged it on his screen so I could see that it was the photo Jen had shown me. "This section of the game site is like a mini-Pinterest, where you can post pictures of things you like or are a fan of." Sid's, or rather Skalle's, pinboard included logos from *The Nightmare Before Christmas*, *The Book of Life*, and *Coco*; screenshots of anime characters; and the photo of the lake. "Look. No street signs showing, and no houses or other buildings in view. No boats for her to spot a name. No people. Not even the dog! I posted it because it's probably the best picture I've ever taken, but it could have been any lake in this part of the country."

"It is pretty generic, now that I'm not comparing it to the real thing."

"Exactly! Would you have recognized that picture if you'd seen it online?"

"It might have looked familiar," I said, "but I can't honestly say I would have identified it as our lake."

"I made up a game name and everything. *Skalle* is Swedish for *skull*, and *Beinagrind* is Icelandic for *skeleton*. Nobody would ever get my real name out of that. And even if they did, it wouldn't matter. *Sid Thackery* doesn't show up on any census, phone listings, utility bills, car titles, nothing. And sure, I do use a picture of a skeleton as my character's sigil, but it's not an actual picture of me."

"Sid, would it have made a difference if you had used an actual picture of yourself?"

He paused for a moment. "Okay, probably not. But I just want you to know how careful I am, which is extremely careful. I never thought anybody would link Skalle to us, and I don't know why she came looking for me."

"That's the best part," I said. "She said she needs a detective."

"Oh my spine and femur," he said, putting his skull into his hands.

"Did you really tell her you're a detective?"

"No! Well, maybe. I never said that precise word, but . . . Look, Runes of Legend has these quests that parties have to complete. Some of them are battles, some are puzzles, and some are mysteries. After a while, I started taking the lead on the mystery quests, because Erik Bloodaxe—he's kind of our chief—Erik Bloodaxe realized that I'm good at them."

"You should be, with all your experience." Sid and I had solved several real-life mysteries, a fact that still baffled me.

He looked pleased for a moment before continuing. "Anyway, after each quest, we end up back in the Questing Dragon. That's the virtual tavern where we get experience points and prizes.

There's also a chat function for roleplay. And in that chat room, in the guise of Skalle, I may have said I'd solved other, well, other things."

"You called them cases, didn't you?"

"Well what would you have called them?"

"I don't know. Misadventures? Fiascos?"

"Hey, don't run yourself down. You're a good detective, too, even if you won't use that word either."

"Thank you," I said, though I wasn't convinced. "You didn't give details about our . . . Okay, about our cases, did you?"

"Of course not. It would be too easy for somebody to check out those stories on the web, and that would lead back to you. And honestly, I didn't think anybody actually believed I'd solved a real case—I mean, everybody lies on the internet."

"That's what Jen's mother said."

"Her mother came with her? How old is Jen? What did she look like?"

I did my best to describe them both.

"Jen must play Odina, who's our skald. Odina is really smart and remembers all kinds of details from previous quests. I got a feeling she was young, and her character's backstory includes a domineering mother."

"I couldn't tell if Ms. Cater was domineering or not."

"That doesn't matter. Most teenagers think they have domineering parents, at least some of the time."

"Fair." I'd probably believed that myself at various points in my life, though if Madison had had similar thoughts, I didn't want to know about it.

"I wish I could have seen her," Sid said wistfully, then put a hand on his chin and drummed his phalanges. "Now I'm worried about Odina. About Jen, I mean. Did she tell you why she wants a detective?"

"No, and I didn't think I could get away with asking questions about a person I'd supposedly never heard of."

"Yeah, I guess not. I can't ask her in-game, either. If I even hinted at knowing she was looking for me, she'd know that you know more than you said you know. You know?"

I was trying to parse that line of thought when Sid said, "Georgia, do you want me to quit the game?"

"Sid, we've had this discussion. I'm not your boss or your mother." Though Sid had lived with my family since I was six, we were still negotiating exactly how our relationship should work, but we'd definitely decided that I was not in charge of him. "Whether or not you keep playing is up to you."

"It is?"

"It is. And if I were giving orders, I'd say that even though I was thrown for a loop by Jen showing up, there's been no harm done."

"I guess not."

"So are you going to keep playing?"

"I'm not sure. I think I'll sleep on it, metaphorically speaking. We're kind of on hiatus right now anyway, so I wasn't planning to play tonight."

"Okay then."

Madison stuck her head out of her room and said, "Are you guys still fighting?"

Sid looked at me hopefully. "Are we?"

I said, "No, we're good. Sid, you did a solid job covering your tracks. Jen being able to find you was just a fluke." An unsettling fluke, but no more than that.

"Good." Madison came all the way into the living room. "Can we eat now?"

CHAPTER FOUR

By the time dinner, cleanup, and two episodes of *Midnight, Texas* on DVD were over, I was ready for bed while Madison and Sid—neither of whom had to work the next day—put a movie in the DVD player and pulled out their electronics for gaming. Though we'd been in Overfeld for several weeks, they were still reveling in the privacy of the cabin.

At home in Pennycross, there was a seemingly never-ending parade of my parents' pet graduate students, who they counseled and fed at all hours and sometimes housed as well. That meant Sid was often stuck in his attic room, and since the grad students typically camped out in the living room, Madison had to be quiet so as not to disturb them. I was enjoying the isolation myself, though as I pointed out to them, we were only getting such a good deal on the cabin because it belonged to one of my mother's former pets, who was spending the summer traveling through Europe with his family.

The only lingering effect of Jen Cater-Brame's visit was some extra caution on my behalf. Though I didn't really think she'd come sneaking around the cabin at night, when I checked to see that the doors were locked, I also made sure that the curtains were drawn tightly so that nobody could get a peek at us, especially not at our bony companion.

I honestly didn't know what would happen if an outsider ever learned of Sid's existence, but over the years, I'd imagined any number of nightmare scenarios involving government agents aiming to weaponize Sid, scientists experimenting to create an army of super-skeletons, religious zealots who'd try to destroy him, or even Hollywood types trying to lure him into the special effects industry and/or a talk show. What I couldn't imagine was an outcome that ended well for any of us.

"Don't worry, Mom," Madison said, realizing what I was up to. "Byron will let us know if Jen what's-her-face comes back. Right, Sid?"

Sid sniffed—purely for effect, of course. He wasn't overly fond of the dog because their first encounter had left teeth marks on his femur, and Madison was always trying to parlay peace between them. "Sleep well," he said. "And don't worry about Jen. Next time we play, I'll keep an eye socket on her and let you know if she acts differently."

I was hoping that was the end of a disquieting incident. I should have known better.

When I got up the next morning, Madison was still asleep, as befit a teenager on summer vacation. I'd expected Sid to be ensconced in his room reading or on his computer, but instead he was at the kitchen table and had my breakfast of cereal and juice waiting.

"Good morning!" he said brightly.

"Good morning. I wasn't expecting this."

"Just wanted to save you a little time so we can get to Overfeld as soon as possible."

"We?" Then I remembered. It was the day I'd promised to take Sid to work with me.

"Did you forget? Or do you think it's too risky after what happened yesterday?" His joints loosened visibly with pending disappointment, but he added, "I'll understand if you've changed your mind."

"Yes, I forgot, but no, I have not changed my mind."

"You're sure?"

"Absolutely."

He popped back together.

"The way I figure it, either Jen believed us yesterday or she didn't, but even if she were to show up on campus and barge into my class, she wouldn't suspect you were Skalle, right? Though the next time you come up with an in-game name, you might want to pick something that's not quite so on the nose. Or nasal cavity, in your case."

"I'll keep that in mind. Now eat your breakfast!"

What I didn't tell Sid was that if Jen was suspicious of us, I'd rather he be at school where I could keep an eye on him. As for Madison, she was right. Byron would alert her if Jen came around again. After I finished eating and wrote a quick note to let Madison know that Sid was with me, Sid folded himself into his bacon-patterned suitcase.

Our concession to the unlikely possibility that Jen was in a tree keeping us under surveillance or had a drone flying overhead to take photos was that we kept the suitcase closed in the car. Normally either Sid or I unzip it during drives so we can talk. This time, we decided to stick with the paranoid approach.

One of the other disadvantages of the cabin was the long commute to work. Though we were living in the town of Overfeld, it was on the very edge of the town line. Once I made it down the gravel track to the closest actual road, I still had a forty-minute drive to Overfeld center, where Overfeld College presided genially over the town green. The college and the town had been founded at the same time, which meant there wasn't the usual division between on campus and off. Shops, restaurants, academic buildings, and dormitories were all mingled together. The large central park—with its footpaths, classical Greek-styled gazebo, and lively colony of jet-black squirrels—was shared by town and gown, though neither contingent was much in evidence at that time of the morning.

Since the college didn't offer undergraduate classes in the summer, the faculty parking lot was nearly empty. Most of the regular faculty members were off on vacation or doing fieldwork, and the few that were left were working on research and papers and such—which meant they didn't have to be there as early as I did.

The cars in the lot likely belonged to the other staff involved with the session I'd been hired for: an enrichment program for high school students whose parents were eager to embellish their off-spring's future college applications. Not that I blamed them. If I'd been able to afford it, I would have tried to talk Madison into signing up for the program. She'd just finished her sophomore year, which meant it was past time to start planning for college. Unfortunately, the program cost more than what I was making for teaching.

Not that I was complaining. I was earning as much as I usually got for a summer semester, with a considerably lighter teaching load. As a bonus, since the idea was to introduce students to college life, or at least college lite, the curriculum was all exploratory classes with discussions and workshops and so on, but no actual tests or grades. In other words, I didn't have to spend a good chunk of my week reading and scoring student papers.

Combining that with the deal I was getting on the cabin, it meant that Madison and I were having the closest we'd had to a summer vacation in years. Getting to bring Sid along had made it just about perfect.

When I got into Kumin Hall, I saw that most of the sleepy-looking scholars were still in the cafeteria, ravaging the breakfast buffet. I waited behind a couple of students to get a cup of coffee, then made my way over to the auditorium across the hall where we'd all be assembling in a few minutes for morning announcements.

The back two rows were filled with the program's instructors, who were looking perhaps even more sleepy than the students.

"Good morning, Georgia," said my friend Charles Peyton. As was his custom, he was dressed in a smartly tailored suit, despite the relaxed dress code for the program. The chinos and short-sleeved top I was wearing were about the average for attire—Matt, the music teacher, was in a T-shirt and wrinkled plaid Bermuda shorts. I wasn't sure if Charles preferred the almost archaic styles because of his work as a historian, or if he'd become a historian because he liked the style.

"Good morning all," I said, taking an empty seat and stashing Sid's suitcase safely out of the aisle. "How are the Andorians today?"

The program's marketing materials referred to gifted and/or talented scholars, so a young *Star Trek* fan had immediately dubbed them Andorians from one of the species in that universe. By the end of the first week, everybody was using the name.

"Ready to soak up knowledge and wisdom," Charles said. He was one of the dorm monitors who slept over with the students, both to chaperone them and to take care of any emergencies that took place overnight. I'd been asked if I wanted to do the same when I was hired, but while the extra pay would have come in handy, the idea of being trapped with dozens of high school students just hadn't appealed to me. Charles, on the other hand, seemed to be having a terrific time. Then again, I'd known Charles for years, and I'd rarely seen him when he wasn't enjoying himself.

So I may have sounded skeptical when I said, "Really?"

Treva Youngblood, one of the other dorm monitors, cackled. "They're all as ill as hornets, is what they are." Though she had a thick Southern accent when speaking English, I'd been told it completely disappeared when she spoke French or Spanish. She was teaching both languages for the summer.

"Perhaps a touch disgruntled," Charles allowed. "There was a problem with the electricity in the dorm yesterday evening, and we were without power for several hours. Dinner preparations were ruined, but that could be solved with an emergency pizza delivery. The students' inability to charge their electronics was more vexing. Their texting and use of social media was seriously curtailed."

"I'm sure they loved that. Did maintenance get the power working?"

"Eventually," Matt said. "The problem was, most of the Andorians had gone to bed by that point, and when the power came on, so did the lights. Which woke most of them up again."

Paul, the art teacher, said, "Don't expect them to be their best and brightest today."

"As if they were ever that bright." Zach taught math, which was the least popular subject offered, and he took the lack of enthusiasm personally.

"At least they got the power fixed," I said.

"For now, anyway," Matt said. "The electrician wasn't sure what went wrong, and he said not to be surprised if it happens again."

Charles looked solemn. "I'm afraid Overfeld is showing its age."

Looking at the worn-out upholstery and battered paneling in the auditorium, and knowing what the classrooms looked like, I had to agree. "Maybe administration is waiting until after this session is over to spruce things up."

There were shrugs, but not much interest. All of us were adjuncts who'd been hired for the summer program, and since Overfeld almost never used adjuncts during the regular term, we'd all be gone in a few weeks. The only full-time employees involved in the program were Heath Ridley, the program's officious director; Mo Heedles, the administrative secretary who managed things by working around him; and Neil Farmer from HR, who'd actually hired us all, but who stuck to his office most of the time. President Valentin Fernandez wasn't around every day, but he was taking a personal interest, and I saw he was up on the stage with Ridley and Mo.

We chatted about the week ahead as Andorians started trickling into the auditorium. Up on the stage, President Fernandez and Ridley were fiddling with the microphone, apparently with no success. Mo gave it a couple of solid whacks, too, but the only result was some sharp barks of static.

Finally Ridley said loudly, "I'm afraid we're having some problems with the sound system, so I'll just have to use some of the projection techniques Ms. Quinn in the drama department has been teaching you guys." There was polite laughter, and a loud snicker from Treva. Mo handed Ridley a piece of paper, and he read out the usual kinds of things: the music classes were hosting a jam session that evening, badminton nets and supplies would put up in the quad that afternoon for anybody interested, the art class would be having a demonstration later in the week, and the movie that night would be *Loving Vincent.*

At first I'd been surprised by the variety of entertainment options that were provided as part of the program, but it had been explained to me that the kids were there more for enrichment than for education. Besides which, they were enough younger than college students that their parents expected a fair amount of supervision. The more entertained they were, the less supervising was required.

Those announcements were par for the course, but then President Fernandez took the microphone, which was less common. He was a trim, distinguished-looking man whose hair was still jet black but, like Overfeld itself, was starting to show his age. I'd never seen him in anything more casual than a suit, though his style was more contemporary than Charles's.

"Good morning, scholars," he said. "I wanted to apologize for the problems with the power in the dorm last night. I'm assured that it's been repaired for the moment, and we will be bringing in electricians to make sure everything is in tiptop shape for the evening."

Normally I wouldn't have expected a college president to make that kind of apology, but it was the first time Overfeld had offered the program, and I'd heard talk that Fernandez had pushed the board to give it a try, so he was particularly anxious that it should succeed.

Ridley took over long enough to remind everybody they were due in class in fifteen minutes, which was the cue for us instructors to head upstairs to the classrooms. Charles insisted on carrying Sid's suitcase up the steps for me, which wasn't necessary, but which was appreciated.

I'd been really enjoying the Writing Workshops I was teaching. Adjuncts typically get hired to teach introductory classes, while the tenured and permanent faculty members have more opportunities to teach within their specialties. That meant I'd taught basic composition so many times I could do it in my sleep, so any change was a pleasure. Plus I had a particular fondness for the workshop format.

True, I had to balance the kids who were writing about the torment of being a privileged suburbanite when what they craved was the freedom to be a privileged New York City dweller against the kids who only wrote TV-show-based mash-ups like *Doctor Who* versus *The Walking Dead*, but as long as the students were willing to take and give feedback politely, I was happy to give them free rein on subject matter. Some days I provided writing prompts of one kind or another, but they weren't required to use them, and I didn't object if a prompt inspired a piece of *Werewolf Hunter* fan fiction.

None of the students were in my classroom yet, which gave me time to get Sid set up in a chair at the front of the room. Actually he set himself up, but I stayed close by to create the illusion that I was doing something.

Once he was comfortable, he said, "Showtime!," gave me a quick wink despite having neither eyes nor eyelids, and with a smile on his skull, stiffened up. He loved having a chance to see new people, even if he couldn't actually interact with them. So for the next few hours, he would be playing the role of a non-living skeleton in order to act as a visual writing prompt for both of my workshop sessions.

I'd pulled that trick a few months earlier at my previous job when I needed to explain why I had a skeleton with me on campus, but even though it had been a spur of the moment improvisation, it had worked out remarkably well. Moreover, my boss had loved it, and when she gave a recommendation to President Fernandez at Overfeld, she'd mentioned it to him. He'd specifically asked me to do it there, too.

Sid had been looking forward to his star turn all summer and had practiced not moving or speaking for long periods of time. The not-moving was tough, and the not-speaking was even harder, but he pinky swore he was up to the challenge.

With him situated, I went to get myself settled for class and found a handwritten note on my desk:

Hope you don't mind—thought I'd stop by to observe today.

It was signed with a casual yet elegant *DH*.

Unfortunately, I had no idea who *DH* might be. I ran through the names of the administrative people I'd dealt with at Overfeld and was making my way through the other adjuncts working the program when students started to arrive, but no *DH* came to mind. I'd just about decided the note had been left by accident or was meant for somebody else.

Then, just before nine, Professor Davidson Hynes strolled in.

The Professor Davidson Hynes.

CHAPTER FIVE

Professor Davidson Hynes's classic papers on cross-disciplinary and experiential learning were still required reading for anybody who took Instructional Design. I'd never met him in person, of course, but I'd seen him in videos, and there were pictures of him in any number of journals I'd read. And while I'd known he was still at Overfeld—he was the school's unqualified star and had helped solidify Overfeld's reputation—I'd assumed he was taking the summer off along with the rest of the faculty to do research or hobnob with other world-renowned scholars on the coast of France. Okay, probably not the coast of France, but maybe at the Bodleian Library at Oxford or the Trinity College Library in Dublin, or at least the Widener at Harvard.

What I did not expect was for him to come into my classroom wearing a rumpled pair of khakis, a long-sleeved gray T-shirt, a black vest, and scuffed sneakers.

He flashed me a quick smile, then walked toward the back of the room to take a seat in the last row.

I mentally cussed at myself for not realizing who *DH* was. And I imagined real mental cuss words, too, not just the bone names I used because of long exposure to Sid. Speaking of Sid, I couldn't decide if it was a good thing that I had him along or not. On the one hand, using a skeleton to inspire creative writing could be considered both cross-disciplinary and experiential, but on the other, I had a skeleton with a puckish sense of humor in my classroom.

As the last Andorian filed in, I smiled in what I hoped was a cross-disciplinary, experiential manner and started to say, "People, today we have a special—" But before I could finish, Professor Hynes shook his head and put a finger to his lips. Obviously he didn't want me to introduce him. Since class members were already looking at him curiously, it seemed an odd choice. Maybe he was worried that his presence would intimidate the Andorians, but I doubted that even gifted and/or talented high school students would know who Professor Hynes was. Then again, he was the expert. The world-renowned, much admired expert, and if I kept thinking that way, I was going to freeze solid and stand there for an hour and a half without moving, just like Sid.

I took another breath and gave that smile again, "People, today we have a special writing prompt. This is my friend, Sid." I put my hand on Sid's skull and continued with my spiel. It had sounded like a great introduction the last time I'd used it, but today it just sounded awkward. I ended it with, "I invite you to use Sid as a jumping-off point for a new project. It can be a short story, a chapter in a novel, an essay, a poem, even a song lyric. Whatever you like. We'll spend the first half of class writing. Then after the break, we'll form a circle for feedback. You can join in if you want to share your work, or you can keep writing. Any questions?"

There were, of course. The Andorians were high achievers, some because of real interest and some because of a determination to do everything perfectly in order to get into the right college, so there were always questions. But soon they were pulling open their laptops and tablets to get to work. Meanwhile, Professor Hynes had pulled out a Moleskine notebook and an actual fountain pen.

I was doing my best to forget about Hynes's presence, but it wasn't easy, and not just because of the scratchy noise his fountain pen made. Though I'd been observed in my classroom any number of times, both before and after earning my PhD, the observers generally weren't people whose names were cited in hundreds—maybe thousands—of academic papers.

Sid still hadn't moved, thank goodness, but somehow I knew he was frequently looking in my direction. Since he could read me as well as I could him, he had to know I was as nervous as—Well, as nervous as a lowly adjunct whose teaching was being observed by a world authority on pedagogy. Usually I kept busy while my students worked on their projects, but this time, I was afraid to even try to type anything because the only words that were going to come out were *All work and no play makes Jack a dull boy.* Instead, I pretended I was reading a journal article on the screen of my laptop.

After over an hour of torture, I announced, "Okay, why don't we take a few minutes to get a snack or stretch our legs? Be back here in fifteen."

I was hoping I'd be able to speak to Professor Hynes during the break, but a couple of students stayed behind to chat and several others pulled out their phones to do whatever it is they'd been dying to do during class. Obviously, conversation with Sid was impossible, and when I looked questioningly over at the eminent professor, he shook his head with a smile. So I took the opportunity to go to the bathroom to check my hair and wonder if I should have dressed better that morning or gone the other way to be as casual as Hynes was.

As I'd expected with a fifteen-minute break, it was twenty minutes before all the students were back in the classroom. Most of them wanted to keep working, but about a third were ready to workshop their material, so we circled up desks for a discussion. Professor Hynes scooted his desk up, too, but instead of joining the group, he placed himself behind me. It was possibly the most aggravating thing he could have done, and I could tell Sid was glaring at the man on my behalf, even if nobody else realized it. On the good side, eventually I forgot he was there and could focus on my students. In fact, I got so involved that one of them had to remind me that it was time to end the class.

Professor Hynes made his exit while the Andorians and I were putting the desks back into their original configuration, but as the classroom emptied, I found another note from him, this one shoved into Sid's mouth. I tamped down my irritation—of course the professor had assumed Sid was inanimate—and opened it.

Interesting techniques. Have to observe another class, but let's
talk over coffee in my office today at 5.

DH

"Do I look like a bulletin board?" Sid whispered without moving his jaw.

I looked around in alarm, but we were alone. I closed the door, just in case. There were windows, so Sid still couldn't move, but he was an accomplished ventriloquist. It's not like he had lips he needed to hold still while he talked.

"What does he want?" Sid asked.

"He wants to talk over coffee at five."

"Didn't you promise to have Madison at Wizard Gary's at five for the Yu-Gi-Oh! tournament?"

"Coccyx, you're right. I'll have to drop her off early and then come back here."

"Or you could tell him you're busy."

"Are you kidding? It's Davidson Hynes! When will I get another chance to talk with somebody like Davidson Hynes?"

"What's so great about Davidson Hynes?"

I launched into an explanation of why it was such a valuable opportunity.

"Fine, fine," Sid finally said. "He's famous and all that. I still think it was rude to show up in your classroom with no warning and to then set a time to meet without consulting you."

"Yeah, a little. I'd probably be annoyed if it were anybody else."

"Are you sure he isn't going to try any funny business? Meeting a young woman alone, after hours?"

"Sid, he's Davidson Hynes!"

"And I'm Designated Backup. I'm coming with you."

There wasn't time to argue. I only had an hour to get lunch in the cafeteria before my second class of Andorians arrived, and as soon as that was over, I had to get back home, fix an early dinner for Madison, make sure Byron was taken care of, drive Madison to Wizard Gary's Game Store, and then get back to campus and try to find Professor Hynes's office. With all that to juggle, it just seemed easier to bring Sid along, or at least part of him. I did leave most of his bones back in the cabin but carried his skull, one of his hands, and his cell phone in his new tote bag.

My mother, who has a fondness for crafting, had taken an old bowling ball bag and painted brightly decorated sugar skulls on both the back and front. Then she cut out the eye holes and hot-glued in thick panels of netting that Sid could see out of without letting anybody see him. Smaller panels on the sides and the bottom gave him a first-rate view of the world, and his hearing was sharp enough that he could hear what was going on, too. The hand was so he could text me an excuse for leaving the meeting or even call 911 should things go badly. Not that I really expected anything—as far as I knew, there'd been no ominous rumors about Professor Hynes—but it never hurts to have backup.

It took a while to locate Professor Hynes's office, since he hadn't thought to tell me where it was. I should have realized it would be in Stevenson Hall, the oldest and most carefully maintained building at Overfeld, where President Fernandez and other campus luminaries had their work spaces. When I got there, it turned out that Sid's concern for my safety had been unfounded. Charles arrived at the office just ahead of me.

"Georgia," he said. "I take it you, too, were honored with a visit from Professor Hynes."

"He showed up out of the blue at my nine o'clock class. Did you get any warning he was coming?"

"Not a peep. I consulted Mr. Ridley, and he tells me that Dr. Hynes prefers to make impromptu visits." He lowered his voice. "He also assured me that—"

Before he could finish, the door to the office opened, and Professor Hynes said, "Wow, you guys are right on time. Come on in. Sorry we didn't get a chance to do official introductions before, but I was running late." He held out a hand to me. "Davidson Hynes. Call me Dave—everybody does."

"A pleasure to meet you," I said.

"It's Georgia, right?" He offered a hand to Charles. "And Charlie?"

"Charles."

"Oh, okay. Charles." He waved us toward a low, dark blue couch and took the armchair opposite.

"Let me get you guys some coffee." There was a carafe on the table in front of us, and he poured into the three cups waiting. "You're in for a treat. This is kopi luwak."

The name meant nothing to me, but it did taste very good.

"Jamaican Blue Mountain peaberry is my everyday java," Professor Hynes said, "but everybody deserves a splurge. You only live once, right?"

"Absolutely," I said, nodding vigorously, even though I didn't know what Jamaican Blue Mountain peaberry was, either.

"I hope you like it black," he said with an apologetic chuckle. "I'm really into the flavor of the beans, myself."

"Actually, I prefer sugar, though if you don't have any, I can manage," Charles said. His tone was entirely polite, but there was an edge in it I wasn't used to hearing from him. Besides, I'd seen him drink black coffee plenty of times.

"Sure, no problem. To each his own, right?"

While Hynes rummaged around in a cabinet, I took a look around, and from the gentle movement inside his bag, I suspected Sid was doing the same.

The eminent scholars I'd encountered in the past tended to adopt a certain look for their offices: lots of leather-upholstered furniture, heavy wood desks, and wall-to-wall bookcases over-flowing with works in their field. And of course, there was usually a batch of framed diplomas and certificates, along with whatever awards they'd won.

Apparently Professor Hynes had a different interior designer. His furnishings were made of teak, with simple lines, and he only had one bookcase, though it was well-filled. The pictures on the wall were photographs of himself and others in exotic locations all over the world. At least they looked exotic to me, since I rarely made it out of New England.

All of the room's furnishings were considerably more plush than what I'd seen in the classrooms and the faculty lounge, and unless I missed my guess, the walls had recently been repainted. In addition to the sleek modern furniture, he had one older-looking piece, a carved wooden chest by the door.

He must have caught me looking at it because he said, "The coffee chest is a beaut, isn't it? Antique, of course. One of my students sent it to me from India—she knows how much I love my beans—but of course I keep my blends in airtight containers."

He waved at the row of stainless steel canisters inside the cabinet.

"Of course," I said.

"And here's the sugar." Naturally he served sugar cubes, nothing so common as paper packets or even a sugar bowl.

Once Charles had his coffee well sweetened, Hynes took another satisfied sip from his own cup, then said, "So, I had a great time watching you two work today, and I thought you might be interested in my take on your styles."

"Wouldn't it be more appropriate to share your observations one-on-one?" Charles said.

"Oh, hey, no, this isn't a formal performance review or anything like that. We're all academics here, right? I've just been at this a while, you know, and I've picked up a few tricks."

"I'm always happy to talk shop," I said.

"Talking shop. That's all this is," Hynes said with a grin, but he pulled out his notebook from his shirt pocket. Most people didn't refer to notes when they talked shop.

"Georgia first. You know I really dug the way you adapted my ideas."

"Your ideas?"

"The physical writing prompt? It was a Native American sculpture I used, not a skeleton, but it's close enough to get some decent results."

"I wasn't familiar with your doing that, actually."

"Really? It's described in my last book." He wrinkled his brow and looked toward the bookcase, and I realized an entire shelf was filled with copies of his own work. "No, it was the one before that. Anyway, a physical prompt is super for experiential learning, but have you considered making it more tactile? Letting people handle the skeleton? Bone has this feel, you know. It is an authentic skeleton, isn't it?"

"Oh Sid's real, all right. I thought about letting people handle him, but the fact is, a human skeleton in that condition is worth several thousand dollars. That makes me a little leery of risking damage." In fact, Sid was pretty insistent that I not let many people handle him. He was understandably protective of his bones—it's not like he could grow a new one if one broke or went missing.

Hynes wrinkled his brow again. "Okay, then, I guess I see your point, though I think you're missing a bet. Anyway . . ."

He consulted his notebook again and went on to say mostly nice things about the way I ran the discussion among my students. It's just that every compliment was followed by a question and several suggestions. It was cute that I called the skeleton Sid, but didn't I think that personifying him was off-putting? Yes, it was great that I gave my students so much freedom, but didn't I think more structure would be worthwhile? And of course the program was for enrichment, and we weren't required to grade, but wouldn't it help the students if I gave them an estimate of what their grades would be if they were in an actual college course? Sure, he loved seeing the students give feedback to one another, but had I tried keeping a tighter control on that, because as the instructor, of course my feedback was the most meaningful. Though he listened to my reasons for doing things the way I did, he wrinkled his brow a lot.

Hynes's last comment was, "I noticed that during that little feedback circle of yours, the students interrupted one another a couple of times."

"They get excited," I said with a shrug.

"I know how you can fix that. You've heard of a talking stick, right? It's a way to keep a discussion fair—only the person with the talking stick can talk."

"I've heard of it, but I don't think—"

"Here's an even better idea. Maybe you don't want anybody holding the whole skeleton, but you could use one of the bones as a talking stick. Like the femur or something. No, better yet, the skull."

"A talking skull," I said. "That would be different." Sid nudged my leg gently. "But again, that skeleton is a valuable item, and the skull is particularly vulnerable."

The wrinkled brow returned.

"I could get a plastic skull and use that."

"I suppose," Hynes said, his brow still dissatisfied. "It wouldn't have the same heft, would it? They wouldn't get to feel the weight and the texture of an actual human skull. The real thing would provide a more experiential encounter."

"Maybe you didn't notice, but I had two students who re-fused to even look at Sid—I don't think they'd want to hold a piece of him."

"You have to encourage your students to try new things, Georgia." Before I could rebut that, he said, "Just think about it. Overall, you're doing okay. Now, Charles."

It felt incredibly awkward sitting there while Professor Hynes critiqued Charles's lecture, both because he thought lectures were too old-school and because he thought Charles's use of language and attire were too formal.

Charles, to his credit, listened politely and, unlike me, didn't try to argue a single point. When Hynes concluded with, "You see where I'm coming from, don't you, Charles? Be experiential, be cross-disciplinary. It's the right way to go."

"I will certainly take it under advisement," my friend replied.

"Hey, that's all I'm asking." He looked up at the clock on the wall. "Wow, this has been great—comparing notes and all—but I've got dinner plans, and I've got to run. Let's do this again before the summer's over, okay?" He ushered us out, locked the door behind us, and strode away, leaving Charles and me standing in the hall.

Once I was sure Hynes was gone, I said, "Okay, that wasn't what I was expecting."

"You mean you weren't expecting faux informal camaraderie or feedback that consists of recitations of decades-old catchphrases?"

I blinked. "Wow. How do you really feel?"

"Do you disagree? Do you also find my teaching style too stiff and formal?"

"Are you kidding? Your students hang on your every word because you really bring history to life. You're a great teacher!"

"Thank you. For my part, I don't in any way agree with his assessment of your skills. You are far more innovative than he is. The man has clearly been living off his reputation for years. And that image he projects. Pfui!"

"He was pretty snotty about your clothes."

"I don't care if he dislikes my choices—taste varies. What I mind is his pretense of being casual when in fact he's a sartorial hypocrite. Those rumpled khaki pants? J.Crew. The T-shirt? Hugo Boss. And though I never shop there, I'm fairly certain his vest came from Armani. Even his 'kicks' were Balenciaga—I'd wager a guess that they cost upwards of eight hundred dollars."

"Seriously?"

"Georgia, you know how I dress. Do you think it's accidental? I know men's clothing. I admit Hynes might have found some of those garments on sale, at a thrift store, or even on eBay, but to wear so many designer items that are designed to look like he just threw them on?" He scoffed. "Trust me, that's a carefully assembled ensemble. I wouldn't be surprised if he purposely wrinkled those pants before putting them on. And that coffee!"

"I thought it tasted good."

"It should, at five hundred dollars per pound."

"How much?"

"At least that, and you don't want to know how it's produced."

I felt vibrations from my bag, and I suspected that in another minute, Sid would know exactly how kopi luwak was produced.

"The only good thing about this colossal waste of time—" Charles stopped. "Pardon me, Georgia, time spent with you is never wasted."

"Thank you."

"I only wish it had not been tainted with our having to listen to that man drone. Fortunately, as I was starting to tell you earlier, the other good thing is that Mr. Ridley assures me that Hynes has no influence on hiring, no matter what he might think. His *feedback* can be safely ignored, and that is precisely what I intend to do."

CHAPTER SIX

Charles had to head back to the Andorians' dorm for dinner duty, but between Professor Hynes picking such an awkward time and my not wanting to drive all the way back to the cabin just to turn around and come right back again, I was at my leisure to enjoy the pleasures of the town of Overfeld. It didn't take long. The only places open were restaurants, bars, the grocery store, and the bookstore. I'd already eaten, didn't want to drink, and was stocked up on groceries. I was stocked up on books, too, but Sid and I still managed to spend an hour browsing in the bookstore. It was particularly fun for him, since he usually had to shop online or via a proxy. Since he was still in the bag with the peepholes, I had to keep my phone in hand to receive his texts about which shelves and books he wanted a closer look at, which got a little tiring, but I figured I owed him a treat after he'd been such a terrific writing prompt. No matter what Professor Hynes said.

When we left there, I planted myself on a bench opposite Wizard Gary's. It was a lovely evening, not humid and just warm enough. Sid and I even managed to hold a conversation. I put my phone up to my ear to make it look as if I was talking on it, and he kept his voice low enough that nobody else would be able to hear him.

"Do you want to fuss about Professor Hynes?" he asked.

"No, I think I covered it pretty well with Charles. I do feel like an idiot for not realizing sooner what a phony he is."

"You were starstruck. It happens."

"I guess. I'm just glad Charles was there to give me a reality check."

"He's a good friend. I wish . . ."

"What?"

"I wish I could get to know him myself."

"You could try to make friends with him online. He's pretty active on a couple of adjunct Facebook groups."

"Yeah, but to do that, I'd have to pretend I was an adjunct, which would mean making up some sort of backstory and lying my butt off. Which, come to think of it, I already have. I mean, I am totally butt free!"

I laughed politely, but then said, "You're still upset about your friend coming to find you, aren't you?"

"Yes and no. Yes, I'm upset, but no, Jen isn't really my friend. Or rather, I'm not hers. How can I be her friend if I lie to her all the time?"

"Do you really lie to her? Or do you just not tell her the whole truth?"

"What's the difference? I read somewhere that the best way to lie is to only tell part of the truth."

"That's not wrong, but in my experience, nobody tells their friends the whole truth."

"Really?"

"Look at Charles. I love the guy—he's smart, and kind, and generous, and just wonderful. And he's a good teacher, too—I wasn't lying when I told him that. But I think he's nuts for living the way he does."

"You mean the squatting?"

"Exactly." In all the years we'd been friends, Charles had never had a real home. Instead he squatted in the offices of absent professors, in unused classrooms, or in buildings left vacant during construction. I'd even provided a refuge for him one time, letting him use my father's office while he was on sabbatical. Charles somehow managed to handle grooming and eating and other necessities, but it couldn't have been easy. This summer, as least, his role as dorm monitor came with a private bedroom with its own bathroom.

I said, "He must make as much money as I do, and I keep a roof over Madison's and my heads. Just barely, and with a lot of help from my parents, but we get by. I don't see why he can't do the same when it's just him. He could get a roommate, or spend less on clothes, or something."

"Might there be some other reason he hasn't told you?"

"There could be, but I'm not going to ask because it's none of my business, and I'm not going to tell him that I think he ought to rent an apartment like most people because it's not my place to do that, either."

"But you're still friends?"

"Absolutely. Good friends, in fact."

"So Jen and I can still be friends? Real friends, even if I don't tell her about my osteo-centric body type?"

"As a real friend who is well aware of your bony magnificence, I would advise against it."

I'd been so intent on our conversation that I didn't see the person approaching. In fact it was Sid who saw her first, and whispered, "Somebody's coming!"

I looked up, and recognized the young woman we'd just been talking about.

Remembering that I still had a phone held up to my ear, I said, "Okay, that sounds good. We'll talk later. Bye." I faked hanging up, and said, "Hi. Jen, isn't it?"

"Jen Cater-Brame," she replied, "and you're Georgia Thackery."

"That's right."

"I saw your daughter inside playing Yu-Gi-Oh!"

"Is the tournament ending?"

"I don't know. She was playing with a different group than I was. They talk a lot when they play, so they're slower. Plus they talk after the game. People don't talk much with me, so I leave as soon as I win."

"Then I take it that you won."

"Yes."

"Congratulations." She didn't respond. Or move. "Would you like to sit down?"

"Okay." She took a seat as far away from me on the bench as was possible without toppling off. "My mother is going to pick me up, but she's at a meeting. She may be late."

"Then we can wait together."

The next three minutes were entirely devoid of conversation, and the silence might have continued if I hadn't felt Sid nudging me from his bag. "Did you have any luck finding your friend Skalle?"

"He's not a friend," she said flatly.

I cringed inside, remembering how Sid had been beating himself up just a few minutes earlier.

Jen continued. "I don't really know him, and he doesn't really know me. We just game together. And no, I didn't find him."

"That's too bad." Another long minute of silence. "Can I ask you something?"

"Why do people ask that? Because obviously you want to ask something, and most people would be curious to find out what it is, so they'd say yes anyway."

With most people, I'd assume that was a rhetorical question, but Jen really sounded as if she wanted to know. "It's a verbal transition—a way to either change the subject or bring up a new subject if the previous one has been exhausted. Think of it like a new paragraph or chapter in a book."

"Oh. That makes sense. Go ahead and ask your question. If it's something I don't want to answer, I won't."

"Fair enough. Why do you want to find Skalle—or rather the person who plays Skalle—when you don't consider him a friend?"

"I told you that before. I need a detective, and I'm eighty-five percent sure Skalle is an investigator of some sort in real life. He could be a police officer or a reporter, but I think a private investigator is more likely. He never misses a scheduled game, and I don't think a police officer or reporter would be able to control his hours that well, and he's hinted that he's not constrained by the usual limitations concerning chains of evidence and warrants. I suppose he could be retired, but if so, he retired young. He knows slang and memes too well to be an older person."

She'd thought it out very thoroughly. About the only possibility she hadn't considered was that Skalle—meaning Sid—was an ambulatory skeleton with a sleuthing habit. I couldn't really blame her for not considering that a likely possibility. "Why do you need to consult a detective?"

"Because of Erik Bloodaxe."

"Who's that?" I thought I remembered Erik Bloodaxe being one of the other characters in Sid's and Jen's gaming group, but of course, I wasn't supposed to know anything about that.

"He's a member of our party in Runes of Legend. Of course, that's just his in-game name. The real Erik Bloodaxe was a Norwegian king in the tenth century. It's the one in our game that I'm worried about. He's missing."

"How do you know he's missing?"

"He hasn't logged on to Runes of Legend in days. We need him for the quests because he's our best fighter, and he promised to be there every night this week. Something must be wrong."

"People have all kinds of reasons for not showing up for something."

"I know that." She started counting them out on her fingers. "He could be sick, he could have had a family emergency, his computer could have crashed, his house could have burned down, his power could be out from bad weather, he may have missed a utility bill payment. There are other, less likely, possibilities as well."

"What about the possibility that he just hasn't been in the mood to play?"

"That's not it," she said with utter conviction. "The game is important to him. Maybe as important to him as it is to me."

"Can't you just find another fighter character?"

She thought about it for a minute. "Are you familiar with RPGs?"

"Sure. I've spent many late nights with dice and character sheets."

"Oh, face-to-face games," she said, her tone vaguely sympathetic, while still implying that I'd probably used stone tablets for my character sheets. "Have you ever gamed online?"

"Only casual gaming." Phone apps like Bejeweled Blitz and Animal Crossing: Pocket Camp were addicting enough for me. I'd been unwilling to spend the time and effort it took to learn to play anything more immersive. "No MMORPGs."

"Then you probably don't realize what it's like to be a female gamer online."

"You're pretty much outnumbered by the guys, aren't you?"

"Not as much as it used to be, and not as much as people think, but it's hard to know because a lot of girl gamers use male character names."

"As part of the roleplaying?"

"Sometimes, but mostly for self-protection. Girl gamers take a lot of abuse from guys. Dirty jokes, comments that are intended as flirting, disgusting remarks. It can lead to stalking online, and sometimes even in real life. I adopted a male identity myself for a long time. Only I got tired of lying."

I didn't have to see Sid to know he was nodding along with that sentiment.

"So I started playing female characters, but then I ran into the same issues that other girl gamers experience. I had to leave half a dozen parties on Runes of Legend because of toxic behavior before I found the one I have now. It's got just the right combination: two male, three female. We've got a strong fighter, a magic user, a tracker, a healer, and a buffer. Everybody shows up when they promise to, and nobody ever says anything mean. It's perfect. That almost never happens in gaming. It's like gold."

"I can imagine." The closest I'd come to that experience was a study group I'd been in during grad school. I'd learned so much with those people, and we had so much fun. Then one of my fellow students transferred to another school, and somehow her departure threw off the balance. The group broke up a month later. I'd been heartbroken.

"I know we all felt the same way about this group, and we were all very excited for The Saga of Thorbjorn and Leipt-Egil. It's a site-wide event, with a limited time period, and we all committed to playing every night during saga season. When Erik Bloodaxe didn't show up for Friday night's session, I was surprised, and when he didn't show up again on Saturday, I was shocked. When he didn't show up on Sunday, I knew something was wrong, and I had to find him."

She sounded so convinced that I didn't try arguing with her. "But you don't know his real name?"

"I don't really know *anything* about him. He was always so nice that I didn't realize how private he was. I know what shows he likes and the books he reads and the movies he enjoys, but I don't how old he is, or if he has a job, or if he's married. Nothing. That's when I went looking for Skalle instead. He did leave a few clues about his real life, particularly that picture of the lake, but of course that turned out to be a false lead."

"Why were you looking for Skalle in person? Can't you just ask him for help in-game? Isn't there some sort of chat or private message feature?"

"Of course, but it's against the rules."

"What rules?"

"The rules of Runes of Legend state that the rooms in the Questing Dragon and the raven missives—those are the chat feature and private message feature respectively—are only to be used for in-game roleplay, not for exchanging personal information of any kind. Real-life topics like politics, religion, or social issues are forbidden."

"And they monitor everything you say?"

"Not that I'm aware of. How could they?"

"Then how would they know if you broke the rules?"

"I would know."

I looked at her, but she was completely serious. "You're unusually conscientious."

"People tell me that, but I don't understand what they mean. My not understanding people happens a lot. That's probably why I don't make friends easily. Some people say I'm a nerd."

"You say that like it's a bad thing." I smiled when I said it, but what Jen said next made me stop smiling.

"My mother says it like it's a bad thing. She thinks I'd have more friends if I didn't spend so much time gaming and reading. I try to explain that the only friends I have are through gaming and reading, but she doesn't understand that."

I didn't know how to respond. On one hand, I didn't want to criticize another parent's opinion or decisions unless they were actively harmful. On the other, telling a child that her personality and habits were undesirable bordered on mental abuse. What I settled for was, "That's too bad."

"She means well, and we have a compromise. I spend the first part of the summer at some kind of camp so I can try new things and meet new people. Then I spend the rest of the summer at home gaming and reading. This year I went to drama camp."

"How did that go?"

"I didn't enjoy acting, but I did appreciate the shows, and it was fun working backstage. So I'm glad I went."

"If you like doing tech, your drama program at school is going to love you. Somebody dedicated to backstage work is a rare and precious commodity."

"Really?"

"Oh yeah. My daughter Madison does theater at her school, and they usually have to beg people to work the crew because most people want to be onstage."

"I'll consider that, once school starts back up. In the meantime, I think the acting lessons will help my online roleplay. I can imagine what a character would do and write about it—I just can't act it out in front of people."

Conversation lapsed after that, but it was a more comfortable quiet. After a while, my phone buzzed, and I found a text from Madison.

MADISON: *Winding down soon. Ice cream?*

GEORGIA: *Sure. Meet me there. I'll go get a table.*

I put my phone away and said, "Madison has an ice cream craving, so I'm going to claim a table before the rest of the gamers come out." I stood, and even before Sid bonked my leg, I had an idea. "Would you like to join us?"

She looked surprised, but pleased. "I'll have to check with my mother," she said, reaching for her phone to text. After a couple of minutes, she said, "She says she'll pick me up there."

"Great."

Jen hadn't asked where we were going, and I hadn't bothered to say because there was just the one ice cream place in Overfeld: Morricone's. Fortunately, it was terrific. They made their own ice cream and cones, and their hot fudge was so good that I could almost have eaten a bowl of that without the rest of the sundae.

We got there just ahead of a group of teenagers who'd hoped to snag the last table. Despite that and the line to order, Jen said, "It's a lot quieter than usual. When the college is in session, the line sometimes goes out the door."

Morricone's decor was what I think of as college town chic. Bright colors on the walls, plain wooden floors, boldly patterned upholstery, and a rotating selection of work from local artists hung all around. In addition to ice cream, they sold a variety of gourmet teas and coffees, though I didn't see kopi luwak on the chalkboard menu.

"If you'll save the seats, I'll go get in line," I said. "I know what Madison wants."

"I get it. You brought me along to hold the table. That's sensible."

"No, I brought you along because I like you."

"Really?"

"Really." And because she seemed the type to suspect compliments as being superficial, I added, "You're interesting to talk to because you see things differently from most people."

"Oh. I suppose I do."

"What kind of ice cream do you want?"

"I'm not sure. I prefer to taste a few flavors before I decide. But if you'll tell me what you want, I'll get it for you. You'll have to pay for your own, of course."

"Of course. And I would be happy to pay for yours, too." Before she could question my motives, I said, "I invited you, so the usual etiquette is that I should pay, unless that would bother you."

"No, it wouldn't bother me." She took the money and Madison's and my orders and joined the line.

My phone buzzed, and I knew without looking that it was Sid texting from inside the bag.

> SID: *And I thought your parents' grad students were weird.*
>
> GEORGIA: *They are. She's a different flavor of weird.*
>
> SID: *But I like her. Thanks for giving me a chance to find out what she's like in person.*
>
> GEORGIA: *You're welcome. I like her, too.*

I wasn't overly surprised that Sid wanted to know Jen better. He'd rescued me as a child, encouraged me when I went through my own shy and awkward period, and believed in me when I was trying to decide if I could raise a child on my own. I had no idea if he'd had a weakness for young women in trouble when he was still traditionally alive, but I knew what he'd been like ever since he woke in his present osteo-centric form.

Madison came into the store a minute later and squeezed her way to the table I was still guarding against people who were eyeing the empty chairs covetously.

"Hi, Mom! You want to hold the fort while I brave the line?"

"No need. Jen is getting our ice cream."

"Jen? The one who came looking for Sid?"

I nodded toward the line, where Jen regarded a tasting spoon with determined concentration before putting it into her mouth. "She finished her game early, and we were chatting when you mentioned ice cream, so I invited her to come along."

"Huh," she said, taking a seat. When she noticed the bag on the chair next to me, she lowered her voice. "Sid, are you in there?"

A firm tap from inside the bag was her answer.

She tapped the bag in return. "You know what, we ought to learn Morse code."

There was a beep from her shorts pocket, and she pulled out her phone to find a message.

> SID: *Texting is easier.*

"Fair."

"Anyway, I hope you don't mind extra company," I said.

"I guess it's okay."

"That sounds less than enthused."

"Jen is kind of odd."

"Yeah, I got that impression."

"I asked my friend Bakshi about her. He says she's a regular at Wizard Gary's, but she'd been out of town or something, which is why I hadn't seen her there before. She looked over at me a couple of times, so I knew she recognized me, but she didn't speak to me. She didn't really speak to anybody. I kind of felt sorry for her. I've only been playing there for a few weeks, and I think I've got more friends than she does."

"Maybe she has friends who weren't there tonight."

"Bakshi says not. She's a good player, though. She regularly beats everybody but Nasir, and that's just because Nasir has a killer deck. But she kind of keeps to herself."

"I think she's lonely, and her mother doesn't really get nerd culture."

"That's rough. Anyway, I heard some of the other players making fun of her. I didn't join in, if you were wondering."

"I wasn't, but I'm glad you didn't. It's tough when even other nerds don't like you."

"Yeah, you're right. A game store should be a safe zone for all nerds. Did you find out why she needs a detective?"

"I did, but let's talk later." Jen was on her way back to the table with a tray of ice cream.

The two girls greeted one another politely, then Jen said, "There was a dollar and sixty-four cents change, but I put it into the tip jar. If you prefer not to tip, I'll give you a dollar and sixty-four cents to make up for it."

"Tipping is fine. I'd have done the same."

She nodded solemnly and started handing out the treats. "Here's your hot fudge sundae, extra fudge, with nuts. Madison, here are your two scoops of chocolate with chocolate sprinkles. Your mother called them jimmies, but that term is only used closer to Boston. Say a two-hundred mile radius."

"Sorry, I forgot," I said.

"It's okay. I understood what you meant."

"What did you get, Jen?" Madison asked.

"A scoop each of dark chocolate and raspberry. I like to alternate bites of each for contrast."

"I'm all about the chocolate," Madison said. "How'd your game go tonight?"

They traded comments that were comprehensible only to those who played Yu-Gi-Oh! Or rather I assumed that was why it was incomprehensible to me—there was always the chance that they were making stuff up just to troll me, but I was pretty sure that Madison didn't know Jen well enough yet to pull that kind of prank with her.

We were nearly finished with our ice cream when I saw Jen's mother come in the door of Morricone's and head our way.

"This is a surprise," she said, sounding as if it wasn't an entirely pleasant one. "Professor Thackery, isn't it?"

"Just Georgia is fine." I pulled Sid's bag off of the fourth chair at the table and put it in my lap. "Would you like to have a seat?"

"Thank you." She did so. "Jen, I hope you weren't bothering these people about that friend of yours again."

"Why would I do that? They already told me they don't know him."

"We ran into each other at Wizard Gary's," Madison explained. "Mom and I have a regular postgame ice cream habit, and we brought Jen along."

"That was very kind of you," Judy said.

"I was explaining my method for beating a superior Yu-Gi-Oh! deck to Madison," Jen said. "Is it all right if I finish?"

"Of course."

The girls lapsed back into Yu-Gi-Oh!-ese, and Judy and I nodded at each other. After an increasingly awkward interval I said, "So you had to work late tonight? Jen said you had a meeting."

"That wasn't for work. It was for a citizen's action committee."

"Hope that went well, then."

"Do you?" she said sharply.

"I'm sorry, am I missing something?"

"It's just that most of the faculty at the college know about my work."

"Oh, I'm not full-time faculty. I'm an adjunct. That's somebody—"

"I know what an adjunct is." She didn't quite snap, but she came close.

There was a vibration from my bag, which I knew was Sid expressing his annoyance. I was kind of annoyed, too, but I tried to keep it out of my voice when I said, "Since you understand adjuncts, then you'll understand why I'm not up on current events in town. I'm just here for the summer program for high school students."

"Which is ludicrously overpriced."

"Okay, maybe we shouldn't talk about the college. Read any good books lately?"

"Are you implying I don't read? I'll have you know I'm an avid reader, and not just the latest trashy beach books."

I took a deep breath and decided I was done being polite. "Now if I ask if you've seen any good movies or TV shows, you'll accuse me of thinking you're lowbrow. Ditto music. I'm definitely not going to bring up religion, politics, or computer operating systems, and I better not talk about sports, either, since I don't know which teams you hate and which you support. How about the weather? It's very nice weather. I like weather. Do you like weather?"

Judy puffed up enough that I was expecting either an explosion, an indignant exit, or a combination of the two, but instead, a giggle popped out. She put her hand up to her mouth, but more giggles emerged anyway.

After a minute, I joined in.

The girls, who must have stopped talking at some point, were staring at us both as if we were insane.

"I'm sorry," Judy finally said. "I've got a knee-jerk reaction when it comes to that college, but I shouldn't take it out on you."

"You can jerk your knee all you want. I've got no particular attachment to the place. By fall, I'll be somewhere else." Not that I wouldn't jump at a full-time job at Overfeld if it were offered, but there was no reason to tell her that. No reason to expect it would happen, either, I thought ruefully. Maybe Charles was right and Professor Hynes didn't influence hiring decisions, but then again, maybe he did.

"I was born and raised here in Overfeld," Judy said, "and it just grates on me that the college seems to run this town. You see, the town charter was written with them in mind. The selectmen of that era were so excited to have an institution of higher learning that they decreed that Overfeld wouldn't have to pay property taxes on any of their real estate, even if it's being rented out to other businesses."

"Harvard has a similar deal," I said, "and I suspect the powers that be in Cambridge don't like it, either."

"Of course they don't. Do you know how many buildings Overfeld owns? I'm not just talking about the campus. They rent out half a dozen buildings in town, including Wizard Gary's, but don't have to contribute a penny to help finance the infrastructure that they take advantage of. That's not fair.

"In the past, the college would voluntarily donate to the town coffers, but for the last ten years, they've been giving less and less. This year they barely reimbursed us for the cost of the extra traffic details needed at graduation. It's ridiculous! But since over half the town selectmen are alumni, nothing ever changes, and the rest of us in town are stuck with some of the highest property taxes in the state, while the college gets off scot-free. So you can see why I'm not a fan."

"Absolutely." Without knowing more of the background, I wasn't going to say I agreed with her, but I was willing to be sympathetic.

"Still, it wasn't right to take it out on you, especially when you're only working here temporarily, so I apologize."

"I appreciate that, and I'm happy to accept your apology."

Normally I would have gone on to ask more about her work or family, but I was still a little wary and was just as glad when Judy said, "Well, we need to be getting home. Thank you again for inviting Jen."

"It was our pleasure," I said.

We left Morricone's together, then turned in different directions to head toward our respective cars.

Since it was dark, without much traffic once we got out of town, Madison held Sid up so he could look out the open window and enjoy the scenery and the breeze from the open window. It made a cozy sight, at least to us. Anybody else might have felt differently. It also made it much easier for us to fill Madison in on why Jen needed a detective.

"I should have realized that she'd be worried about Erik Bloodaxe," Sid said. "It's like Jen says—the guy has been completely reliable since we started the party, but last week, he just didn't show. We managed to get through the first quest on Friday but took more damage than we should have because we didn't have our best fighter. On Saturday, we only got halfway through the second quest and couldn't get any further without Erik. When he didn't come Sunday, we didn't even try to keep going.

"Odina—meaning Jen—kept showing up at the scheduled time on Monday and Tuesday, and I did, too, but the other two party members gave up after Sunday. If it hadn't been too late, I think they'd have joined other parties. I was disappointed, too. Saga season is a big deal in Runes of Legend, and it would have been my first one. But I just got mad at Erik—I didn't stop to think something could be wrong." His skull rolled in Madison's arms so he was looking in my direction. "Georgia, I realize missing persons aren't really our specialty, but I really think we should see if we can help."

"Sid—" I started to say.

"I know, Overfeld isn't our town, and you've got work and Madison to deal with."

"Hey!" Madison said.

"No offense," Sid said, "but you are your mother's first priority."

"Okay, I can accept that," she said.

"Sid—" I tried again.

"And I know you've been enjoying having time to relax and swim and all that, but this is so important to Jen. Maybe I'm not her friend, but she's mine, if that makes any sense."

"SID!"

He shut his jaw with a loud snap.

"I think you're right," I said. "I think we should try to find Erik Bloodaxe."

"You do?"

"I do. Jen and Erik are your friends, so if there's trouble, I think we should help."

He grinned widely, which shouldn't have been possible, but he did anyway. "Thank you."

But I had to say, "Putting our good intentions aside, I don't even know where to start."

"Then we're in luck," Sid said smugly. "I already have a lead!"

CHAPTER SEVEN

Having dropped his bombshell, Sid paused for us to provide adulation.

"Sid," I said, "I know you're pausing for adulation, and I promise to provide said adulation, but only after you tell me what your lead is."

"I'm going to hold you to that. So here's the deal. I told you that I signed up for Runes of Legend when we were visiting Overfeld back in the spring, but I didn't tell you what drew my attention to the game. You remember how I went with you on your interview to provide moral support?"

"I remember you begging me to bring you along because you were nervous about staying in the hotel room alone, and you didn't want to stay in the trunk of the car."

"Tomato, tomahto. At any rate, you brought my skull along, which was obviously good luck because you got the job."

"Obviously. My credentials and interview skills were beside the point."

"Maybe not entirely. Anyway, you put your bag on the table next to you when you were filling out that stack of paperwork."

"Right. That was in the faculty lounge in the Dobson Building."

"I couldn't see much from there—you could keep that in mind when you put me down, you know."

"Well it's not like I could carry a purple sugar skull bag with me on a job interview."

"I like this bag! It's stylin'!"

"I like it, too, but it's not appropriate for every occasion." I had a more formal black bag for job interviews, and while it was big enough to fit Sid in, just barely, the only way he could see out of it was through a small hole in one seam that I'd promised not to repair as long as he agreed not to enlarge it. "Besides, it was a faculty lounge, and not a particularly nice one. There wasn't much to see."

"Which I will have to take your word for because I saw very little of it. I was aimed toward a window, and there was somebody with an open laptop in front of the window. All I could see was the back of the laptop and an inch or so of neck. It looked like a male neck—there was an Adam's apple."

"Okay."

"But it was getting dark, and his screen was reflecting onto the window behind him, and in that reflection, I could see he was playing Runes of Legend."

"Okay, I'm with you."

"I watched him for a while, and the game looked interesting."

"I'm still not understanding why this is a lead."

"Because the guy's username was showing. It was Erik Bloodaxe."

"You're kidding."

"Nope. When we got back to the hotel, I checked out the game, made an account, and started playing. A week or two later, I was perusing the boards looking for a party to join, saw that Erik Bloodaxe was recruiting for his party, signed up for it, and the rest is history. Or at least legendary."

I tried to picture it. "Wait, if you were looking at the screen's reflection, doesn't that mean the words were backwards?"

"Well, yeah."

"You can read backwards?"

He shrugged as best he could with only his skull available. "You'd be surprised at the skills you can master when you're stuck in a bag with nothing better to do."

"Fair point. Anyway, that means you know already who Erik Bloodaxe is."

"Not exactly. I only saw his in-game name on the screen."

"But at least you know what he looks like."

"Not so much. All I could see was an inch of neck. He was Caucasian, not much of a tan, and didn't have a beard."

"That's not a lot to go on, Sid."

"I know, but fortunately, he was sitting right behind you."

"How is that fortunate?"

"You know who you were sitting in front of, don't you?"

I tried to visualize that moment, but failed. "Was he behind me the whole time?"

"No, only for fifteen minutes or so."

I tried again. "I'm sorry. I have no idea who it was."

"But he was right behind you!"

"Coccyx, Sid, it was three months ago. I'd worked half a day, then driven a couple of hours to get to Overfeld for the interview, had the interview, waited for a while for them to confer, got the job, talked money, and then had to fill out paperwork. And since no school does it the same way, it's always both tedious and confusing. I wouldn't have noticed if Chris Pratt was doing a strip tease behind me."

"Still," he said, "it's a solid lead. We know that Erik Bloodaxe teaches at Overfeld."

"We know he works there. Other employees are allowed in the faculty lounges, too."

"Does that mean I'm not entitled to adulation?"

"I'll allow a medium-sized adulation. How would you like it expressed?"

"Dance party?"

"Why did I even ask?"

Normally I enjoy a good dance party, especially with no neighbors around so we could play the music extra loud, but it had been a long day, so while we did dance, I stopped after three songs to get ready for bed, and by the time I was done, Madison had to quit, too, so she could tend to Byron.

Sid could have danced all night, and still have begged for more, but he is patient with our fleshy weaknesses. Besides, I think he was eager to get to work. If there's one thing he loves as much as a good dance party, it's to generate pages and pages of files for what he calls our cases—which I decided I might as well refer to as cases, too. Sid announced he was going to go through all the game transcripts he'd saved for any comments from Erik Bloodaxe that might help us pinpoint who he was. Then he was going to compare that information with the list of personnel, faculty, and adjuncts at Overfeld. That kind of tedious work would have driven me insane, but Sid was delighted by the prospect.

When I came into the living room to wish everybody good-night, Sid was tapping happily away in the living room while Madison channel surfed.

Something Jen said had been niggling at me. "Madison, have you ever run into sexist stuff in online games?"

"Sure. Who hasn't?"

"Really?"

"I mean, most of it was just 'Ha ha your character can make my character a sandwich,' but sometimes I get a guy who tries to flirt. Really badly. One jack wagon kind of stalked me—always showed up when I was online and sent me private messages. He kept asking what my real name is and where I live."

"Madison! Why didn't you tell me?

"Inept flirting and so-called jokes are easy to shut down."

"And the stalker?"

She waved it away. "That was a long time ago, when I first started playing MMORPGs, and I didn't tell you because I was afraid you'd want me to quit. Now I mostly play with a regular group of people, the way Sid does, and it's not a problem."

"But you'll let me know if it becomes one, right?"

"Sure."

"Really?"

"Really, but what would you do if somebody was bugging me?"

"If you could find out his real name, I could get one of your Aunt Deborah's boyfriends to have words with him." My sister was currently dating both a police officer and a campus security guard. They were great guys but would cheerfully paste on badass faces for a good cause, especially if that good cause would please Deborah. "Or I could send Sid over to pay a visit in the middle of the night."

"I vote for Sid," Madison said.

"That does sound like more fun. But don't go getting into trouble just to give me a chance to unleash the wrath of Sid."

"Who am I unleashing my wrath on?" Sid said, looking up from his keyboard. "I didn't know I had wrath."

"You'd have wrath if you found out somebody was harassing Madison online."

"Somebody's harassing Madison? Where is the ossifying piece of sacrum? Let me at him!"

"See? Plenty of wrath."

"Nobody is bothering me," Madison assured him. "Mom is just trying to figure out the MMORPG world."

"It's very confusing. I'm an old-school gamer. Dice and graph paper and fat rule books, lounging in somebody's living room with pizza boxes and soda cans everywhere."

"That isn't really an option for me," Sid said. "I never drink soda."

That was almost a joke, but I caught the wistfulness behind it. So I stopped by to kiss him on top of his skull on my way out of the room. I was really glad we'd decided to hunt for Erik Bloodaxe.

CHAPTER EIGHT

I was less glad about hunting for Bloodaxe the next morning. Sid had once again fixed my breakfast for me and was waiting at the table to show me what he'd done while I slept. Or rather to give me a summary. The massive file he'd put together contained every single comment Erik Bloodaxe had ever made that might indicate something about his identity.

He'd also made a list of each Caucasian male working at Overfeld College, either currently or during the month when he first saw Erik's screen reflection. To be excruciatingly thorough, he included men who were bearded but who had been clean-shaven at some point in the recent past, according to their social media. The list included Charles and Professor Hynes, though at least he'd put them at the very bottom of the probability chart.

"Sid, I am in awe of your attention to detail, but what am I supposed to do with this data? Are you expecting me to approach likely candidates and ask, 'Have you watched *Guardians of the Galaxy* at least once a month ever since you got it on DVD?' or, 'How far along are you in watching *Game of Thrones* versus reading the books?' or even, 'Do you prefer fighting with an axe or a sword? Do you think your in-game fighting style more reminiscent of the Dread Pirate Roberts's in *The Princess Bride* or Aragorn's in *Lord of the Rings*?'"

"Hey, is it my fault Erik's a really private guy? I mean, I thought I was being circumspect, but Skalle is an open book compared to him. The media and book stuff is all I could find, but it seems like most of those would make great conversation starters."

I took a big swallow of cereal to keep from saying anything that might refer to the fact that Sid's experience with starting conversations was somewhat limited. He couldn't help that, after all. I settled for, "I'll do my best."

"And you won't be doing all the work. I'm going to tackle their social media. That ought to help us check some people off of the list."

"Sounds like a great plan," I lied.

As it turned out, I really was able to eliminate a few people as the day went on. Charles was easy—I'd been the one to tell him Overfeld was hiring, and that was after I got the job. Therefore he wouldn't have been in the faculty lounge at the same time I was.

As for the rest, it helped that we adjuncts were spending a fair amount of time together. Before the morning announcements, for which Mo dug up a portable mic since the auditorium's sound system was still on the fritz, I mentioned that I was looking forward to the next Marvel superhero movie and found out that Matt had never seen any of the previous ones, not even *The Avengers* or *Black Panther*.

Over lunch I quoted lines from *The Princess Bride* but mostly got blank looks, and the one person that did recognize it later said that he didn't like *Lord of the Rings*. When somebody commented that it felt chilly outside, I solemnly intoned "Winter is coming," to see how many *Game of Thrones* fans were around. There were several, but they only knew the TV show, not the books. That meant I crossed off some people, and, as a bonus, got to geek out about the show.

In the meantime, Sid was hitting social media hard and emailed updates as he eliminated people for one reason or another: one wasn't familiar with the shows and movies and books Erik Bloodaxe liked, another had an uncommon aversion to online gaming, a third was addicted to online gaming but not Runes of Legend, and two of the Overfeld professors who were spending the summer on campus had been in the middle of a beard-growing battle the day I'd had my job interview.

Normally I'd have headed home after my afternoon class, but Ridley had called a meeting to discuss the upcoming Parents' Day. So all of the instructors gathered in the faculty lounge in Kumin Hall to hear what the plans were.

"Before we get started with the actual arrangements," Ridley said, "I want to discuss some of the problems we've been having with the physical plant here on campus."

"You mean the power going out in in the dorms?" Treva said. "Or the sound system in the auditorium?"

"What about the missing badminton birdies?" Mike brought up. I hadn't heard about that one.

"And there was an issue with the drainage pipe in the laundry room," Charles said.

Ridley waved it all away. "You guys know this is the first time we've done the Enrichment Program, so of course there are going to be glitches. What we don't want is for students to get the wrong idea about them. More importantly, we don't want their parents to get the wrong idea. So I'm asking you guys to be careful when mentioning any of the problems when you're anywhere students can hear, and whatever you do, don't discuss them with the students. Downplay them, change the subject, whatever it takes to distract them. Okay?"

"Are you sure that's the right approach?" I asked tentatively. As I'd told Judy the other night, I had no reason to be overly loyal to Overfeld, but I still wanted my students to be satisfied with their experience, and Ridley's plan seemed like the worst way to go about it. "I've got a daughter in high school, and the last thing she and her friends want is for things to be sugar coated or covered up. Being frank with them usually works better."

"Dr. Thackery, isn't it?" Ridley said, looking at Mo for confirmation. "I hear what you're saying, and I certainly don't want you to lie to the students. I'm just hoping you guys can point out the good things that are going on rather than dwelling on minor problems. What's that old song? Accentuate the positive, eliminate the negative. That's all I'm asking you to do."

He didn't sound like he was asking so much as telling, but I nodded anyway. Honestly, I didn't think it mattered how we spun the incidents. The kids were going to notice, and they were going to talk amongst themselves, and if Madison's crowd was any example, they were going to go on social media and spread the word. I really hoped the administration could get matters under control soon, before the program's reputation was irrevocably ruined.

"Now," he said, clapping his hands, "let's talk Parents' Day." He did so for considerably longer than I wanted to listen. For the grand finale to the session, parents were invited to visit and see what academic wonders their kids had been up to. The drama and music programs would be performing, the art class would have a showing of their work, the science kids would be demonstrating and hosting poster sessions, and so on. My writers were going to produce a magazine with their best work, with layout and illustrations provided by graphic design students.

It was all good stuff, but I didn't really need to know the details of the meals and parking, and I'd already gotten the kids started on picking out their best writing because I'd been told what was expected when I interviewed for the job. Neil Farmer, the Human Resources guy who'd walked me through all the paperwork back in the spring, had given me a thorough explanation of job expectations.

Memory is a funny thing. Thinking about how helpful Neil had been brought my memory of that day back, and I flashed on a mental picture. There had been five of us filling out paperwork in the faculty lounge: Matt, Treva, Paul, Zach, and me. Neil had been in there, too, because he'd stuck around to see if any of us had any questions.

I was delighted, and not just because the meeting was finally coming to an end. I realized I'd just trimmed our enormous list of Bloodaxe candidates to five.

CHAPTER NINE

"Are you absolutely sure those were the only people in the room?" Sid demanded.

The first thing I'd done when I got back to the cabin was tell him about my recovered memory. Well, first I'd kissed Madison and patted Byron, and promised them both that dinner was on the way, but then I talked to Sid.

"Not absolutely," I said. "Somebody could have walked in while I was distracted. Let's say eighty percent sure."

"Okay then. Let's consult the file." His finger bones fairly flew across the keyboard.

"You don't have to check on Treva. She doesn't have an Adam's apple."

"Fair. Okay, you already spoke to Matt. He doesn't watch superhero movies."

"Right. And Paul didn't recognize my quotes from *The Princess Bride*."

"So that leaves Zach Thales and Neil Farmer." Sid put pictures of both men on his screen, then enlarged them.

"Are you trying to decide if you recognize Erik Bloodaxe's neck?"

"It's worth a try." He stared for quite a while. He can, in fact, stare longer than anybody else I know. True, he doesn't have eyes, but that means no eyelids, either, so he can go for hours. This time, he stopped after a couple of minutes and shook his skull. "Nope, I can't tell. But I'm thinking it was this guy." He pointed to Zach.

"How come?"

"According to his social media, he games a lot online, plus he's younger. And Neil Farmer looks kind of boring."

"Neil is nice. He mostly stays in his office, but he's come out to deal with problems a couple of times."

"Georgia, his profile picture is of him in a suit. It's Facebook, not LinkedIn! Face it, Georgia, he's a stiff."

"Some of my favorite people are stiffs."

"Like who?"

I looked at him pointedly.

"Oh, very droll. Skeleton equals a dead guy equals a stiff. Well maybe I'm a stiff, but I don't act stiff, and I never wear suits."

"You rarely wear anything, so that's not really relevant. I think we should check them both out."

"Bet it turns out to be Zachary."

"You're on! Winner picks out the movie for our next movie night?"

"You call that a bet? How about some real stakes? Four movie nights."

"Bring it, Bone Boy!"

"Oh, I'll bring it. Get ready to watch the four best osteo-heroic movies ever made."

"I'm thinking rom-com. So many to choose from . . ."

"Excuse me," Madison said. "Why don't I get to pick the movie?"

"Because we're tired of *Frozen*," Sid said.

I added, "I really think you should let it go."

Our intellectual banter continued through dinner and beyond, though I'm sorry to say that the jokes didn't get any better. We were trying to pick out a movie to watch afterward when my cell phone rang. It was the landline at my parents' house.

"Hello, Thackery Annex," I said.

There was a chuckle from the other end. "Hello, Georgia."

"Hi, Phil." I'd called my father Phil for most of my life, for a semi-random reason that he delighted in telling people, especially other academics. I'd inherited my ambition to academia from him and my mother, both of whom were English professors. Unlike me, however, they'd achieved tenure long ago and had been teaching at McQuaid University ever since. "How's life in Pennycross?"

"Noisy, I'm afraid."

"Too many grad students?"

"Too many suitors. Deborah and her pair of beaux were here for dinner last Sunday."

"Both of them? That must have been interesting."

"They were on their best behavior, but they just can't resist their competitive impulses. When Dab casually mentioned that we really ought to repaint the dining room, Louis immediately offered to do the job for us. Then Oscar said he'd be happy to replaster the ceiling. Before we knew it, they'd one-upped themselves into doing the painting, the ceiling, and sanding and refinishing the floor. I believe there was mention of wainscoting and trim, too, but I'm letting Deborah oversee the details. They've all been over here every night this week, measuring and arguing over paint choices. They're planning to spend all weekend working on the project."

Deborah had been dating both guys for several months, and so far, had shown no inclination to choose between them. In theory, it was all very adult and modern, but in fact, each guy took every opportunity to show why he was the better man. Hence the home renovation mania.

"That sounds both noisy and smelly," I said.

"Which leads me to the reason for this call."

"You don't want me to come to Pennycross to help, do you? You know how bad I am at that kind of thing." I could change a light bulb and most of the time, knew which kind of screwdriver to use. Anything more complicated tended to end badly. "But I'll drive down if you want me."

"Actually, we were hoping for the opposite. Your mother and I think that lounging around a lake sounds like a much more pleasant prospect than listening to dueling hammers."

"You want to come up here for the weekend?" I raised my eyebrows at Madison and Sid, and they both nodded enthusiastically, and in Sid's case, audibly. "We'd love that. When can we expect you?"

"We thought we'd get an early start and be there by lunchtime tomorrow."

"Terrific."

I hung up, looked around the room, and sighed.

"I'm afraid we're going to have to pass on the movie. We've got some straightening up to do." The place didn't look bad, but it wasn't camera-ready, either.

Before I decided what to do first, there was a ping from my cell phone as a text arrived from my mother.

> MOM: *Don't you dare spend all evening cleaning.*
> *It's Friday night, and you should be relaxing.*

I laughed, showed the screen to the others, and replied:

> GEORGIA: *Yes, Mother dear.*

"She knows me well," I said. "You two arm wrestle over which movie we're going to watch, and I'll make popcorn."

I knew there'd be enough time for a little cleaning in the morning, and even if Madison slept in, Sid would be willing to help out.

As expected, my parents arrived in time for lunch, and as per usual, they brought along a carload of groceries. There'd been times in the past when I'd resented their providing supplies, as if they were implying I couldn't pay my own way, but I knew they didn't mean anything by it. They just liked feeding people. The groceries they brought us probably cost less than what they'd have spent feeding a bunch of grad students for the weekend.

Once we'd enjoyed the sandwich fixings they'd brought, we all headed for the lake. Since it was the weekend, there were other people around, so Sid wasn't able to swim, but I carried out his top half in a wicker laundry basket so he could at least join in on the conversation. Though several boaters and a pair of kayakers came by, nobody got close enough to notice, and if they had, I had a towel handy to drape over him.

The rest of us took a dip in the lake. Then my parents, Sid, and I settled on lawn chairs in the shade while Madison and Byron kept playing in the water.

"How are you enjoying teaching at Overfeld, Georgia?" Phil asked.

"I'm having a good time. I've got two sections of writing workshop, and it's nice to not be teaching basic composition for a change. And no grading papers all night long! I do give feedback, but it's nothing formal. So that part's great."

"Which implies that some other part isn't so great," Mom said.

"I guess Overfeld's just not quite what I expected."

"How so?" she asked.

"It's got such a great reputation that I was expecting something more upscale. The physical plant is kind of grungy, to tell you the truth."

"Well, I suspect the college endowment has never matched their reputation. After all, Overfeld has always specialized in teaching people how to excel in academia, and academics rarely have the financial means to make extravagant donations to their alma maters."

"Some Overfeld grads do very well for themselves," Phil objected. "Perhaps they just aren't as generous as other alumni."

"Meow, Dr. T!" Sid said.

He had a point. That remark was a bit catty for my usually genial father.

"Your father still holds a grudge because Overfeld turned him down," Mom said with a grin.

"Maybe a little one," Phil acknowledged.

"You applied for a job at Overfeld?" I asked.

"No, I applied for admission as an undergrad back in the day, but I didn't even make it onto the waitlist."

"Wow." Though he'd never bragged about it, I knew Phil had won a full scholarship because his grades were that good.

"Don't get me wrong," Phil said. "I have no regrets. I couldn't have had a better college experience than I did at Amherst."

"And not just because he met me there," Mom added.

Phil patted her hand affectionately. "Though of course that was the greatest gift and certainly the most educational. But Overfeld was *the* school for those of us seeking a career in the classroom, not just as researchers. Had I managed to get in, I would have had a very different career."

"Like Davidson Hynes has?" I said.

"Oh, Professor Hynes was already blazing his path when I applied. I was particularly enthusiastic about working with him. Instead I had to settle with following his career at a distance. I have no regrets, but one always wonders how things might have gone differently."

Mom said, "Professor Hynes might soon have some regrets of his own if the rumors we've been hearing are true."

"What rumors are those?" I asked.

"That Overfeld is on the verge of bankruptcy."

CHAPTER TEN

"Are you serious?" I said.

Mom said, "Nothing has been announced publicly, but from what I've heard, most of the faculty members have dusted off their curricula vitae and updated their resumes in order to spend the summer networking at other universities to see what openings are available. We've had half a dozen visit McQuaid."

"I'm shocked. Okay, the place could use some paint and some electrical work, but it's Overfeld! Nobody there has said anything about the school being in trouble." Then again, they'd hardly tell an adjunct something like that, and it certainly explained why they'd hired adjuncts for the summer program instead of using their own people. I'd assumed it was because we were cheaper, and because the rest of the faculty had better things to do with their time: conferences, research, trips to Disney World. It hadn't occurred to me Overfeld's tenured professors would be hunting for new jobs.

"I've never heard of a college going bankrupt," Madison said as she and a soggy Byron plopped down on the grass next to Sid's basket. "Is that a thing that happens?"

"Sometimes," I said. "Mount Ida in Newton, Mass. shut down this past spring, and I read something about Newbury College in Brookline having troubles, too."

"Such a shame about Mount Ida," Phil said, "but don't count Newbury out yet. I've met President Chillo a few times, and he's both intelligent and dedicated."

"Still, according to an incredibly depressing man at Harvard Business School, there are going to be a lot of college closings in the next few years," Mom said. "He's predicting that half of the colleges in the country will be going bankrupt over the next ten years. Half!"

"Do you think that's true?" I asked.

"It's impossible to know for sure, but I'm afraid his research seems solid. Mergers are on the rise, too. Mount Ida might have been saved if a merger with Lasell hadn't fallen through, and I hear Wheelock in Boston is merging with Boston University. But even if mergers like that save some of the schools, I'm afraid a lot are going away forever."

"Why?" Madison asked. "Why now?"

"It's a combination of things. The main issues are the declining birth rate and rising tuition, both of which result in fewer students going to college. That means competition for students is fierce, and if a college doesn't have the right majors—meaning the popular ones—students go elsewhere. With a buyer's market, students can be pickier about amenities like on-campus health clubs and better food in the cafeterias, and those things are expensive to provide. I've even heard speculation that since our basic teaching paradigm of lectures from the front of the room hasn't changed in centuries, it's past time for a change."

"Academia does change," Phil said, "albeit slowly. Look at Professor Hynes's work."

I nodded but didn't say anything. Despite Charles's reassurances, I was still embarrassed by the tone of the feedback Hynes had given me. I hadn't told Madison or my parents about the encounter and didn't want to bring up it then, either. There's nothing like spending years as an adjunct to make one doubt one's gifts as an academic. At least Sid believed in me—I'd heard a definite snort from his basket when Phil mentioned Hynes's name.

Phil stood. "Enough of that. Why don't you continue to relax while I get dinner started? I hope everybody's hungry! Except Sid, of course."

My father was a wonderful and enthusiastic cook. When I used the charcoal grill that came with the cabin, I usually went with burgers and hot dogs, or maybe a splurge on steaks, but nothing so simple would do for Phil. Oh, he was still cooking steaks, but before cooking them, he dry rubbed them with something he refused to divulge. He also grilled teriyaki chicken and assorted vegetables on skewers, potato wedges and corn on the cob, and even a skillet cobbler. Given that there were only four of us eating, there were going to be enough leftovers for me and Madison to gorge on for the rest of the week, plus plenty of beef bones for Byron. Of course, I suspected that had been Phil's plan all along.

The next day started out the same—my father cooking while the rest of us watched him—but after the dishes from the brunch omelets were washed and put away, Phil said, "You know, I wouldn't mind taking a peek at the college. We've driven past there a few times, but I haven't actually been on campus since I visited during high school. Would you mind, Georgia?"

"Sure, why not? I don't know how many buildings we'll be able to get into because they didn't issue keys to us summer instructors, but I can show you around the outside, at least."

"Splendid!"

Mom and Madison said they'd rather spend more time by the water, and Sid decided to stay inside and use his computer in peace. Normally he spends most of the night online, but with my parents in residence, I'd given them my bedroom, and he'd given me his. We'd all assured him that it would be all right for him to use his laptop in the kitchen or living room, but he'd insisted on just reading instead. I'm sure the bag of new books my father had brought along had nothing to do with that decision.

There was a comfortable buzz of people in the center of town—not so many as to be crowded, but enough to feel convivial. Even the campus wasn't as deserted as I'd expected for a Sunday afternoon. Clusters of Andorians were scattered around the quad: reading, talking, texting other people while sitting together, and, of course, playing hacky sack. It was an unwritten rule of colleges with even minimal outdoor space that when the weather permitted, there had to be at least one game of hacky sack going on at any given time.

Kumin Hall was locked, as expected, but we could at least look in the windows, and afterward I gave Phil the cheap tour of the rest of the campus.

"It's such an attractive place," Phil said. "I hate the idea of it shuttering its doors."

"Even if they didn't accept you?"

"An academic shouldn't hold grudges, Georgia," he said solemnly. Then he chuckled. "Who am I talking to? Nobody holds grudges like an academic. I've been snubbed by someone because I had the temerity to question one of his footnotes seven years before." He told me the story but then went back to saying, "Still, it's as you said. This is Overfeld. Having it close down would be the end of an era."

We were heading past the dorm being used for the Andorians when we found our way blocked by a parade of students carrying bags and bundles. Their expressions ranged from annoyed to more annoyed to downright mutinous. The program's dorm monitors were herding them along while keeping determinedly cheerful faces in place.

As the last student passed, I got the attention of Lisa Quinn, the drama teacher, who was bringing up the rear. "What's going on?"

"No big deal," she said brightly. "It's just that the air conditioning isn't working as well as it should be. The weather forecast says there's a heat wave coming, so we're moving the Andorians to another dorm so they can be more comfortable."

"Really?" I'd checked my weather app that morning and hadn't seen anything about a heat wave. Given that and Lisa's overly wide smile, I suspected that she was taking Ridley's words about accentuating the positive to heart. Since I didn't want to spoil it for her, I said, "Well, I'll leave you to it. See you tomorrow!"

She trotted after the students.

"I see what you mean about the physical plant needing work," Phil said. "Ah, Georgia, if you could have seen this place in its heyday. Overfeld was a picture postcard of a New England college campus. It looked far more like what people think of as the Ivy League than most Ivy League schools ever did. The buildings, the furnishings, the grounds—all were kept meticulously. It was a bustling campus—enrollment was at an all-time high—but it still felt oddly serene. There was an air of passionate devotion to the liberal arts here, and the students and faculty didn't care that other schools were more famous. They knew they were educating future professors for universities all over the country. In fact, they were just this side of smug."

"Wow." I compared that mental picture with the way the school looked now, with poorly maintained older buildings and a handful of soulless modern buildings that were far less attractive, even if they did have more working power outlets. "What happened to the place?"

"I've heard a dozen different explanations. Some say the board of overseers invested the endowment unwisely. There's talk of disputes with various unions, and of course, town-and-gown issues. Perhaps it's their specialty—as your mother said, their alumni typically don't have a lot of money to give back. Or maybe they didn't modernize quickly enough and have yet to embrace distance learning. One friend of mine insists the school is too big while another says it's too small. It could be the location, which is too bucolic for many tastes and can be isolated in the winter. And of course, as the pool of matriculating students shrinks, all schools have to spend more time and money on recruiting, as well as offering more generous scholarships, which makes it harder to meet expenses. Most likely, it's a combination of all of those." He shook his head sadly. "Once a school starts to decline, it's very difficult to slow that process, let alone reverse it."

To cheer ourselves up after such a sobering discussion, we went across the town green so Phil could visit the bookstore. Like me, he's never met a bookstore he didn't like, and we spent a happy half an hour browsing. Knowing that he's nearly as fond of ice cream as he is of books, I then casually mentioned there was an excellent ice cream place nearby. He picked up on my subtle hint immediately.

Once again, Morricone's was doing land-office business, and by the time we'd gotten my strawberry in a cup with chocolate syrup and he had his cake batter in a cone with rainbow sprinkles, plus a gallon of dark chocolate to take home to Mom and Madison, there were no tables available. We were going to hunt up a bench out on the green when I saw that one of the tables had but a single occupant: Charles.

"Phil, you remember my friend Charles, don't you?" We'd all had lunch together in Pennycross a couple of times. I squeezed my way to his table. "Hi, Charles! Good ice cream weather?"

"Georgia, Phil. What a pleasant surprise! Would you two care to join me?"

"I was hoping you'd ask." After we sat down, I realized all Charles had on his table was a bottle of water. "You came to Morricone's to get water?"

"I'm waiting for a takeout order," he said. "A rather large one, so it's going to take a while."

"Having a party, Charles?" Phil asked.

"More along the lines of a bribe. There's been an issue with the Andorians' sleeping accommodations, and it was thought that a large selection of ice cream might soothe their irritation."

"We saw Lisa on the quad, and she said something about the air conditioning going out," I said.

"Ah, yes. Air conditioning."

I looked at him. "It's not the air conditioning, is it?"

He looked around to make sure nobody was in earshot, then lowered his voice. "I wish it were something that simple. The truth is that one of the Andorians complained of itching this morning, and when Treva investigated, she found that the girl's bed was infested with bed bugs."

"Ew!" Bugs of all descriptions creep me out, and the idea of them in my bed was the absolute worst.

"Exterminators were brought in immediately, and they say it may be an isolated case, but then again, it might not be. It is hoped that by moving everyone to another dorm, one which has been thoroughly inspected and cleared, we will avoid further insect incursion. Treva is laundering all of that student's effects, and her own as well, just in case."

"Why the story about air conditioning?"

"Director Ridley doesn't want word about the infestation getting back to the parents. They'd pull their scholars out of the program, demand large sums of money back, and worst of all, go onto every social media avenue available to let the world know that Overfeld's dorms are unsanitary." Charles looked unhappy. "The way I understand the life cycle of bed bugs, it's just as likely the problem originated with the Andorian. She said she'd been traveling this summer, and she could have picked them up from a hotel her family stayed in along the way. They can attach themselves to clothes or nest in suitcases or—"

"I don't need to hear any more about their travel habits," I said. I was going to be scratching myself all day as it was.

"At any rate, I request that you keep it sub-rosa. I think it likely that word will get out no matter how circumspect we are, but perhaps we'll get lucky."

He didn't look hopeful, and neither was I, but I'd do my best to keep it quiet.

Since Charles was more plugged into Overfeld gossip, I thought I'd see if I could pick his brain about my favorite candidate for the alter ego of Erik Bloodaxe. "The admin crew must have loved having to come in on Sunday to get this all taken care of. Did Ridley come himself, or did he send poor Neil Farmer?"

"Ridley was here, but of course it was Mo who handled the logistics. She was going to come get the ice cream herself, but I insisted on taking care of this one small task. Running into the two of you proves that virtue is often rewarded."

"So Neil didn't get hauled out on a weekend?" I persisted, knowing that even if Charles thought it odd I was asking about somebody I barely knew, he was too well-bred to say so.

"It wasn't an option. He's been on vacation all week, and I believe he'll be gone most of next week, too, though he intends to be back for Parents' Day."

"Oh, I hadn't realized he was out. I hope he's gone someplace fun."

"I spoke to him Friday last, just before he left, and he was quite looking forward to it. He was planning a trip to New York City to take in some shows and then had a selection of odd jobs to perform at his home."

"The travel part sounds like fun, anyway," I said. The staying-at-home piece sounded more promising in terms of being able to talk to him.

Charles asked Phil about his work, and we went on to exchange news about McQuaid, since we'd all worked there at one time or another. I was just about finished with my ice cream when Charles looked up and frowned.

I turned to see Professor Hynes walking in. I'd have been happy to pretend I hadn't noticed him, but Phil said, "Surely that's Davidson Hynes."

"I believe it is," Charles said stiffly.

"Have either of you had a chance to meet him?"

Charles looked at me. The man is uncommonly discreet. Since I obviously hadn't told Phil about the discussion we'd had with Hynes, then I must have some reason for my omission, and he wasn't going to spoil that for me.

Phil was looking at us both curiously, so I said, "Actually, we did. Just the other day."

"And?"

"He wasn't what I expected," I said, echoing my earlier comment about Overfeld itself. I explained how Hynes had invited himself into my classroom, and the feedback he'd bestowed upon me. "I don't think he was impressed by my work."

"Is that so?" Phil said mildly.

"Pfui!" Charles said indignantly. "It is we who were not impressed by him. Not only does he have no business passing judgment on our skills, he certainly has no right to do so inaccurately. Georgia is, as we both know, a gifted instructor."

"Quite right," Phil said. "I think I would like to meet the great man." Hynes had made it through the line and was looking for a vacant seat. "Call him over, would you, Georgia?"

For a minute I flashed back to a time when Phil had reamed out one of my elementary school teachers who had misgraded one of my math tests, and I was hoping he wasn't going to repeat that. I should have known better.

I stood and waved. "Professor Hynes, would you like to join us?"

Hynes made his way to the table. "Georgia! Charlie!" He sat down. "I'm sorry, you prefer Charles, don't you?"

Charles nodded tightly.

"Dave, I'd like you to meet my father, Dr. Phil Thackery. Phil, this is Dr. Davidson Hynes."

They shook hands.

"A pleasure to meet you, Professor," Phil said.

"Please, call me Dave. Everybody does," Hynes said. "So a doctor. Medical, or one of us academics?"

"Academic, but hardly in your league," Phil gushed. "I'm in the English department at McQuaid."

"McQuaid . . . Yes, that's a nice little school. How's it going over there?"

"Suffering from our success, I'm afraid. Enrollment is up once again, so another building project just broke ground on campus. Another couple of years of dodging construction workers and machinery." Phil chuckled. "I shouldn't complain, not when so many older universities are having financial woes."

Hynes held onto his smile, but I could tell it was a strain. "English, you said? What's your specialty?"

Phil talked a little about his current research, then said, "But enough about me. I have to confess, I'm an ardent admirer of your work."

"Really?" Hynes puffed up. "That's always good to hear."

"Oh, yes," Phil said. "My mother was in academia, too, so I heard of your research when I was just a child. I followed your work throughout high school and into college." He patted my hand. "And now Georgia has a chance to learn from you. It must be gratifying to have yet another generation of young devotees. What a legacy!" He chuckled again.

I was having a hard time keeping from throwing in a chuckle or two of my own and was fairly sure Charles was in the same boat, but Hynes didn't look like he was going to be laughing anytime soon.

Phil said, "Are you working on anything new these days, Professor?"

Hynes smiled unconvincingly. "I'm afraid I can't talk about my current study in public yet, but I've got some papers in progress."

"Really?" Phil said. "Still writing, still doing research. That's quite remarkable, isn't it?"

Back at the counter, a pair of employees brought out several bags filled with gallon containers of ice cream.

"I believe my order is ready," Charles said. "Have a pleasant drive back to Pennycross, Phil, and give my best to your lovely wife. Georgia, I'll see you tomorrow." Then he raised his voice, as one does when speaking to an older person whose hearing is going. "Nice to see you again, Dave."

Before Hynes could respond, Phil said, "I'm afraid Georgia and I have to get going as well. We've got ice cream for my wife and granddaughter and don't want it to melt. It's been an honor, sir, an absolute honor."

Hynes still couldn't think of anything to say, and when we were partway to the door, Phil turned to me and said, "My word, Georgia, it's like meeting a piece of history."

It was all I could do to get out of the place without bursting out laughing.

Once we were outside, Phil said, "Georgia, I misled you earlier when I said nobody holds a grudge like an academic. I am now reminded that a father's ire is even more powerful."

CHAPTER ELEVEN

Soon after we got back to the cabin and served up ice cream to Mom and Madison, it was time for my parents to load up their car and head back to Pennycross. Deborah had texted them that the guys had finished redecorating their dining room, so they knew the coast was clear. I hugged both of them goodbye, but I may have hugged Phil a little longer than usual in gratitude for his epic takedown of Professor Hynes.

Once they were gone, I told Sid what Charles had said about Neil Farmer.

"That's great," he said.

"What about your favorite candidate?"

He made the sound of a juicy raspberry—I have no idea how he managed it without a tongue. "Zach is out of the running because of the way he dissed the *Lord of the Rings* movies on Facebook. He said the hobbits weren't believable. There's no way Erik would say something that boneheaded. And trust me, I know boneheadedness."

"So I win the movie nights?"

"Yes, and you can gloat on the way to Neil's house. Come on!"

"You want to go right now?"

"Why not? If this is the part of the vacation when he's doing home repairs, he might be there. I found his address online."

"Did you not get his phone number?"

"Um, I'm not sure."

I just looked at him.

"Okay, yes, I got his phone number, but I think this would go better in person."

"How? Even if he's there, what do I say? 'Excuse me, but do you have a moment to talk about our game and roleplay?' He'll think I'm an evangelist for the church of MMORPG."

"I think we can come up with something a little more subtle," Sid said. He drummed his finger bones noisily against his skull, and after a minute, snapped his phalanges. "I've got it. Tell him you're thinking about buying a house near his, and you wondered what the internet service is like because—and this is the subtle part—you play online games."

"Okay, that's moderately subtle, assuming that he's willing to admit he does the same."

"Why wouldn't he be?"

"Some people look down their noses at grown men playing games. Neil could be embarrassed or worried about his professional reputation."

"That's ridiculous."

"I don't disagree, but I've seen academics hide all kinds of hobbies and interests because it could affect their work life. Online gaming, historical recreations, even an archeologist who didn't tell anybody she was a mystery writer. And she was smart to keep it quiet. As soon as she got outed, she lost a research grant."

"But Neil isn't an academic."

"True, but he works in an academic setting, and Human Resource guys probably have their share of prejudices. So I'll try, but if he doesn't own up to being a gamer, there won't be a lot I can do."

"That's when you turn up the sex appeal." Madison had just returned from walking Byron.

"Excuse me?" I said.

"Come on, Mom, you're not that old. You must remember how it's done."

"Thank you so much for that ringing endorsement, but we don't even know that I'm Neil's type."

"There are pictures of him with a former girlfriend on Facebook," Sid said, "so you're the right gender. That's a plus."

"Just switch out those jeans for something tighter, and change your top. That royal blue sleeveless one looks great on you."

"While I appreciate the compliment, I don't think—"

But Sid was defying reality to make Bambi eyes at me, which I have yet to learn how to resist.

"Fine," I said, "I'll change." As befitted my new role as femme fatale, I even put on lipstick. Madison decided to stay home because she thought it would be harder for me to flirt with a daughter watching and incredibly awkward for the one I was flirting with.

Needless to say, Sid was coming along. I wanted to just bring part of him, whereas he wanted his whole self involved, so we compromised. His skull, hand, and phone went in the sugar skull bag, while the remainder of his bones rode in the floor of the car, covered with a blanket.

With GPS and Sid acting as navigator, we finally found the place. Neil's house was more isolated than my cabin, and the narrow road leading to it was even longer, albeit better paved.

"This is nice," I said once I made it to the end of the driveway. It was a neat clapboard house, centered in a precise square of lush green lawn that was bordered on three sides by thick trees. "There's no car in the driveway. I bet he's still in New York."

"Coccyx. Wait, maybe his car is in the shop, and he got an Uber back here. He could be inside right now, waiting for an attractive lady visitor."

"Theoretically possible, if highly unlikely. I'll ring the bell."

"Take me, too!"

"Of course." As I walked toward the front door, I felt Sid wriggling his skull around in the bag so he could look in all four directions.

"He needs to mow the lawn," Sid said softly, so only I could hear him.

"He can't very well do that from New York. Which is where he probably is."

Sid just sniffed in reply.

I climbed the steps to the front porch, rang the bell, and waited for a couple of minutes before saying, "He's not home."

"Try it again."

I did so and waited longer. "Sid . . ."

"Just one more time."

Since it was easier than arguing, I rang a third time. No response. "Satisfied?"

"No. Hey, there aren't any houses nearby, right?"

"Right."

"Then let me look around."

Before I could argue, the car door opened and the rest of Sid came lumbering toward us. As soon as it was close enough, it reached for his skull and popped it into place on the end of his spine. Then the entire skeletal package started making a circuit of the house, looking in windows as he went, while I waited for him on the porch.

"Well?" I asked when he came back into view.

"Nothing helpful. I spotted what looks like a home office, but it's just ordinary stuff."

"As opposed to?"

"A man cave? A shelf filled with Runes of Legend merchandise or a Viking poster or some sort of game-related decorations? But there's nothing that couldn't come right out of an Office Depot ad."

"Any signs of life?"

"No, but he left a lot of lights on."

"A lot of people leave lights on when they're gone for a while, or they set a security timer. Face it, Sid. Neil is on vacation. I know you wanted to solve this more quickly for Jen's sake, but we're just going to have to wait until he gets back to see if he's really Erik Bloodaxe."

"Maybe there's a clue to his online identity hidden in a closet or something. I've got my lock picks in the car, so I could get in easy."

"Sid, I don't think we should break into Neil's house."

"Nobody will see us, and there's no sign of a security system."

"That's not the point. Even ignoring the fact that it's illegal, breaking in would be a terrible invasion of Neil's privacy. If we had any reason to believe he was hurt or in trouble or anything like that, or if we strongly suspected him of doing something immoral, maybe we could justify it, but everything looks fine. It just wouldn't be right."

"Oh." He considered it. "You're right. If Neil Farmer really is Erik Bloodaxe, then he's my friend, and a friend would never do something like that."

"That's the way I see it anyway."

"A man's home is his castle."

"Exactly."

"And his car isn't here, so we can't search that."

"Also true."

"What about Neil's office?"

"Excuse me?"

"A man's workplace isn't his castle, is it?"

"Not exactly, but what are the chances he'd have something related to his gaming at his office?"

"When you had an office, you brought in posters and personal knickknacks, enough to show a little of your personality. Why wouldn't Neil do the same?"

"Would a friend sneak around another friend's office?"

"Why are you asking me? This friend stuff is new to me. What I do know is that Jen is worried, and she's my friend, too, so I want to help her. That means identifying Erik Bloodaxe as soon as possible. I don't want to wait around doing nothing until Neil gets back from New York."

I thought about it. "Okay, I suppose it won't hurt to take a peek in his office. But just a peek. No going through all his drawers, no trying to get onto his computer, nothing like that."

"Agreed."

"And we can't go today. Phil and I tried to get into Kumin earlier, and it was locked, so the Dobson Building is bound to be, too."

"Ahem," he said. "Expert lock picker here."

"Yes, you could probably get us in, but there were a lot of Andorians out and about when Phil and I were there, and they might notice a skeleton picking a lock."

"Good point. Tomorrow then?"

"Tomorrow it is."

We headed back home and spent the rest of the evening eating leftover teriyaki chicken and reading, which would normally have been a perfect end to the day. Instead, I was restless.

At first I thought it might be because I was worried about sneaking into Neil's office, but I really wasn't. Sid and I had done crazier things in the past and gotten out okay. What was really bothering me was what Mom had said about half the colleges in the country shutting down over the next few years. If that happened, half of my job opportunities would disappear, and I'd be competing with formerly tenured professors for what was left. Was it any wonder that I would allow myself to be distracted by the quest for Erik Bloodaxe?

CHAPTER TWELVE

The next day did not begin well. When I wheeled Sid into the auditorium, the other adjuncts were looking decidedly glum.

"What's wrong?" I asked Matt.

"We're not supposed to talk about it," he said, "but anybody can see that the Andorians already know." Still, he lowered his voice to a whisper. "Did you know we found bed bugs in the dorm?" He scratched his shoulder.

"I heard," I said, resisting the urge to move away from him.

"They said we're all clear now, but—" He scratched his leg.

Director Ridley came by, looking worse for the wear, and on his way past hissed, "Stop scratching!"

It was the exact wrong approach. By the time the students came in, we were all scratching ourselves.

After the usual batch of announcements, including more tidbits about Parents' Day, Ridley took the microphone to reassure everybody that while yes, there had been a trivial insect problem in the dorm, it was all taken care of, and there was no cause for alarm, and if any bugs did show up, exterminators would be called immediately, but that wouldn't happen because magical wombats had spent all night catching and eating any stray six-legged beasts.

Okay, he didn't say the last part, but he might as well have because the students would have been just as likely to believe that as they did what he actually said.

There were questions galore, and half the students seemed to be typing away on their phones. With all that, we were late getting into our classrooms, and the parents of one of my best writers came to take their kid away from our plague-ridden den during lunch.

To add insult to injury, when classes ended for the day, we found flyers posted on every available surface in the quad declaring that the powers that be at Overfeld College needed to Pay Their Share. I had no doubt that Jen's mom Judy was involved.

I hadn't been lying to Judy when I said I had no particular loyalty to the school, but knowing that Overfeld was in such financial trouble did make me considerably more sympathetic when I saw President Fernandez walking by, looking as troubled as if he'd lost his last friend.

After that, what I really wanted to do was to go back home and take a soak in the lake while still fully dressed. Not that I really believed any bed bugs had gotten into my clothes. It was more that I wanted to stop scratching. But I couldn't do that to Sid, who'd spent the whole day in his suitcase waiting for a chance to sneak into Neil's office.

Which we did, only to find that Neil Farmer wasn't on vacation after all.

* * *

I managed not to throw up when I realized what I'd been breathing in. In my defense, I'd had no idea what a dead body smelled like. The ones I'd encountered before had been . . . well, *fresher* was the only word I could think of, though somehow it didn't seem appropriate. Now that I knew, I didn't think I'd ever forget.

I grabbed Sid in a quick hug. "Are you okay?"

"There's no time for that. I'm getting into the suitcase, and we're getting out of here before anybody else comes up those stairs and you get into trouble."

"Why would I get into trouble? Are you saying he was—How did he die?"

"He was murdered. Stabbed. The knife is still in him."

"Then we can't run away."

"Why the patella not?"

"We have to tell the cops. The sooner the body is found, the more likely they are to be able to find evidence to catch the killer."

"We'll call in an anonymous tip."

"Mo knows we were in the building. If an anonymous tip comes in an hour later, she's going to put the pieces together."

"Well you can't tell them you picked the lock! For one, you didn't—I did. For another, the police will arrest you."

"I know, I won't tell them anything like that. Just give me a minute to think." It was actually more like ten minutes, but eventually we came up with something that I thought would keep me from getting involved while making sure that the poor man's body didn't lie there, undiscovered, for much longer.

With Sid safely in his suitcase, I went back downstairs to the admin office and said, "Excuse me, Mo, but that smell you told me about? I think it's coming from upstairs, and it's really bad." Sid had held the door to the office open for a few minutes to make sure enough of the reek wafted down the stairs that my noticing it would be credible.

Mo followed me back down the hall and made a face as she agreed that something was rotting on the second floor. I was afraid she'd want me to go upstairs with her, but she said she'd call the maintenance department right away and get them to check it out. I was more than willing to let her make the call. The further away I was away from Neil's office, the happier I was. I wouldn't have minded leaving the building entirely, but the other admin folks were so curious about what it could be that I decided it would look more natural if I were equally curious. So I shared coffee with Mo and her colleagues while they speculated and shared stories of the worst things they'd ever smelled. I did not, however, accept the renewed offer of a donut. I couldn't stand the idea of eating anything.

Just as Mo finished describing the time a skunk snuck into the crawlspace under her house and died, making an odor so bad she and her husband thought it was a gas leak, a harried-looking maintenance man showed up. I started to accompany him and Mo, but Mo waved me back, saying there was no need for both of us to suffer, and I went gratefully back to my coffee.

It took what seemed like an awfully long time for Mo to come running back, looking as pale as Sid had been. Without answering her friends' questions, she grabbed the phone, dialed 911, and managed to choke out that a body had been found before breaking down into tears.

The police arrived swiftly, and after the officers investigated enough to know that it was a serious call, more officers and scientists were summoned. Campus security came, too, as well as President Fernandez and Director Ridley.

Other than trying to comfort Mo, who'd known Neil for a long time and liked him, I mostly just tried to stay out of the way. I could feel gentle nudges from Sid's suitcase, and I guessed he wanted me to check and see if Mo knew anything about Neil having enemies or playing online games, but I ignored him. It wasn't something I could ask without a reasonable excuse. Despite my reluctance to push, she had plenty to say about Neil: that he'd always been so nice to her, and it had been so sad that he lived alone, and that he'd given her a ride home right before his vacation. When one of the other admins wondered if that meant Mo had been the last person to see him alive, it sent her into a fresh bout of tears.

It felt awkward to stick around, but I didn't think I should leave. I was pretty sure most people would stay when a dead body was found. I was desperate for my behavior to seem natural, even in such an unnatural circumstance. Plus I thought the police might want to talk to me, and I mentally went through my story about smelling the body over and over again.

After a long while, a uniformed officer came to speak to Mo, the other admins, and me. He seemed satisfied by my explanation of why I'd been in the building. When I told him that I'd only met Neil a couple of times, and hadn't actually gone into his office, he took my contact information and sent me on my way.

I craved nothing more than to get home where I could take off my clothes and shower because I was convinced I could still smell decomposition, but I did take a minute to text Charles before starting the drive home. I wanted to be sure he and the other dorm monitors kept the Andorians as far away as possible from Dobson, though they'd almost certainly noticed the unusual amount of activity and the influx of police vehicles. Charles responded right away to thank me, ask about my well-being, and assure me that he was at my disposal should I need him.

I texted Madison, too, but just to apologize for being so late and to let her know that we were on our way back to the cabin.

With that taken care of, I couldn't wait to load Sid into the car and get away from the campus. As soon as we were moving, Sid unzipped the case and peeked out.

"Now that we've got a minute, are you still okay?" I asked him.

"I think so. Mostly I'm glad I don't have a stomach. If I did, I'd have barfed all over the body."

"Was it that bad?" There hadn't been time to ask for any details before.

"Coccyx, Georgia, it was awful. No offense, but bones are so much neater. Skin-covered flesh is fine, too. It's the transition from one to the other that gets messy."

"I'm going to take your word for it," I said, trying hard not to imagine what Sid had seen.

"I'm sorry, I shouldn't have said anything."

"No, I'm sorry. If you could handle seeing it, I should be able to handle hearing about it. You tell me whatever you need to tell me." I didn't want him holding it in and allowing it to haunt him.

"If you're sure . . ."

"It can't be worse than what I'd imagine."

"Okay then. The smell got worse as soon as I walked in, but at first I didn't see him—the body I mean. Then when I turned on the lights, I saw stains on the desk. It was blood, but it was dark, so I still didn't realize what it was I was seeing. It wasn't until I got right up to the desk that I saw him on the floor."

"You said before that the knife was still in him."

"In his throat."

"So he was face up?"

He nodded. "Not that anybody would have recognized him. It was . . ." His voice dwindled away.

"I heard one of the police officers say he's been dead for a while." No wonder the smell of decomposition had permeated the second floor. "If Neil was your gaming buddy, that explains why he hasn't been showing up."

"Oh, Neil was Erik all right."

"Why are you so sure?"

"That knife in him? I recognized it. It's Erik Bloodaxe's sword."

CHAPTER THIRTEEN

"Erik Bloodaxe is an online character. How could he have a real-life sword? And you said it was a knife."

"I had time to think about it while we were waiting for the cops, and I don't believe it was a knife. I could only see the hilt, but I'm sure it was a miniature sword, or maybe a letter opener made to look like a sword. And not just any sword. You see, Erik Bloodaxe won the Ship's Blade in the game—that's a sword with the hilt carved to look like a Viking dragon boat. It's not particularly historically accurate because Vikings were known as axe wielders, not swordsman, which is why he's Erik Bloodaxe and not Erik Bloodsword—"

"Focus, Sid."

"Sorry. I'm still rattled."

"Of course you are." I reached into the bag and patted his skull.

"Anyway, the Ship's Blade is a powerful weapon, and you have to survive a tough quest to obtain it, and only certain classes can even wield it. Owning the Ship's Blade is a huge deal in the game."

"Okay."

"The hilt sticking out of Neil's throat is an exact replica of the hilt of the Ship's Blade, meaning official Runes of Legend merchandise. That's not something you can pick up just anywhere."

"Purely for the sake of argument, how do we know the miniature sword didn't belong to the killer?"

"Because the Ship's Blade comes with a matching metal stand, and that stand was on Neil's desk. I can accept a killer bringing the knife along with him, but nobody is going to lug around a heavy stand. It had to have been Neil's, and that can't be a coincidence. Neil Farmer was Erik Bloodaxe."

Madison was waiting for us, looking concerned, but when she started to hug me, I waved her off. "You don't want to touch me, sweetie. I stink, and Sid does, too. As soon as he's out of his suitcase, take it out back, and let it air out."

"And don't let the dog pee on it," Sid said as he started to emerge.

I didn't think it was going to be a problem. Byron had taken one whiff of me, snorted in disgust, and retreated to Madison's room.

"Does this mean you two know about the body found at the college?" Madison said.

I stopped on my way to the bathroom. "How did you find out?"

"One of the maintenance people is my friend Bakshi's uncle, and Yvette's sister is a local cop. I've got another couple of connections, too, and if there's anybody left in Overfeld that doesn't know, it's because they haven't been online."

"I forget how small a town this is. Yes, a body was found, and I'll tell you what I know when I get washed. Assuming that you don't already know everything by then, that is."

I used up all of the hot water before I was sure I didn't smell like putrefying flesh, which would have been a dirty trick to play on Sid if cold showers bothered him. In fact, he didn't usually shower—he uses peroxide to keep his bones looking bright. This time was an exception. As soon as I got out of the bathroom, he went in. My clothes went straight into the washer, with extra soap. I knew I was overreacting, but between the bed bugs and the smell from the body, I'd rarely had a better excuse to seek maximum cleanliness.

Once that was taken care of, and I was dressed in clean shorts and a T-shirt, I sat down to tell Madison what had happened.

"I should have known you'd be right in the middle of it," she said once I was done. "You know, other mothers play bridge or collect pottery or learn new languages."

"Are you implying that finding dead bodies is my hobby?"

"Not so much implying as asserting. How many is this now?"

"It wasn't intentional," I said so I could avoid counting them out. "And anyway, Sid found this one."

"Hey, I'm not judging. If investigating murder is the way you roll, that's the way you roll."

"I'm not planning to investigate this one. We were just looking for the poor guy. Now that we know who he is, the cops can take over."

"Did Sid agree to that?"

"We didn't discuss it."

"And you really think he's going to keep his nasal cavity out of it? When it's somebody he knew, and he found the body himself?"

"Did he say something while I was in the shower?"

"No, but he went into his room and was doing something on his computer, so I figured he was getting started. And what are the chances that you'll let him investigate without you?"

"You know, it wouldn't hurt for you to be wrong about something once in a while."

"I'll remind you that you said that the next time I get a calculus test back."

I had to resist the impulse to thump her skull the way I do Sid's. She had nerve endings and might not appreciate it.

After that, I was expecting Sid to emerge and jump metatarsals-first into the case, but instead, when he came into the living room, his bones were hanging loosely. And while it should be impossible for a bare skull to have an expression that isn't a smile, Sid still looked terribly sad.

"Georgia," he said, "you've lost friends, haven't you?"

"I have."

"What did you do?"

Belatedly I realized that Neil/Erik was the first person Sid knew who'd died, at least since he died himself. "Come sit down with me." He flopped onto the couch, and I took one of his bony hands in mine. "It's never easy to lose a friend, Sid. Remember when my friend Doris Ann died earlier this year?"

"Doris Ann the librarian?"

I nodded. "She wasn't a young woman, and she'd been ill, so it wasn't the same as with your friend, but it was still hard to accept."

"You cried for her. I can't do that for Erik."

"I know, but you can remember him, and that's more important."

"What about a funeral?"

"I don't know where he'll be buried, but if it's local or if there's a memorial service on campus, I'll go and take you in the sugar skull bag."

"Is attending a funeral what I'm supposed to do?"

"It's not about what you're supposed to do—it's about what you want to do. Mom always says funerals are for the living."

"That lets me out," he said with a ghost of a smile.

"Okay, Bone Boy, funerals are for the survivors. Meaning that if it would make you feel better to go to a funeral, then we'll work it out, but if you can't or don't want to go, you can pay your respects in other ways.

"Like what?"

"You remember how I didn't go to Doris Ann's services because I couldn't afford to go to Ohio? I could have sent flowers or a card or food for the family. But Doris Ann had told people she wanted money sent in her name to the library she worked for, so I did that."

"Then I want to do something like that for Erik. I mean, for Neil."

"As soon as we find out more, we'll take care of it."

"Is there anything else?"

"Well, one of the things I always try to do is to let people know. When Doris Ann died, I called mutual friends and spread the word online."

"Coccyx, Georgia! I've got to tell Jen! And the rest of the party, too. They need to know."

"How?"

"I'll send them all a message via Runes of Legend and have them come online tonight."

"That sounds like a good idea. You set it up while Madison and I warm up some leftovers."

He still wasn't really smiling, but his bones were back where they belonged as he clattered off. By the time Madison and I got dinner onto the table, he was back.

"I got confirmation notes from everybody in the party," he said. "Except Erik, of course. The party just won't be the same without him."

With most people, I would have thought that mourning a game character instead of the actual person was tacky at best, and incredibly self-centered at worst, but it was different for Sid. Erik Bloodaxe had been his friend far more than Neil Farmer had been.

I said, "Why don't you sit with us while we eat and tell us about him?"

Now he smiled for real, and he started telling us tales of the mighty Erik Bloodaxe.

CHAPTER FOURTEEN

We rushed through dinner, and Madison volunteered to do the cleanup so that Sid and I could go online.

"Are you sure you want me listening in?" I asked. "These are your friends, not mine."

"But you're my best friend, Georgia. I want you here."

"Then I'll be happy to stay with you."

He checked the clock. "We've got a few minutes, so before we get started, I better give you a little introduction to the party. Gudron is our laeknir. That's a healer. Kiersten is our rune weaver—a kind of magic user—and she's great with fireballs and magic missiles. Jen is Odina, our skald—that's a tracker—and she uses a bow and arrow. And as you know, Erik Bloodaxe was our axe-toting berserker, our tank character."

"Got it. Gudron heals, Kiersten uses magic, and Jen/Odina tracks. What does your character do?"

"Skalle is a trickster, which is a buffer type."

"Meaning you come between what and what?"

"Not that kind of buffer. I make characters more buff. When I declaim, it increases my party's abilities and decreases the abilities of our enemies."

"What do you declaim?"

"Alliterative verse, of course. It's a Viking-based game."

"You do that on the fly?"

"I have some pre-existing poems, but sometimes I make them up as I go."

"I want to see some of those."

"They're not that good," he said in a way that made me think he was quite proud of them. I was definitely going to ask to see them at some point.

"Anyway," Sid said, "you can see this is pretty much a perfect party. All the basic character classes are represented, and Jen's right—there's no sexist crap. We get along great, everybody shows up on time, and we have the same attitude toward the game."

"Which is?"

"We take it seriously, but only as long as it's fun. Heavy on the roleplay, light on grinding through quests just to level up."

"Sounds like a good time to me."

"Yeah," he said sadly. "I hope this isn't the end of it. Without Erik Bloodaxe, the party is too weak on offense to get much further." He shook himself noisily. "Anyway, let's get logged on." He started clattering away on the keys. "I'm going straight to the Questing Dragon to set up a private chat room." He zipped past a screen with a map, clicked on a town, then a dragon sign hanging on a building, and then into a tavern scene where a grizzled character filled tankards.

"Nice graphics."

"Yup. But I'm trying to get into character now, so if you don't mind . . . ?"

"Sorry."

Sid's—or rather Skalle's—avatar showed up in the bottom corner of the screen. Sid had chosen a slender, red-haired avatar with a long aquiline nose, with his skeletal sigil painted on his chest plate. The main view of the screen was designed to make it look as if Sid was sitting at a rough wooden table with four empty chairs. In front of each place was a tankard of ale or mead or some appropriate virtual libation. After a few minutes, other avatars blinked into place in the other chairs. Fortunately, Gudron, Kiersten, and Odina were labeled onscreen, so I'd be able to follow along. The fifth chair remained empty, and I didn't need Sid to tell me that it should have been Erik Bloodaxe's spot.

The players started sending messages immediately.

GUDRON: *Seriously, Erik is blowing us off again?*

ODINA: *Your words are strange to me. Please speak in the tongue of this place.*

GUDRON: *Fine! It seems our erstwhile companion has once again left us to fend for ourselves, making our intended quest impossible.*

GUDRON: *And out of character, now. I'm out of here. No offense, I love roleplay as much as the next person, but that's not the only thing I'm here for. I'm not going to waste time logging in if Erik isn't going to bother showing up.*

KIERSTEN: *Mayhap he has met with some misfortune. We should arrange a gathering at a more favorable time.*

SKALLE: *Wait! I have dire news about our missing companion.*

ODINA: *???*

Sid paused, as if trying to decide how to word it. Then he started again.

SKALLE: *I know this is against the rules, but I just can't do this in roleplay. I'm going to have to talk about real world events, and I'll need to speak out of character.*

GUDRON: *It's okay with me.*

ODINA: *Agreed. Kiersten?*

KIERSTEN: *Go ahead.*

THE SKELETON MAKES A FRIEND

SKALLE: *I've been worried about Erik Bloodaxe for a while now. He's always been so dependable. As some of you may have guessed from things I've said, I've got some experience in investigation. So I started sniffing around the New England area to see if there were any incidents that might explain Erik's repeated absences.*

ODINA: *I was afraid something had happened, too, and I tried to look for him. Did you find him?*

SKALLE: *Sadly, yes. According to my sources, a man was stabbed to death in a place called Overfeld, New Hampshire. I have reason to believe this man was Erik Bloodaxe's IRL identity.*

GUDRON: *Are you sure?*

SKALLE: *Fairly sure. The man was stabbed with a miniature sword from the Runes of Legend collection. It's a replica of the sword Erik won in the Quest for Helva's Bane.*

GUDRON: *Could it have been the murderer's?*

KIERSTEN: *You think Erik is a murderer?*

SKALLE: *The sword was definitely the dead man's. He had the matching stand on his desk.*

ODINA: *When was he killed?*

SKALLE: *He was last seen alive Friday afternoon.*

ODINA: *Then he didn't blow us off after all.*

SKALLE: *No, he didn't. I thought you three would want to know.*

KIERSTEN: *Thank you.*

GUDRON: *Look, I don't want to be mean, but how do we know you're telling the truth?*

KIERSTEN: *Why would he lie?*

GUDRON: *Trolling. People make up all kinds of stories online.*

ODINA: *He didn't make up the murder. I heard about it. A man was stabbed on the campus of Overfeld College. You can Google it.*

KIERSTEN: *I believe you.*

ODINA: *It's okay if you don't. You should always check these things out.*

There was a pause. "I guess they're Googling," I said. Sid nodded, waiting.

GUDRON: *The report I found said he was stabbed with a letter opener and doesn't describe it.*

KIERSTEN: *Same here.*

ODINA: *I have a friend who works on that campus, and I could ask her for confirmation, but you'd have no particular reason to believe me, either.*

"I wonder who Jen's friend on campus is," I said.
"That would be you, Georgia."
"Oh. That's sweet."

KIERSTEN: *This is nuts. I believe you. Both of you.*

GUDRON: *I guess I do, too. Do the police know who killed him? Or why he was killed?*

SKALLE: *Not yet.*

ODINA: *Are you going to try to find out?*

GUDRON: *How could Skalle do that?*

ODINA: *Remember what he said. Skalle is a detective in
            real life. At least, I think he is. Are you, Skalle?*

"Coccyx, Georgia, what do I say now?"

"Tell them as much of the truth as you can. And who knows?
Maybe they've got information that will help."

He drummed his finger bones on the table for a minute before
going back to the keyboard.

SKALLE: *I do investigative work, but I can't really say
            more.*

GUDRON: *Sorry to be mean again, but this sounds kind
            of bogus.*

"She's not wrong," Sid said. "It does sound bogus. Because, as
you know, it is. Any suggestions?"

"Tell her you can't say more."

He did, and nobody responded for a while, though I could see
ellipses displayed over the other three avatars. "What do the ellipses
mean?"

"It means they're talking privately, without me being able to
listen in."

"I feel like I did in junior high school, when people would
pass notes around me. I was always paranoid that they were talking
about me."

"This time I'm not being paranoid. I'm sure they're talking
about me. Cross your finger bones that they don't log out." After
several minutes, the ellipses disappeared.

GUDRON: *Okay, let's say that we believe you. What are
            you planning to do?*

SKALLE: *What do you mean?*

ODINA: *We think you should investigate.*

Sid looked at me. "Georgia?"

"If you want to tackle this, I'm with you."

"You're sure?"

"Sure as sacrum."

The decision wasn't as offhand as it sounded. It wasn't just because sleuthing was my hobby, at least according to Madison, or because Sid was remarkably nosy for somebody who didn't even have a nose. What really convinced me was the fact that it was Sid's friend who'd been killed. Sid had always had my back, so how could I do any less for him?

SKALLE: *I'm not unwilling, but for all we know, the police might already have a suspect in mind for Erik's murder. Wait, should I call him Erik or his real name?*

KIERSTEN: *Use Erik. That's how we all knew him.*

SKALLE: *Okay then. The police are going to follow procedures to investigate Erik's death: forensics, canvassing for witnesses, digging into his finances and his known associates. They'll be better at all of that than I would be.*

GUDRON: *So you aren't going to do anything?*

"I can hear the skepticism dripping from her voice," I said.

"She's got a very acute bull-hockey detector," Sid said, but he said it fondly. "What do I say now?"

"Tell her you could lose your job if anybody found out you were investigating."

He hesitated. "I hate lying."

"Sid, your job is to help out with this family, right? If anybody found out that an ambulatory skeleton was up to anything, do you think you'd be able to do that?"

"I get it. I'm not technically lying."

> SKALLE: *I do want to help, but it's complicated. I could lose my job if word got out that I was investigating. Jurisdiction issues are a minefield.*

To me, he said, "Jurisdiction issues really are tricky. I never said they're tricky for me personally. I mean, I know I'm fudging, but—"

"It's for a good cause, Sid." I patted his scapula comfortingly.

> SKALLE: *Whatever I do, I have to do on an unofficial basis.*

> GUDRON: *Then you aren't going to do anything.*

> SKALLE: *I didn't say that. I'm just saying that I don't have the usual police resources at my disposal. I do have my own resources, though.*

> ODINA: *What kind of resources?*

> SKALLE: *The four of us, to start with.*

> GUDRON: *What good does that do? We didn't even know Erik's real name until today.*

> SKALLE: *True, but over the past few months, we've spent hours together. I know we were in character, but it seems like he must have let something slip about his real life.*

> ODINA: *I tried to think of something before, when I was trying to find him. There was nothing.*

SKALLE: *There might not be anything that said who he was, but there's a lot about what he was. I once read an article that said that the character one plays in RPGs says a lot about them.*

GUDRON: *Like what?*

ODINA: *Like the fact that you're very suspicious, Gudron, and tend to keep your distance, which probably indicates that you've been lied to in the past. Perhaps traumatically so. Kiersten hates conflict, so I suspect she's seen too many arguments in real life. Skalle makes a lot of jokes, but I think he's lonely. And it must be obvious to everybody that I can be socially awkward.*

KIERSTEN: *Wow. I guess we do know all that.*

GUDRON: *Yeah. What about Erik?*

KIERSTEN: *He was a good leader for the party. He took responsibility, yet let everybody have their say.*

GUDRON: *He was thoughtful. One time I mentioned I have a snake phobia, so he vetoed any quest that had reptilian monsters.*

ODINA: *He didn't care about the game prizes. He divided up treasure he could have kept as his own. He only cared about being a hero. I know, anybody can be brave in a game, but I think he wanted to be brave in real life.*

KIERSTEN: *Does any of that help, Skalle?*

SKALLE: *I'm not sure. You guys keep thinking, and if you come up with anything else, send me a message in game.*

GUDRON: *Will do. And now I've got to get going.*

KIERSTEN: *Before we leave, I was thinking that we should have a memorial for Erik. I mean, a virtual one. How about this same time, a week from Saturday?*

GUDRON: *Agreed.*

KIERSTEN: *I'll be here.*

SKALLE: *Count me in.*

Both Gudron's and Kiersten's avatars blipped out, but Odina was still there, looking at Skalle.

ODINA: *There's something I should tell you. I was sure you were a detective, and since I couldn't find any clues as to who Erik was, I went looking for you.*

SKALLE: *In real life?*

ODINA: *Yes. I should have brought it up here, but the Questing Dragon is supposed to be for roleplay.*

SKALLE: *I've broken that rule pretty thoroughly tonight.*

ODINA: *That's okay. It doesn't bother me as much when other people break rules, just when I do. I've been told I need to loosen up more, so maybe seeing others doing things for a good reason will help. At any rate, I wanted to apologize for violating your privacy, or at least trying to.*

SKALLE: *You were coming to me for help, and you trusted me not to be some kind of nutcase. Those are both huge compliments.*

ODINA: *I suppose that's true.*

SKALLE: *I'm sorry we can't meet in person. There are
           reasons, but I can't even tell you the reasons.*

ODINA: *That's okay. Everybody has rules they have
           to live by. I did want to ask if you really took
           that picture you posted. The one of the lake.*

SKALLE: *Yes, I took it.*

ODINA: *I'm glad.*

SKALLE: *Why?*

ODINA: *I used it to find the house I thought you were
           living in, though I'm told I made a fool of
           myself because obviously you weren't there.*

SKALLE: *I didn't mean to lead you on a wild goose
           chase.*

ODINA: *That's all right. I don't mind if you can't tell
           me everything, but I would mind if you lied.*

SKALLE: *I can't say I'll never lie to you, but I'll try not to.*

ODINA: *That's okay. Let me know if I can help you
           investigate.*

Her avatar disappeared.

"Oh my spine and femur," Sid said with a heavy sigh. "That was tough."

"You did a great job."

"You think? I don't have much experience interacting with friends."

"Excuse me? You've been my best friend since I was six years old. You played pirate treasure and mystery island games with me; you drank pretend tea at my teddy bear tea parties."

THE SKELETON MAKES A FRIEND

"Pretend tea is still my favorite."

"You listened when I had teenaged angst and grad student angst and maternal angst. You're a terrific friend, Sid."

He grinned a remarkably sweet grin but said, "It's different with us. I mean we are friends, but we're not *just* friends. We're more like family, don't you think?"

"Yeah, we are." We really were, even if not by blood.

He flashed that grin again, but just for a second. "You, and Madison, and the Doctors T, and Deborah. You're all family, which is wonderful, but it means I don't really have friends."

"Jen was right—you are lonely."

"Coccyx, Georgia, I wish you hadn't seen that."

"I wish I'd seen it before."

"No, no, no! I love living with you and Madison, your parents are great, and verbal sparring with Deborah is always a pleasure. It's just that sometimes I want more. And given my flesh-free lifestyle, I can't make friends the usual way, so all I've got is online friends, which is fine. But I still want to be a *good* online friend, even if I don't always know how to go about it."

"Oh Sid—" I wanted to tell him that he was wrong, but honestly, he had a point, and I didn't think it would be right to lie to him, which told me what I needed to say. "Yes, you do still have a lot to learn about being a friend, but that's okay. Even good friends make mistakes sometimes."

"Yeah?"

"All the time. Now I don't know Gudron and Kiersten well enough, but I do think that you and Jen can be friends, even if at a distance. Maybe you can't go out to the movies or attend each other's birthday parties, but there's no list of requirements for somebody to be a part of your life. Just as long as I'm still your *best* friend."

"Cross my chest cavity and hope to die again."

"All right then. Since we're on the case, do you want to start talking possibilities?"

"No, not tonight. I'd rather think about Erik some more."

"Do you want me to sit with you?"

"If you don't mind."

So I did, reading while he leaned against me. After she realized we'd gotten quiet, Madison came in with a book of her own and sat on his other side. Even Byron put his head at Sid's feet, without even taking a nibble.

Sid had said he couldn't cry, and he shouldn't have been able to, but I could have sworn I saw a tear drip down one cheekbone that night.

CHAPTER FIFTEEN

It wasn't until I arrived at Kumin Hall the next morning that it struck me that somebody in that building could have killed Neil Farmer. Sure, there might be something in his private life that had provided the motive, even something from his online gaming world, though I hoped for Sid's sake that neither Jen, Kiersten, nor Gudron were involved. But since Neil had been killed in his office, on-campus suspects were the obvious choice.

At first, I thought I was more suspicious than the other adjuncts because when I got to the auditorium, they were clustered together, talking a mile a minute. Then I heard what they were saying and realized that they were busy eliminating one another from suspicion.

"It's a tragedy, but I hardly knew the man," Treva said. "Neil did the screening interview, then sent me off to see President Fernandez and Ridley. The only other time I ever saw him was when I was filling out paperwork."

"Same here," Matt said. "Except we had coffee together because Fernandez and Ridley were running late the day I came in."

"What did y'all talk about?" Treva asked.

"Weather. The town. Insurance."

"Insurance?"

"Neil was in HR, and negotiating insurance was a big deal for him. He seemed nice enough."

"I found him to be both efficient and kind," Charles said. "It was he who suggested I take the dorm monitor position so I wouldn't have to make other living arrangements for the summer.

I took him out to lunch one day as a thank-you. He was quite pleasant, albeit reserved."

"Well, no matter what he was like, that was a terrible way to die," Treva said, shaking her head. Then she spotted me. "Hey, Georgia. Is it true you found the body?"

"Not exactly," I said. "I, um, smelled it."

"You want to run that past me again?"

"I went to use the bathroom in Dobson, and I noticed a bad smell coming from upstairs. I didn't know what it was until somebody went into Neil's office." The somebody had been Sid, not Mo or the maintenance guy, but I wasn't going to mention that. "I didn't see anything, if that's what you're asking."

"Even if you had, nobody would want you to relive a sight like that," Charles said.

Everybody expressed agreement, but I suspect some of them would have been glad to know more. I might have wanted to hear some of it myself, if I'd been in their position. As it was, having heard what I had from Sid, I was happy to remain fuzzy on the details.

"Have the police arrested anybody?" I asked.

"Not that I'm aware of," Charles said. "After your thoughtful warning last night, a pair of officers came to speak to me and the other dorm monitors to check on the security arrangements. I appreciated their concern for our safety."

"Are you sure it was for *our* safety?" Treva asked. "They might have been trying to figure out if any of us monitors could have gotten out to do away with that poor man. Or maybe they were looking at the Andorians."

"They're barely more than children," Charles protested.

"That may be, but kids younger than they are have killed before. I'm not accusing, mind you. I can't imagine any of the Andorians having spent enough time with Neil to have a reason to kill him, but the police might think that way."

"It's probably somebody from his personal life," Matt said. "I dated a cop for a while, and he said they always look at the victim's significant other first, then the family, then close friends. Most of the time, they don't have to look any further than that."

"He wasn't married," I said.

"How do you know that?" Treva said, looking suddenly suspicious. "Did you know him better than we did?"

"Mo told me when we were waiting for the police. She didn't think he was dating anybody either."

"Then they'll move on to his family," Matt said.

"Couldn't it have been a theft gone wrong?" Paul asked. "When I was working at Barnard a few years back, some people broke into the admin building overnight and stole most of the computers and printers."

"Or a serial killer?" Lisa put in.

"It does seem as if we've had a lot of murders on New England campuses in the past few years," Treva said. "Isn't that right, Georgia?"

"Excuse me?"

"Oh, come on, everybody's heard about what happened at Falstone earlier this year. And there was some hinky stuff at Pennycross, too, wasn't there?"

"Treva!" Charles said. "I'm surprised at you. Yes, Georgia has been unfortunate enough to be witness to some terrible events, but—"

"Get down off that high horse, Charles. I'm not saying anything that we don't all know."

"I don't know anything about any of this," Paul said.

Lisa said, "According to my friend Sara Weiss—"

"Forget what Sara Weiss says," I said. "I'm right here. If you've got questions, you can ask me. Unless you're asking me if I'm a serial killer. If I were, I certainly wouldn't tell you."

There was an uneasy ripple of laughter.

"I don't know what Sara told you," Charles said, "but I can assure you that Georgia's role in all these matters was entirely heroic. She helped solve the murder of a friend of mine, an adjunct like ourselves."

The other adjuncts looked moderately impressed, and Matt added, "I did hear that Georgia's kind of an amateur detective. That cop I dated knew a cop in Pennycross and said she found a missing heir, too."

"You make it sound like a bigger deal than it was," I mumbled, feeling heartily embarrassed.

Fortunately, I was rescued when Ridley, Mo, and President Fernandez came in and headed for the podium. Ridley looked harried and irritated, Mo's eyes were red from crying, and President Fernandez seemed to have aged a decade since I'd last seen him. Even his suit was looking creased. We adjuncts quieted down as students started coming in.

Charles sat next to me and whispered, "I hope you don't mind my defending you, Georgia, but I felt someone had to correct whatever version of the facts that Sara Weiss has seen fit to spread around."

"I appreciate it, Charles. I'm just not comfortable with people talking about me so much."

"All part of being an adjunct, I fear. One cannot escape the gossip."

He was absolutely right. We were a gossipy bunch. In fact, most of the time I enjoyed a good gossip session as much as the next adjunct. It's just that I was concerned about my sleuthing hobby being as well-known as it was beginning to be. It was hard enough to keep finding adjunct jobs year after year, and I didn't want to jeopardize my seemingly endless quest for a tenured or at least a permanent position by making myself notorious. In the eyes of some administrators, the fact that Sid and I had solved murders didn't make up for the fact that I might damage a school's reputation in the process. As it was, I was banned from teaching at Pennycross again, even though my parents had tenure there.

Back on the podium, Ridley didn't even bother to start with the usual movie and badminton announcements. Instead, President Fernandez took the microphone first. He took a deep breath and visibly gathered himself to stand taller.

"Scholars, I'm sure you're already aware that the body of a member of our Overfeld family was found here on campus last night. His name was Neil Farmer, and while I doubt most of you had dealt with him personally, I thought you should know that he had an important role in the Enrichment Program. It was Neil who screened the hundreds of CVs to choose the best possible instructors for you, and he worked with Ms. Heedles and Director Ridley to handle the logistics of our day-to-day operations. Though it was not part of his usual role, when the admissions person assigned to deal with your paperwork went out on maternity leave a month earlier than expected, he stepped in to handle paperwork and financial arrangements as well. So even though the majority of you never met him, I would ask us all to observe a moment of silence in his honor."

After a few minutes, Fernandez continued. "I strongly believe that Mr. Farmer would have wanted us to finish out the program. Not only would it be a hardship for many of your parents if we shut down early, but your instructors are determined to keep making this the best possible experience for you. So we will keep our schedule intact."

I was glad to hear that, both for financial and investigative reasons.

"As you've no doubt heard, Mr. Farmer was murdered, but you should not be concerned about your safety. We've brought in extra security to ensure your welfare, and the police will have a more active presence on campus as well.

"Speaking of the police, I understand officers came to the dorm yesterday evening and asked if any of you had seen anything suspicious to let them know. I would like to echo that request."

A student I recognized from my writing workshop raised a hand. "How can we help if we don't know when he was killed?"

Ridley made a face, but Fernandez said, "The police are still running tests to determine that, but I can say that the last time he was seen on campus was the Friday before last." Other hands came up, but Fernandez said, "I understand your curiosity, but at this point, there's nothing else I can tell you about the investigation." He waited until the hands went back down. "Your classes will be held as usual today, but should any of you wish to opt out, you are welcome to return to the dorm or to engage in quiet activities on the quad. Also, several of our campus counselors will be making themselves available should you wish to talk to them. Oh, and one other thing. The program administration offices have been temporarily relocated to this building so the police can complete their work in Dobson." He consulted his watch. "Classes will begin in ten minutes."

We instructors left immediately, and as we headed up the stairs, Matt said, "I'm surprised. I thought Fernandez would gloss it over. It's not like the Andorians knew the guy."

"Maybe not, but they knew he'd been found dead," Treva said. "It's better to be upfront about it."

I rather agreed with Treva, and I thought the tribute to Neil had been well done. I only wished that Sid had been there to honor his friend.

CHAPTER SIXTEEN

Most of my students did come to class, though a few came late. The humorous writing prompts I'd been planning to provide would have been wildly ill-timed, so instead I asked for volunteers to work on laying out the literary magazine we were putting together as our contribution to Parents' Day, and I let the rest work on whatever they wanted. They were quiet at first, but by the end of our class they were nearly up to their usual volume.

There was plenty of talk about Neil at lunch, enough so that I would have taken notes if I hadn't been trying to avoid any more discussion of my detective proclivities. To my relief, and perhaps because Charles was keeping watch, nobody mentioned them, at least not then.

It was after my afternoon class, in which the mood was almost normal, that the subject of sleuthing was raised again, and from an unexpected source.

After the last student left and I was packing up my things, President Fernandez came into my classroom.

"Dr. Thackery, do you have a minute?"

"Of course."

He closed the door before taking a seat at one of the student desks. "Please," he said, waving me to my own desk. "I don't wish to intrude, but it's come to my attention that Neil Farmer's murder is not the first one you've been in the proximity of."

"I'm afraid it's not," I said, my heart sinking as I wondered if I could get out of my rental agreement at the cabin.

"And I understand it was your observation that led to the discovery of Neil's body."

"It was, though somebody else would have noticed soon. It was getting to be pretty . . ." Stinky didn't sound polite. "It was pretty noticeable."

"Yes, I went to the building myself." He leaned forward. "You and I haven't spoken much, but given past events, I did want to make sure that this incident hasn't triggered any disturbing memories for you."

I hadn't expected that, and I was touched. "I'm fine."

"I know you're only in Overfeld temporarily, so I was worried you might not have an adequate support system."

"My daughter is here with me, and—" I stopped myself before mentioning I had my best friend in residence, too, "and I have friends among the other adjuncts."

"I'm glad to hear that. Feel free to avail yourself of the campus counseling services if you should want someone else to talk to. Or call me at any time if there's anything I can do." He pulled a card out of his pocket and handed it to me. "That's my personal cell phone number on the back."

"Thank you."

"While I'm here, I should commend you for your splendid work. I've had nothing but good reports."

"Then I take it you haven't spoken to Professor Hynes."

"As little as possible," he said, then looked embarrassed, as if realizing he'd been less than diplomatic. "Please forget I said that. I'm not at my best today."

"Who would be? This on top of the other glitches here on campus would be enough to put anybody off his game."

He sighed deeply, and for a moment the exhaustion showed. Then he stood and offered a hand. "Let's hope that the worst has passed. Again, if there's anything I can do, don't hesitate to ask."

Chapter Seventeen

As if President Fernandez's visit hadn't been enough of a surprise, when I got to the faculty parking lot, I got another. Jen Cater-Brame was sitting on the hood of my battered minivan.

She slipped off immediately and said, "I was careful. I didn't scrape the paint or make a dent. I'm not very heavy."

"That's okay, I'm sure it's fine. It's an old car anyway. Were you looking for me?"

"Of course. Why else would I sit on your car instead of on a bench?"

"Fair enough. How did you know it was my car?"

She gave me a look that said she wished I'd stop asking stupid questions. "I saw it at your cabin. A green minivan with Doctor Who and anime bumper stickers, and a deep scratch along the right side."

I should have known anybody observant enough to recognize our lake from a picture posted online would have been able to spot my car.

Jen said, "I knew you'd be parked in the faculty lot, and I guessed at how long you would take to get here after classes ended. You were a little later than I expected. I'm not criticizing you for that, of course. You didn't know I was waiting."

"I'd definitely have come sooner if I'd known you were. What can I do for you?"

"I came to tell you something."

"Do you want to talk here? Or we could go get ice cream."

She considered. "I don't think this is an appropriate conversation to have over ice cream, but something to drink would be good."

"There's a soda machine in Kumin Hall. We can get something, then find a place to sit."

"That would be all right, but I believe I should pay in this circumstance."

"That would be nice."

Once we had our Cokes in hand, we walked over to the town green and found a bench with nobody nearby.

"I found out what happened to Erik Bloodaxe," she said.

"That's your missing gaming friend, right?" I hoped it was reasonable for me to have remembered the name. Pretending not to know stuff that I actually knew was making my head spin.

She nodded. "He's dead."

"You mean in game?"

"No. In real life. His real name was Neil Farmer."

I tried to looked shocked. I don't think I did all that well, but as I'd learned, despite her attention to detail, Jen wasn't the best judge of normal reactions. "That's the man who died here. On campus, I mean. I sort of found him."

"How does one *sort of* find a body?"

I explained and then asked, "How do you know Neil Farmer was Erik Bloodaxe?"

"Skalle told me."

"Then you found him?"

"No, he told me in game. He really is a detective, despite what my mother thought. He heard about the case via his network of informers and realized it was Erik, and now he's going to be investigating the murder. I can't tell you any more. It's confidential."

"That's fine. I wouldn't want you violating any confidences." I took a swallow of my Coke, and she mirrored me. "All of this must have been a shock to you. Are you doing okay?"

"I don't know. I'm . . . I'm nonplussed."

I nodded, not knowing how else to respond to that.

"I was complaining about Erik missing a game when he only missed it because he was dead. That was inappropriate of me."

"But you didn't know—you couldn't have known."

"I realize that, but it still seems wrong. I mean, it's natural I felt irritation, but it's not proper to be irritated at a dead man. So what am I allowed to feel?"

"What did you feel when you did find out?"

"Shock. Sorrow. But still irritation about the game." She frowned. "No, it's more like regret. I'm unhappy that our party isn't going to be playing together anymore."

"Those all sound like reasonable reactions to me."

"And anger," she said, looking almost startled. "I'm so very angry at the person who killed Erik. I don't think I've ever been so angry."

"People get angry at death."

"Maybe it's because I don't understand it. One moment a person is there, and then he's gone. Where does he go? What does death feel like?"

"Those are questions people have been arguing about for a long time, and I don't think anybody has a definite answer."

"One time at one of the summer camps Mom sent me to, I went horseback riding," Jen said. "I didn't enjoy it. I didn't like the horse, and I don't think it liked me because it threw me off. One second, I was on the horse. The next second, I was on the ground. I don't remember anything in between. Do you think death is like that?"

"I don't know, Jen, I really don't. I don't think anybody does." If it had been Madison or Sid, I'd have reached out a comforting hand because I had no solid answers for her. The only person I knew who might be able to answer questions about what came after death was Sid, except he didn't remember anything about his previous life or his death. But it was Jen, so I kept my hand where it was. "Maybe that's why we get so angry, because we don't understand and we're afraid. Fear makes people angry."

"That makes sense." She sat for a minute longer. "I want to help Skalle."

My first thought was to warn her off, but in that respect, Jen was like any teenager. If I pushed her in the wrong direction, it could make her more determined to get involved. "What do you think you can do?"

"He's not local, so I thought I would talk to somebody on campus and find things out."

"That's an idea." Then I realized something. "Wait, are you asking me for information?" Confidential informant was a new role for me.

"Do you have any? You did find the body."

"I never saw it, but I'm told he was stabbed. The last time anybody saw him on campus was Friday afternoon."

"I knew all of that."

"He was due to be on vacation for a couple of weeks, which is why nobody reported him missing. He wasn't married."

"Is that all?"

"He was a nice guy. I only met him a couple of times, but he was good at his job and willing to help out in a pinch. People tell me he was very quiet and private."

"Why would anybody kill somebody like that?"

"That's the big question, isn't it?"

She finished up her Coke and said, "It's not a lot, but thank you anyway. I'll pass it on to Skalle."

"You do that. And Jen, do be careful who you talk to. What with a killer on the loose and all."

"I'll keep that in mind, but I don't have any campus sources other than you." She paused. "I don't think you killed Neil."

"That's good to know." A bit more certainty would have been nice, but with Jen, I'd take what I could get.

CHAPTER EIGHTEEN

Sid and Madison had the last of the leftover steaks warmed up for our dinner when I got back to the cabin, so I should have realized that they'd been up to something, but I was too hungry to make the connection right away. Besides, I had news for them.

I started with what had been said at the morning announcements, then went on to Fernandez's visit to my classroom.

"He sounds like a great guy," Madison said.

"Yeah, maybe," Sid said. "Assuming that concern for your welfare was his real reason for visiting."

"As opposed to what?" I asked.

"If I'd committed a murder and then found out that one of the people working for me was known to be a brilliant detective, I would certainly want to know what she was up to. Moreover, I'd want to encourage that brilliant detective to call me first if she found any clues."

"Whoa, that's paranoid thinking," Madison said.

"Paranoia is just another word for accepting that one has enemies, young Padawan."

"Padawan?" I said.

"Just a figure of speech," Sid said. "You know, from *Star Wars*?"

"Familiar with *Star* Wars, I am," I reminded him. "Aware of a motive why Fernandez would kill Neil, are you?"

"It's early days yet, Georgia. He could have all kinds of motives."

"Let me know when you find one," I said. "And speaking of Padawans, Skalle may have one."

"Another?" Madison said.

"What do you mean *another?*"

"Yeah, Madison, your mother is hardly my Padawan," Sid said, almost stumbling over his words. "Right? So what do you mean, Georgia?"

Okay, I knew I was missing something going on between them, but I ignored it for the time being so I could tell them about Jen's attempt to interrogate me. "I am having a hard time remembering what it is I'm not supposed to know, and Jen using me as a source only confuses the issue."

"Coccyx, Georgia, I don't want her getting into trouble, running around and talking to people. What if you'd been the murderer?"

"I'm not thrilled about it either. She said she doesn't know anybody else on campus, so I may be the only interview she had planned, but I still spent the drive home trying to decide whether or not I should tell Jen's mother what she's up to. On one hand, it would be betraying a confidence, but on the other hand, it might keep Jen safe."

"Jen trusts Skalle," Sid said, "so let me handle it. All I have to do is get her to promise not to interview any more sources."

"Will that work?"

"Can you imagine Jen breaking a promise?"

"No, which is a relief. Now, with my news out of the way, you can tell me what you two are up to. Because I know sure as sacrum that you haven't been playing in the lake all day."

Madison turned to Sid. "You owe me ten bucks."

"No way, you rigged the bet."

"Did I call myself your young Padawan?"

"No, but you did say, 'Another?' As if she wasn't going to catch that!"

"Might I point out that it was your idea to get dinner on the table? I told you, when a kid does extra chores, parents always know something is up."

"Ahem," I said. "Are you going to try to blame this on Byron next, or is one of you going to tell me what's going on?"

They went back and forth for a moment, mouthing, "You tell her!" "No, you tell her." At least that's what Madison was mouthing. I can't exactly read Sid's lips, since he has none, but I could extrapolate.

Apparently Sid won the battle because eventually Madison said, "Okay, you remember how I knew about the murder even before you two got home yesterday?"

"Right."

"Sid thought—and I thought, too—that if I could get that much information just from casual chatting, then there was no telling how much I could find out if I really went digging."

"And by digging you mean online, right? You didn't go anywhere?"

"Hey, would I let Madison go anywhere unsafe?" Sid said.

"How would I know what your Padawan training program involves?" I snapped.

Sid's eye sockets got big and round, and Madison said, "Should I leave?"

"No, I think we should all discuss this," I said in as even a tone as I could manage. "Sid, while we have established that I am not in charge of you, I am still in charge of Madison. You should not have gotten her involved in a murder investigation without my knowledge."

"I wanted to help," Madison protested.

"I'm sure you did, and you're very brave for doing so, but it wasn't that long ago that you were seeing a therapist because of what happened the last time you got involved."

"Can I at least tell you what I was doing?" she asked.

"I think you should."

"All I did was go on Discord—that's the social media program I use."

"I know what Discord is."

"Okay, I'm in a Discord for Wizard Gary's, and just about all of the other people there are local, so they were already chatting about the murder. They don't have many murders around Overfeld, and people are interested. Half scared, half morbidly curious. So really, almost all I did was follow their posts."

"Almost?"

"I did ask a couple of questions, but nothing overly specific that would look weird. Really."

"Okay," I said, relenting somewhat.

"I probably would have done the same thing even if you two weren't, you know, doing what you do. But knowing that the dead guy is Sid's friend, I wanted to help."

"I'm sure Sid appreciates that." I turned to him. "But I'd be a whole lot less mad if you two had texted me what you were doing instead of fixing dinner and springing it on me."

"You're right," Sid said. "You're right, and I'm wrong, and it won't happen again. From now on, I won't even talk about our cases in front of Madison."

"Hey!" she said.

"That's not right, either. Madison isn't a child, and she has a right to know what's going on in the household. But keeping her safe has got to be our number one priority."

"It is, and it always will be," Sid said. "Pinky swear supreme."

"Okay then. I probably overreacted, and I'm sorry. Sid, why don't you see if you can get in touch with Jen while we deal with the dishes?"

He rattled off, and Madison and I cleaned the kitchen in harmony. We finished up just as Sid returned, laptop tucked under one bony arm.

"It's all set," he said. "She said she wasn't comfortable with detective work anyway."

"I wouldn't think it would come naturally to her." I kind of wished it hadn't come naturally to Madison, either, but that ship had sailed.

"Now let's flesh out our files with what Madison found out."

"As if you'd know anything about flesh," I said but got settled on the couch with Madison. Sid was clearly on his best behavior after our disagreement—he let Byron claim the arm chair even though that meant he had to pull a seat in from the kitchen for himself.

"All right, Madison. Let's have it," Sid said, his laptop open and ready. Never, in all my years in academia, have I met somebody who likes taking notes as much as Sid does.

As it turned out, the amount of data Madison's buddies had provided was kind of scary. I'd lived in small towns before, but never anywhere that so much was known about a resident so quickly. After Madison spilled all she had, Sid added in info he'd found via social media, and then I contributed what I'd picked up at Overfeld.

Once he'd entered everything into his files, Sid steepled his hands in his favorite genius detective pose. "To sum up, Neil was a local boy, the only child of deceased parents. College graduate, but not from Overfeld College."

"Nobody from Overfeld goes to college here," Madison said. "They may work there, but they go to school elsewhere. Jen's mother isn't the only townie who dislikes the place."

I said, "Town-gown conflict is traditional, but I've never heard of anybody killing over it. Besides, Neil had worked at Overfeld for years."

"Seven years," Sid put in.

"So why kill him now?" I asked.

"We're still gathering facts, Georgia. No reaching for conclusions yet!"

"Sorry."

He consulted his file. "Neil was single, and his last long-term relationship broke up over a year ago. He was well-liked at work, though he did keep to himself. Not a member of any local fraternal or charity organizations. No pets."

"That's a relief," I said. "I'd hate to think of a pet left in his house all this time." I petted Byron's head.

"His police record is clean other than parking tickets. He was a social drinker and had no history with illegal drugs. Finances were fine as far as anybody knows, and he bought his house using the inheritance from his folks."

Madison said, "He was squeaky clean, wasn't he?"

Sid went on. "He was scheduled for two weeks of vacation. He was going to take the train to New York City for the first part and spend the rest doing household projects. That Friday was the last time he was seen, and he definitely left campus—he gave Mo a ride home."

"But he was killed in his office, right? What was he doing there?" I asked.

"Nobody knows," Sid said.

"What about his car? Has it been in the faculty parking lot all this time?"

"We don't know that, either."

"The only thing unusual in his background is his gaming, which is pretty benign," I said.

Madison said, "Apparently it was only online gaming. He never came to Wizard Gary's."

"Interesting." Sid tapped his chin with one finger bone. "Why would that be?"

"Are we into the conclusion phase?" I asked.

"Not yet, but I will allow speculation."

"Then I would speculate about what I said before, that Neil didn't want people to know he spent his time online with a virtual axe and sword. Plus one of the advantages to an online game is that you don't have to worry about leaving the house, or getting dressed, or personal hygiene."

"I'll have you know I freshen up before every game," Sid said.

"Trust me when I say you're an exception," Madison said. "One other thing. Yes, a lot of gamers play in real life as well as online, but with an RPG, sometimes it's an advantage to just be online so you can maintain the illusion. People I play with online don't think of me as a high school student with a blonde pixie cut. They see my avatar of a dragon hybrid with green eyes and a forked tongue, and react accordingly."

"What about online friendships?" I said. "I've heard stories about virtual conflicts bleeding into the real world."

"I don't think there's much like that in Runes of Legend," Sid said. "Player characters don't fight one another, only non-player characters, and there were no conflicts in our party."

"Social media?" I asked

Sid shrugged. "Nothing contentious on his Facebook page, his LinkedIn is all business, and I couldn't find a Twitter, Pinterest, Tumblr, or Instagram. Which isn't to say that he wasn't making enemies right and left on Reddit or in some other MMORPG, but we can't find out without access to his computer. I should have taken his laptop from the office when I found him."

"No you shouldn't have! What if there'd been tracking software on it? Let the police deal with that."

"It's not like we have a choice now, anyway." Sid scrolled through his notes. "There's not a lot here to work with. The ex-girlfriend was old news. A secret life as a gamer but in the most heroic of ways. Why was he going to New York again?"

"To visit the Met, go to the top of the Empire State Building, and see *Hamilton* and *Aladdin*," I said. "And while *Hamilton* is a tough show to get into, I don't think anybody would kill over a single ticket."

"Could Jen be a suspect?" Madison asked tentatively. "I mean she almost found Sid. Maybe she did find Erik/Neil, killed him, and was coming after you next."

"As your mother, I encourage you to think out of the box, but as a more experienced amateur detective, I have to point out that Jen has no motive."

"Serial killers don't always have recognizable motives."

"Do you honestly think Jen could be a serial killer?"

Sid said, "We're still speculating, so I'll put it down as a possibility. An extremely remote, unlikely possibility."

Madison said, "I just can't think of a reason why anybody would want to kill Neil. Face it, the guy was boring."

"He was a nice guy," Sid snapped. "Why is that a bad thing?"

Madison blinked. Sid didn't snap very often—in fact, I couldn't think of a single time he'd ever snapped at Madison. I started to intercede, then stopped myself. It wasn't enough for Sid and me to continue working out kinks in our relationship—he and Madison had to coexist, too.

"I didn't say it was bad," Madison said. "It's just that he seems like too ordina—I mean, too nice a guy to be a murder victim."

"Nice guys get killed, too," Sid said softly.

"Oh God," she said, and I knew she'd forgotten that Sid himself had been murdered. "I'm sorry, Sid. I didn't mean . . . Of course nice guys get killed, and I shouldn't have made fun of your friend."

"It's okay," he said.

Even so, it seemed like a good time to put the case aside for the evening. We switched to TV and laundry, and dishing up some of the dark chocolate ice cream from Sunday made for a sweet ending to a cranky evening.

CHAPTER NINETEEN

Wednesday started out much more pleasantly. The weather was clear, the traffic was light, the other adjuncts weren't looking at me as if I were a nutcase, and no dead bodies were brought up at morning announcements. My workshop went well, too—the students were nearly finished laying out their magazine, and I was confident we'd make our deadline the next day. Admittedly, it was a low bar for improvement, but it was appreciated just the same.

I was feeling almost normal until I ran into Mo at lunch. She looked better than she had on Tuesday but still wasn't back to her usual cheerily efficient self.

"How are you doing?" I asked her.

"I'm all right," she said. "My husband made me take a sleeping pill last night, and that helped."

I knew I should grill her for more background information about Neil, but I couldn't bring myself to do it when she looked so unhappy. Fortunately, she seemed to want to talk.

"It still doesn't seem real, you know. Neil was so excited about his trip. He got his ticket to *Hamilton* months ago, and he played the soundtrack over and over again. Then for him to be gone. . ."

"Have the police made any headway?"

"Not a lot. They're pretty sure he was killed Friday night because he was wearing the same clothes I'd seen him in earlier, and they don't think it was premeditated because he was killed with a letter opener he kept on his desk. He just got it a few months ago, too."

"Have they figured out why he was back on campus?"

"No, but I did hear the power was out at his place that night—there was that bad thunderstorm we had—and Neil had his laptop, so maybe there was something he wanted to do online. But why come here? It's not like our Wi-Fi is all that good, and he could have gone to a restaurant or the bookstore."

Now that she mentioned it, I remembered Sid had said that he'd seen lights burning at Neil's house. They must have been on when the power went out and then come back on when it was restored. "Do the police even have an idea of what happened?"

"Not a decent one! First Chief Bezzat thought it was a robbery gone wrong, which isn't totally moronic, except that nothing was missing. Then she started talking about a sexual encounter gone wrong, which is crazy. Neil had dated a few women, but none recently. I'm not saying he never had a one-night stand, but he was a professional and would never have brought a hookup into the office! Why would he when he could have taken her to his own place? Plus, like I said before, he had his laptop. What was that for? To watch online porn for a warm-up? I could tell she had no clue when she started asking if he could have been dealing drugs. Dealing drugs out of a college HR office?" She snorted.

"It doesn't seem very likely, does it?"

"Not at all. And none of those crazy theories would explain why his car was left parked by the train station."

"Is that where it was?"

"Parked in the lot across the street, but that makes no sense, either. Sure, he was planning to take the train to New York, but not until late in the day Saturday, and his luggage was still at his house."

"Maybe he didn't park it there himself," I said.

"You think the killer did it?"

"Possibly, but I can't imagine a burglar, hookup, or drug dealer going to the trouble."

"This is crazy. Things like this just don't happen in Overfeld."

I had no answer for that, so we moved on to the funeral arrangements, such as they were. Neil had only distant family, and his will had specified no formal services, so once the body was released by the police, he was going to be buried quietly. Overfeld was planning a memorial service for him, but they'd decided to wait until the fall.

"That's when the regular faculty and the rest of the staff will be back," Mo explained. "I mean, most of you summer guys didn't really know him."

"No, you're right, we didn't." I did, however, know why he'd been back on campus the night he was killed. Or at least I thought I did.

Once my second writing workshop was busily working, I texted Sid.

> GEORGIA: *I know why Erik came back to Overfeld the night he died.*
>
> SID: *Why?*
>
> GEORGIA: *You remember the thunderstorm that night? Electricity went out at his house, and what do you want to bet the internet was out, too?*

There was a long pause.

> GEORGIA: *Sid?*

No reply.

> GEORGIA: *Sid?*
>
> SID: *Are you saying he died because he wanted to play Runes of Legend with us?*
>
> GEORGIA: *NO!*
>
> SID: *Are you sure?*

CHAPTER TWENTY

I had to get to my afternoon class after texting with Sid about Erik, and if Professor Hynes had picked that day to observe me at work, he'd have found plenty of nits to pick. Maybe the Andorians didn't realize it because they were involved in their projects, but my mind was definitely elsewhere.

Specifically, it was trying to figure out what could be worth killing for in a Human Resources office.

There was lots of confidential employee information in the files, of course: addresses, phone numbers, work backgrounds, family members, maybe even references to criminal records. If anybody was on the school's insurance, there could be data about health issues, including mental health and substance abuse problems. Probably the most sensitive of all would be records of employee compensation. Most adjuncts in a given college were paid the same amount, regardless of experience or education, but staff and permanent faculty were a different story. Unless they were unionized, they negotiated their salaries individually, and most people have a sneaking suspicion that somebody else is being paid more for the same work.

I concocted so many scenarios that I could have kept a dozen writing workshops busy for years. But while none of them were completely impossible, no one of them struck me as more likely than the others.

When class ended, the first Andorian to reach the door stopped, picked something up off the floor, and handed me a large envelope. "This is for you. I guess it got slipped in under the door."

"Thanks," I said, taking it from her. It was an interoffice envelope, the resealable kind with a button and string closure and rows of lines so you could reuse it repeatedly, though my name was the only one written on this one. In the age of emails and texts, I rarely saw them anymore.

As the last of my students left, I sat back down and opened it. Inside were five letters, or rather five photocopies of letters. Each seemed to have been sent from a different person—I couldn't tell for sure because the return addresses and signatures were covered with black boxes, but the fonts and letterheads were different. I started to read the first one:

Dear President REDACTED,

As a loyal alumna of Overfeld, I have agonized over this decision, but I've come to realize that I must tell the truth, no matter how much pain and embarrassment it causes me. When I was a student, I was sexually abused by Professor Davidson Hynes.

I stopped and, while still holding the letters, closed and locked my classroom door. Only then did I feel safe enough to continue reading.

The story is much the same as we've all read in the newspapers. Professor Hynes . . . No, I will not give him that honorific. Hynes started taking an interest in me while I was taking his course in REDACTED. He invited me to meet with him in his office and convinced me that my work was something that he wanted to encourage. I might have been suspicious if he'd been entirely positive—I knew my own flaws—but he salted his compliments with chiding for the times I'd skimped on studying and failed to write a second draft of a paper that would have strengthened it. So I believed—and was incredibly flattered by—his interest.

Our first two meetings were during normal office hours. The third was in the early evening, and we were the only ones in the building. I was uneasy at first, but nothing untoward occurred that time or the next. It was at the fifth meeting that things changed.

When I arrived, he offered me coffee, as he had done every other time. But this time, he sat next to me on the sofa, rather than in the chair across from me, and as we spoke, he caressed my arm, my hand, and then my thigh. He continued to talk as he touched me. He told me what he could do for my career, how he could ensure the brightest of futures for me. I tried to tell him I didn't want it, not that way, but he never stopped. I don't know if you would term it seduction or rape, but I knew, even as it was happening, that it was wrong.

When he'd finished, he sent me on my way, saying only that we would talk soon. But we never did. I saw him in class, but he never spoke to me in any other context again.

I didn't tell anyone it had happened, and I certainly never confronted Hynes. Even if I'd been strong enough to bring it to the attention of the administration, I had no faith that I would be believed. I was a lowly undergraduate, and I had been known to drink and carouse. He was Davidson Hynes, the star scholar of Overfeld College.

Instead I stopped coming to his class. Despite that, he gave me a high grade, which somehow made it worse, as if I'd been paid for services rendered. I spent the next two years avoiding him on campus, and at commencement, I blurred my faculties with a stiff shot of whiskey because I knew he would be on the rostrum for the community to admire him. I wanted nothing more than to forget about what had happened.

But even REDACTED years later, the memory still cuts, and I've come to realize that it's time to speak up. I confess to craving some small measure of revenge, but even more, I've realized that I am unlikely to be Hynes's only victim. So I am writing to ask you to do now what I did not do then—stop Hynes from traumatizing other students.

The signature was blacked out.

"Coccyx," I said softly.

I didn't want to, but I made myself read the other letters, two from other women, two from men. Hynes had used identical techniques each time—encouraging and criticizing students, slowly winning their confidence, and then abandoning them after he was done with them. And every bit of identifying information, names and dates and even the names of the classes, had been redacted.

CHAPTER TWENTY-ONE

I started to shove the letters back into the envelope, but then imagined a situation in which they went missing, leaving me with no proof that they ever existed. So I pulled them back out, took as clear a picture of each as I could manage with my cell phone, and emailed them to myself. Only then did I feel safe to return them to the envelope and put the envelope into my satchel, which I clutched considerably more tightly than usual.

Mo called to me as I walked past the temporary administration office on the first floor. "Did you get that envelope?"

"I got an envelope," I said cautiously. "Was it from you?"

"No, just interoffice stuff that got put in the main box. I slid it in under the door so I wouldn't interrupt your class."

"Thanks. You know, I almost never see these envelopes anymore."

"We don't use that many either, but a lot of the older professors won't do email, so we have to run pickups and delivery every day to keep them happy."

"Got it," I said. "See you tomorrow."

"Hey, are you going to have that magazine ready to go to the printer soon?"

"By this time tomorrow," I said with assurance, though at the moment I couldn't even remember how far along we were.

"Good deal. See ya!"

I started to go, and she stopped me again.

"And Georgia? Thanks for listening today at lunch. It helped."

"Anytime." I mustered up a smile before finally making my escape.

I got back to the cabin in record time. Sid and Madison were just coming inside from the lake.

"Hi, Mom!" Madison said. "I won't hug you because I'm wet. Catch you when I get out of the shower."

"You bet."

Meanwhile, Sid was regarding me with narrowed eye sockets. "What's wrong?"

"I got something slid under my classroom door," I said and tried to get it out of the satchel.

"Georgia, your hands are shaking."

He was right. I had no idea if it was fear or outrage or both. I managed to get the envelope out and handed it to Sid. "Look at what's inside."

By the time he'd finished the first paragraph, he was cursing under his breath in his own particular vernacular and didn't stop with the bone names until he finished the fifth letter. "Where did these come from?"

"Mo said that envelope came via interoffice mail, but I was afraid to ask for details."

"I don't blame you. These letters are political dynamite—they could destroy Hynes's career."

"Ask me if I care! If he's been pulling this kind of thing, he deserves to be fired! Just for starters!"

"Why haven't they already fired him?"

"You know why, Sid. Overfeld must have been sitting on this because it's Professor Davidson Hynes, the most eminent scholar at prestigious Overfeld College. You know sure as sacrum that if it had been an adjunct who did anything like that, he'd have been fired and blackballed after the first letter, and I'd have cheered them on when it happened. But Hynes? Him they protect!"

I was too angry to keep still, so I started pacing around the room. "Not only could this ruin Hynes, it could bring down the whole college. Overfeld is already in trouble, and if it comes out that they've been turning a blind eye while Hynes assaults students, it could be the final straw."

"So why were these sent to you?"

"In that I got them the day after the other adjuncts gave me a hard time about playing detective, I have to think that somebody wants me to go after Hynes."

"As if I'd let you go after Hynes alone."

"Well, nobody on campus knows about the awesome power that is Sid."

"True. But this approach still seems odd. If they wanted to implicate Hynes, why not send the letters to the local paper?"

"I don't know. Maybe an Overfeld grad owns the paper."

"Overfeld grads don't own every newspaper in the state, or the TV stations, or the radio stations. They could have put them up on the web. But they sent them to you instead." He drummed his finger bones on the table. "Do you think this has something to do with Neil's murder?"

"I was so shocked I didn't even think about that, but if it's not, it's an awfully big coincidence that the letters showed up just now."

He looked back over each page. "Any one of these could provide a murder motive—either for the victims or their parents or spouses. For anybody who loved them. But they'd have wanted to kill Hynes, not Neil."

"Unless . . ." I had a nasty thought that Sid wasn't going to like. "Say the administration knew about these letters and somehow convinced the people involved to keep it quiet."

"How?"

"Paid them off, got nondisclosure agreements, played on their loyalty to the school. Whatever."

"Meaning they covered it up?"

"It's a possibility."

"Why would Neil be involved?"

"What if the killer wasn't going to Neil's office? There are three offices in the Human Resources suite."

"Then whose office was he going to?" Sid asked, then snapped his fingers so he could answer his own question. "He wasn't going to an office—he was going to the file room! And I bet there's more information about the arrangements in those files. You know, we could—"

"No, Sid, I am not helping you break into a crime scene that might still be active. Not to mention trying to dodge the extra security on campus." I also wasn't eager to be anywhere near that office again. Maybe they'd been able to air out the Dobson Building successfully, but I suspected I'd always smell decomposition in there whether or not it was actually present. "Anyway, if there's a link between the letters and Neil's death . . . What if Neil was involved in the cover-up?"

"No. No way."

"It would explain a lot."

"No! Neil wouldn't cover up something like this!"

"How can you be so sure?"

"Because I am. There must be another explanation."

Logically, I knew Sid could have been blinded by his loyalty to his friend, but just as logically, an adjunct English professor shouldn't have been trying to solve a murder while working in partnership with an ambulatory skeleton. So I was going to forget logic and go with Sid's gut, or lack thereof. "Okay, maybe it's the other way around."

"Meaning what?"

"Even with dates and other information redacted, these letters look old to me. A couple of them were typed, not printed. So who knows how long they've been rattling around in the files? What if Neil found them and was planning to use them to expose Hynes, and—"

"I thought we decided that Neil was only on campus to play Runes of Legend. So Hynes—"

"It wouldn't have to be Hynes," I had to say, despite my ever-increasing dislike of the man. "It could be somebody who was trying to protect him."

"Fair point. But whoever it was wouldn't have expected Neil to be in the office." He held up a bony finger. "Unless he arranged for Neil's power to go out and waited for him at the office."

"I don't think that works. The only reason Neil went to his office rather than a coffee shop was so he could have privacy for the game, and nobody at Overfeld seems to know about him playing. I think we have to go with the police conclusion—the murder wasn't premeditated, which is why the killer didn't have a weapon and had to grab the miniature sword."

"Agreed," Sid said.

"What if the killer found out about the letters and went to get them to use against Hynes?"

"It could have been a blackmail attempt."

"Good thought. Anyway, Neil caught him sneaking around, wanted to know what was going on, and was stabbed so the guy could get away."

Sid went to the window and held the letters up in the sunlight. "There are no bloodstains that I can see. And trust me when I say there was a lot of blood in Neil's office."

"These are photocopies. It would have been the originals in the files, and those are the versions that would be bloodstained."

"Right. So where did these copies come from?"

I went back to speculating. "Obviously somebody found out about the letters. Call him X. Then, somehow Hynes or somebody trying to shield Hynes . . ."

"Call him Q."

"Okay X finds out about the abuse and the letters. He decides to expose Hynes or possibly blackmail him. Q finds out, and not knowing X has made photocopies, sneaks into Dobson to get the originals out of the files. Neil stumbles in on him, and Q kills him. Now X is scared to come forward because of the murder, so when he finds out there's an amateur sleuth around, he decides to get her involved."

"I guess," Sid said, unconvinced. "Should we jettison the blackmail idea, going on the assumption that an attempted blackmailer wouldn't care about Neil being murdered?"

"Probably. I suppose even a blackmailer could have a conscience, but it's more likely that he'd just abandon the scheme. I think that makes X kind of a good guy."

"Except for putting you in Q's crosshairs," Sid said indignantly.

"I'm only in danger if Q finds out I've got these, and I'm not planning to tell anybody connected with Overfeld or Hynes until we know a whole lot more."

"So how do we figure out who Q is without Q finding out about us?"

I sat back down. "I've got nothing."

"Me neither." He slid the photocopies back into the envelope. "I knew Hynes was scum. Him and his disgusting coffee."

"There was nothing wrong with his coffee."

"Oh yeah? Google *kopi luwak* sometime. And no matter how good his coffee is, he's a creep!"

"Who's a creep?" Madison said.

She was freshly bathed and blow-dried and looked so young, and all I could think of was how I'd feel if I found out somebody like Hynes had abused her. I jumped up and hugged her as if I hadn't seen her in months.

"Okay, that was more enthusiastic than I expected," she said, her voice muffled from being pressed into my shoulder.

I pulled back enough so I could look her in the eye. "Madison, you'd tell me if anybody tried to harass you, right? Sexually, I mean?"

"Are you worried about online stalking again?"

"No, I'm talking about real life. Like if somebody tried to talk you into something you didn't want to do?"

"Of course I'd tell you."

"Promise me!"

"I promise, but Mom, you're freaking me out. What's going on?"

With a few footnotes from Sid, I told her about the letters and, when she insisted, let her read them.

"Man, that is messed up," she said. "Not only is that guy a major creep, but there's no telling how many more people he's pulled this on."

"Why do you think there are more?" Sid asked.

"Because these guys never stop on their own." When she saw my face, Madison added, "I am not speaking from personal experience, Mom, but this stuff is all over the web."

"You're right, if an abuser isn't caught, he'll just keep going," I said. "The thing is, it's rare to have this kind of behavior continue for years without causing at least a few rumors, at least among people in the field."

"So who do we pump for these rumors?" Sid asked, noisily rubbing his hands together.

"I don't think I can go to any of the staff on campus, not until we have a better idea of who might be involved. And I can't use the adjunct network because Overfeld almost never uses adjuncts. Plus there aren't that many who are both plugged into gossip and who I can trust not to tell anybody I'm asking questions."

"Oh dear," Madison said in an exaggerated monotone. "If only we knew somebody with long-standing ties to the academic community, who has connections at universities all over the country, and yet who could be trusted with anything. Or even two such somebodies."

It took me a second, but finally I caught on. "Right. Good idea. I'll call Mom and Phil after dinner."

"Georgia," Sid said proudly, "we should have made Madison a Padawan years ago."

CHAPTER TWENTY-TWO

We'd just about run out of leftovers from Phil's grilling frenzy, so we went simple for dinner: ham and cheese sandwiches, pickle spears, and lemonade served on the picnic table by the lake. Sid even joined us, though he did swath himself in a hooded sweatshirt and sweatpants, just in case somebody came by on the lake. Nobody did, and it was refreshingly peaceful to sit and watch the sunlight fade as we ate. By mutual consent, we didn't speak about the case but tried for more cheerful topics. Which, since it was us, turned into a discussion of which Marvel superhero was the toughest.

Sid and Madison were debating the strengths of Captain America, Black Panther, and Squirrel Girl when I moved far enough away that I could use my cell phone to call home.

"Hello, Georgia," Phil said.

"Hi, Phil. How's the dining room?"

"I admit it does look considerably more elegant. I'll have to send you some photos. One grows so accustomed to how one's home looks that it's hard to realize when it's time to refresh. Fortunately, Deborah provides perspective."

"That and a certain lack of sentimentality."

"Perhaps she's not sentimental when it comes to paint and plaster, but she does still have the first lock she ever picked mounted in a place of honor at her office."

"That sounds like her. Speaking of picking . . . I need to pick your brain about something, and it's extremely delicate."

"Would this have anything to do with the murder victim found at Overfeld?"

"Possibly." I explained what I knew about the murder and the letters I'd been given. "It seems to me that if Hynes has been taking advantage of students for all this time, there has to have been some scuttlebutt floating around. My sources are no good for this, but I thought you might know more."

"If I'd heard even so much as a whisper about this, I would have warned you before I let you set one foot on that campus," he said sharply.

"Of course you would have. I'm not thinking. Those letters really have me shaken up."

"Not to mention the murder."

"Yeah, that, too."

"At any rate, let me consult Dab. I'm sure she knows nothing, either, but she might have some ideas of who we can talk to in order to find out more. I'll try to get back to you this evening, but you know how your mother is when calling people. Once she's on the phone, it's difficult to get her off again."

"I know what you mean." Actually what I knew was that Phil was the one who could talk for hours, but since Mom would be there to keep him on target, I was willing to let him believe the opposite was true.

I hung up and said, "Phil hadn't heard anything, but he and Mom are on the job."

"Good," Sid said. "We need to go watch *Captain America: Civil War* to compare the fighting prowess of Captain America and Black Panther."

"Squirrel Girl is out of the running?"

"Of course not—she's unbeatable. We're trying to decide on the second-place winner."

The issue remained unresolved, even after watching the DVD and all the extra features, but at least the cinematic slugfest helped clear my mind of nastier conflicts.

I didn't hear anything from my parents that night, but when I got up the next morning, there was a text directing me to check my email. I went to Sid's room as soon as I'd read it.

"I just heard back from Mom and Phil," I said. "Zilch."

"Nothing at all?"

"Phil said they heard about some not-quite-unethical ways Hynes has treated other academics, and of course, everybody knows his ego is monumental and that he's the oldest angry young man in the history of angry young men. But there's never been the slightest hint that he's treated students inappropriately."

"Huh." Sid scratched his skull. "Tell you what. I'll hit the web today to search for rumors and innuendos. Maybe other academics don't know anything, but there are sites where students rate their profs, and—"

"I will leave it in your capable metacarpals," I said before he could tell me all the sites he was planning to visit. "I've got to get to work."

That morning's announcements were all about the upcoming Parents' Day festivities, which reminded me that I owed Mo the final layout of the magazine my students were producing. They'd finally decided on a title—*Andorians Ad Astra*—and one of the students had come up with a cover design that everybody loved. Well, eighty percent loved it, and the other twenty percent didn't gag at the sight, which was better than it could have been. In the first class, we focused on proofing pages online. Then I printed the whole magazine so the second class could proof that version. Just as the session ended, I saved a completed file to thunderous applause.

Being a belt-and-suspenders gal when it came to such things, I both emailed the file to Mo and saved it to a thumb drive. Then I printed a copy of the final version, so she'd know if the printer screwed anything up, and headed downstairs to personally deliver both printout and thumb drive.

"You got it done!" she said when I handed it to her.

"We did. Feel free to admire it."

"It looks great," she said as she flipped through it. "The parents are going to go crazy over this. Who knew high school students could be so creative?"

"They're a talented bunch. I wouldn't be at all surprised if some of them go pro someday."

The door to the office opened, and I saw the man I least wanted to see that day: Professor Hynes. He led in a group that included President Fernandez; a blonde woman and a dark-haired woman wearing crisp business suits and heels who looked nothing like academics; and a man maybe ten years older than I was whose khaki pants, white short-sleeved Oxford shirt, and leather messenger bag screamed academia. That last person looked familiar, though I wasn't sure if it was his face or his not-quite-a-uniform.

"This is our temporary administration office," Hynes was saying, "and our able administrative associate Ms. Heedles. You're going to want to talk to her—she knows all there is to know about Overfeld. Mo, this is the delegation from Hardison Business School."

There was a volley of pleased-to-meet-yous.

Then Hynes spotted me, his mouth tightened, and he ostentatiously turned in the other direction. He really hadn't liked what my father had said to him.

President Fernandez looked at Hynes questioningly and said, "Good afternoon, Doctor Thackery." He spoke to the group. "Doctor Thackery is one of the instructors for our Enrichment Program, though unfortunately for us, she's only here for the summer."

"Why temporary?" the dark-haired woman said.

"She's an adjunct," Hynes said with a sneer. "That's like a temp, only with an advanced degree."

"I mean why a temporary office?" she said, looking surprised by Hynes's tone.

Fernandez stepped in. "Since we had to move operations out of the Dobson Administration Building, we decided to take advantage of the time to freshen up the facility. Ms. Heedles and her colleagues will be working here through the fall."

"Why did—?" she started to say, but the blonde woman whispered something in her ear. "Right, that's where—"

"I'm afraid so," Fernandez said. He pointed at the pages Mo was still holding. "Is that the student literary magazine?"

"All ready for the printer," she said, handing it to him. "It looks fabulous."

He turned pages while the others peered over his shoulder, and I kept my fingers crossed that the Andorians hadn't missed any obvious typos.

Fernandez looked pleased, the women looked moderately interested, and Hynes looked in the other direction. The academic-looking man said, "High school students did this all themselves?"

"I made a few suggestions and kept warfare from breaking out over which typeface to use, but yes, this is their baby."

"I'm impressed."

Hynes actually scoffed. "Don't you think it would have been more valuable for the students to focus their attention on their actual writing, and not the minutiae of publication?"

"Not at all," I said. "I find that students respond well to the experiential nature of producing a magazine, and the cross-disciplinary challenge of combining graphics and text makes for a very compelling learning paradigm."

Hynes blinked, and I think he was trying to decide if he'd been mocked or complimented. When I bared my teeth at him, he figured it out.

"Now then," he said with forced joviality, "let's continue on our way."

Fernandez looked confused at the abrupt segue but handed the printout back to Mo and followed him and the others out.

Once the door had shut behind them, Mo said, "So how did you get on the great man's poop list? No, don't tell me. You didn't worship his every word when he bestowed coffee upon you."

"Actually, it's because of when my father was visiting. He may have implied that Hynes wasn't as young as he used to be."

She snickered but said, "Oh, I shouldn't laugh, Georgia. You need to be careful with that guy. He holds grudges like nobody's business, and I've known him to pull a few dirty tricks over the years."

"Yeah? Did you ever get a vibe from him? Like a creeper kind of vibe?"

"From Hynes? No, never. No matter how big his ego got—and it's plenty big—his one redeeming characteristic was always how much he loved his wife. To be honest, she was just as big an egotist as he is and always had this let-me-talk-to-your-manager expression on her face, but they were made for one another. I don't think he ever so much as looked at another woman while she was living. She's been gone a couple of years now, but I think he's still mourning her."

"Wow. I'd feel sorry for him if he hadn't just called me a temp. Not that there's anything wrong with being a temp, but the way he said it sure implied that there is."

"Yeah, he did make it sound like it was the lowest of the low. What a snob!"

"So what was with the tour?"

She looked away. "Oh that. Um, just a visit, I guess."

"Hardison is near here, isn't it? In Northbury?" I maintained a list of New England colleges who might someday want to hire me, either as an adjunct or something more permanent, but business schools were outside my target range, so I didn't know much about Hardison.

"I believe so."

"Is it a good school?"

"I don't really know—I suppose so." She checked through the printout again for no reason that I could determine. "Well, I better get this sent to the print shop. You have a good day." She started fiddling with her computer.

Mo was such an incredibly bad liar that I was almost impressed. I thought about trying to get more out of her, but she looked genuinely flustered, and she really did need to get the magazine printed, so I let it go. "See you tomorrow."

I was halfway across the quad when I heard my name being called. I turned and saw the academic-looking representative from the business school group trotting toward me.

"Hi! It is Georgia, isn't it?"

"Yes. I'm sorry, I didn't get your name."

"Walker Schild."

"Nice to meet you."

He grinned. "You don't remember me, do you?"

I looked at him more carefully, then got a mental picture of the same guy, only skinny, poorly-shaven, and frantic to finish his dissertation. "Oh my spine and femur, you were one of my mother's pet grad students!"

He laughed, and I realized what I'd said.

"I'm sorry, I meant to say that you studied with my mother."

"No, you were right the first time. She did kind of adopt me, as if I were a little lost puppy. I was so broke in grad school that I could have starved if she hadn't kept feeding me. I remember you giving me dirty looks one time because you got home from school and I'd eaten the last of the Oreos."

"That's right. Would it have killed you to have eaten the Chips Ahoy! instead?" Those had been Deborah's favorite, so I wasn't as committed to their preservation.

"Sorry, I've always been an Oreo man. So how are you enjoying the cabin?"

"Wait, am I staying in your cabin?" I'd known the owner was one of Mom's former students, but I hadn't connected the name with the Oreo incident. "It's wonderful, and I really appreciate you giving us such a break on the rent."

"As much as your mother did for me back in the day, I was happy to pay her back a little. I'd have let you have it for free, but she said you'd never go for that."

"And she's absolutely right. But weren't you and your family supposed to be traveling this summer? Or did you fudge that for my mother?"

"No, we really have been in Europe. Some stuff came up at work, and I had to fly back to take care of it. I left my wife and kids in Munich."

"I hope you get to rejoin them soon." Touring another college seemed like an odd reason to have to cut into family vacation time, but it wasn't my business. "It was great seeing you again."

"You, too." He reached into his pocket and pulled out a business card to hand to me. "Keep in touch, and if you run into any issues with the cabin, just let me know and I'll take care of it."

"You bet." Then I looked at the card. "Wait, you're in administration?"

"Yeah, I went over to the dark side of the Force a long time ago." He waved at his clothes. "I only dress like this so as not to scare off the real academics."

"You fooled me," I said.

He grinned. "Give my best to your parents!"

"Will do."

When I got back home, only Byron came to greet me. After I gave him a tummy rub to show him how honored I was by the attention, I found Sid at his laptop at the kitchen table while Madison was on hers in the bedroom. After waving at her, I joined Sid and told him about running into Walker Schild.

"I remember that guy," Sid said. "I used to eavesdrop while he talked through his dissertation with Mrs. Dr. T. He was studying Chaucer. How did he end up at a business school?"

"You got me. Anyway, I also had a lovely encounter with Hynes." I described it.

"What an ossifying piece of sacrum!"

"Definitely, but according to Mo, he's not a sexual predator. She says he was completely devoted to his wife and still is, even though she passed away a while back."

"Actually, Georgia—"

"I know, she could be mistaken, but Mo is pretty sharp."

"Okay, but actually—"

"And sure, she could be lying because she knows about the cover-up, but later I asked her about this tour of the campus the people from Hardison were taking, and when she told me she didn't know anything about it, it was the least convincing lie you ever heard. I'm talking about a performance on the level of Deborah trying to convince my parents she didn't have any homework. There's no way she could have lied to me about Hynes without me knowing. Right?"

Sid just looked at me.

"What do you think? Could Hynes be that good at covering his tracks?"

He looked at me some more.

"What?"

"Can I talk now?"

"Oh. I interrupted you, didn't I?"

"Yup."

"Sorry. You go ahead.

He made a throat-clearing noise purely to make a point, since he has no throat to clear. "As it happens, I don't think that Hynes has been covering his tracks because I don't think he was abusing his students."

"But what about—?"

This time he interrupted me. "The letters are forged."

CHAPTER TWENTY-THREE

"Forged? What do you mean?"

"Phony. Spurious. Fraudulent. Ersatz. They are a sham."

"I know what the word means, but why would five different people make up stories like that?"

"Who says it was five people?"

"The styles and word choice seemed quite distinct."

"I have an explanation for that, but let me start at the beginning. I went online as soon as you left this morning, and I traveled down rabbit hole after rabbit hole, trying to dig up dirt on Hynes. I read until my eye sockets were sore. Nothing.

"Now if it's positive references to the man you want, I can send you links all day long. There are his own papers and journal articles, and he's cited in hundreds more. Then there are biographical sketches, retrospectives, tributes, photos of him presenting papers at conventions, photos of him accepting awards, photos of him teaching classes, photos of him looking meaningfully into the distance. He's got an impressive electronic footprint, though it might please you to know that the overall impression is exactly what Charles said. Hynes's best work is long behind him."

"What about his recent stuff? He told Phil he was working on a couple of papers."

"He's published nothing major in the past ten years. All I can find is where he appears as the second author on some of his students' papers. Sometimes even a third author."

"Ouch!" Sometimes a person listed as the second author had actually worked on a paper or the research that led to it, but not always. Academics routinely give credit to their mentors by naming them the second or third authors of their papers, even if said mentors played nothing but advisory roles. It was a combination of seal-of-approval to anybody who might read the paper and thanks-for-your-help to the mentors. "I mean, it couldn't happen to a nicer guy, but ouch."

"Even so, there are some pockets of academia that still seem to think that his work is the best thing since sliced bread. Not that I eat sliced bread, but I understand it's great. A lot of people refer to him as one of the grand old men of pedagogy, and corporate trainers are huge fans of his teachings. Plus there are citations to his work in quite a few recent books and articles, so he's not totally forgotten, and he still goes to a lot of conferences, which is why it took me all day to go through it all.

"What I couldn't find, no matter how hard I looked, was a single solitary intimation that Hynes might possibly be a sexual predator.

"What I did find were these pictures from Overfeld's website." He slid his laptop toward me so I could see an open file of a photo of Hynes. "There is a carefully staged casual portrait of him in his office in every single college catalog and in a lot of the marketing material. As far as I can tell, they take a new one every year."

On the screen, Hynes was wearing the exact style of rumpled casual clothing he still wore but was considerably younger. The office was the same one I'd been in, though the furnishings at that point were nineteen-sixties rebel mode: Hopi masks and Navaho wall hangings, and chairs covered in paisley fabric.

"Flip to the next," Sid said.

Hynes again, a little older. Same office, but now it was all pop art and bean bag chairs that I was glad he'd replaced before our coffee date.

"Keep going."

Hynes kept aging as the bean bags gave way to futons with tatami underneath, then kneeling chairs, and later a trio of stability balls. The last one must have been taken recently—it had the same furniture I'd seen.

"Other than the chance to watch Hynes age, why am I looking at these?" I asked.

"Notice anything?"

"Only that interior decorators must love him. He'll try any trend that comes down the track."

"Except couches."

"Excuse me?"

"Couches, or sofas, or even loveseats—I'm not sure what the difference is. The point is that he never got one of any of those three types of furniture until about three years ago. Before that, it was all some variation of chair."

I scrolled back through the pictures.

"Okay, no couches, sofas, or loveseats. Why do I care?"

"That first letter says Hynes sat next to her on the sofa. In his office."

"You're right—I remember. But there was no sofa," I said. "Unless that student was here within the past three years."

"Or if that letter was a forgery."

"Maybe the woman was mistaken. Traumatic events can really scramble a person's memories."

"The second letter mentions a loveseat, and there's a couch in two of the others. Georgia, I think they're all forged."

"But they felt so genuine! I know, I'm an English professor, and I should know just how well a writer can evoke emotions in their work, but I would have sworn those letters were real."

"They *are* real, kind of."

I glared at him. "Are they phony or are they real?"

"Both. The letters aren't fake, but they are forged."

I thought for a minute, trying to understand what he meant. "You Googled the text, didn't you?"

"It wasn't quite that simple, but I did Google letters written as part of the #MeToo movement, which led me to a website filled with scanned-in letters from people who'd been mistreated. Pages and pages of them." He got that look that I knew meant he was wishing he could cry. "I was glad I don't have a heart, Georgia, because reading them would have broken it."

"The fact that you say that proves that you don't need one," I said, patting his hand.

"Anyway, about a hundred pages into the site, I found our first letter, or at least the source of it. Somebody had taken an account from an actual victim, retyped it, changed the applicable names to *Overfeld* and *Hynes*, and redacted the dates and other details."

"Seriously?" It was bad enough that somebody had victimized that woman—somebody else appropriating her story felt like another assault. "What about the other letters?"

"They're all on that same site, except for the third. For that one, our forger pulled pieces from two different letters and combined them."

"I could almost admire the thoroughness, if it wasn't from such a piece of sacrum." I ran my fingers through my hair, trying to make sense of it. "So we don't think Hynes—or somebody trying to protect Hynes—was the killer after all?"

"I don't know, Georgia. Even false accusations could give Hynes a motive for murder. If they'd gotten out, his reputation would have been tainted, even if he was later cleared."

"So Hynes isn't a predator, but he could still be the killer. Or the killer could be trying to protect Hynes. Or the killer could be somebody else entirely. This doesn't exactly help us, does it?"

"It's not that bad. The forger basically still has the same plan we thought it was before. Only instead of using you to bring Hynes to justice, whoever it is wants to use you to bring him to injustice."

"If injustice was the goal, why not make dozens of photocopies and plaster the campus with them the way Judy Cater did her protest signs? Even if the teachers and staff didn't believe it, plenty of Andorians would post it on social media, not to mention what would have happened if Judy got a hold of a copy. Instead the forger sent them to me. Why me?"

"It's got to be because of your sleuthing habit. Like it or not, Georgia, you've got a reputation, and he's going to assume you'll be on the case this time, too. Which leads me to the following possibilities." He held up one finger. "One, the forger is the killer and wants to divert attention away from himself." He removed the finger's bones and placed them on the kitchen table. "Two, the forger has reason to believe Hynes committed the murder and hopes that if he draws your attention to him, you'll find the proof to get him convicted." Another finger's worth of bones on the table. "Three, the forger hates Hynes and wants to frame him." He divested himself of more bones. "Four, a combination of diversion and hating Hynes." He was down to the thumb. "And five, a combination of believing Hynes is a killer and hating Hynes. Did I miss anything?"

"Yeah, you missed how we're going to figure out which one of those five possibilities is the right one, not to mention who the forger and murderer are."

"Details!" he said airily.

I thumped him on the skull, aiming carefully to keep from hurting my finger. "There is one thing we can assume. Three of our possibilities include somebody having a hate-on for Hynes, and even in the other two, somebody dislikes him enough to allow him to get arrested. So whoever the forger is, he or she is out to get Professor Hynes, which means we need to take a closer look at him ourselves."

CHAPTER TWENTY-FOUR

Since Sid had already spent a full day looking for dirt on Hynes online, we saw no reason to go back to Google. And once again, we didn't think it would be safe to nose around campus, even though I was willing to bet that Mo knew some stories. Fortunately, this time we didn't need Madison to remind us that my parents were the obvious source of information about academics. I called the house and got my mother, put the call on speaker so Sid could join in, and explained what we'd found out and what we were now looking for.

"Those letters are forgeries?" Mom said. "It never would have occurred to me to doubt them."

"Me, either," I said. "It was Sid who figured it out. I asked him to look for other victims, and instead he found this."

"Well done, Sid."

"Thanks Mrs. Dr. T."

"And Georgia, I'm not surprised you believed," Mom added. "Given what any woman in academia knows, it was hardly a shock."

"Mom? Did something . . . ? Did somebody . . . ?"

"That, my dear, is a conversation for another day. Suffice it to say that while in my case, it was off-color remarks and the assumption that I didn't have a brain in my pretty little head, with the occasional crude invitation, I have encountered a number of women who have experienced much worse."

I'd always been wary myself—a single mother could have been considered a prime target—but when I was younger, my parents always seemed to have a friend at the schools where I was studying and later working. There was nothing like knowing a grad student or adjunct was the daughter of not one, but two well-regarded scholars in the field to ward off predators.

I said, "You and Phil told me you hadn't heard about any blips on Hynes's sexual reputation, but what about enemies? Academic battles, maybe?"

"Certainly, back in the day, but most of the old guard who disputed Hynes's methods are too old to matter anymore. They're either retired, dead, or both. Why would anybody have waited so long to try something like this?"

"They say revenge is a dish best served cold," Sid put in.

"Yes, but I believe this would be more than just cold—this would be frozen." She paused. "You know, there was something that came to mind just recently, but I can't put my finger on it. Hold on, and let me ask your father."

A few minutes later, she said, "Here he is now. I'll put this on speaker."

"Or I could hold my cheek next to yours, and we could share the receiver," Phil said with a chuckle. "It's much cozier that way."

"Geez, Dr. T., get a room!" Sid said.

"We have a whole house full of rooms, and they've all been put to the test."

"La la la, I can't hear you," Sid said, putting his bony hands against his ear cavities, as if that would make any difference. "Just tell me you don't go into my attic."

"No, dear," Mom said.

Sid put his hands down until Mom added, "It's too chilly in the winter and too hot in the summer." And Sid's hands were back at his ears.

I cleared my throat in order to change the subject as swiftly as possible. "Phil, I'm trying to find out if Professor Hynes has any enemies—"

"Any living ones, that is," Mom added. "Weren't you and Jean-Luis talking about an incident earlier this week?"

"That was a dreadful story, and if I'd heard it before encountering Hynes, I'd have crafted my takedown of him more thoroughly, but it happened a long time ago, and I don't see how it could be relevant."

"I'll take it anyway," I said. "If nothing else, I'll understand the man a bit better."

"And gossip is fun," Sid said, having rejoined the conversation.

"You'll remember our saying many faculty members from Overfeld are looking for jobs. An English professor applied at Pennycross, and I was asked what I thought of him. I spoke to him, and while he seemed qualified, it's easy to exaggerate one's abilities in an interview, so I wanted to check his references, one of whom was my old friend Jean-Luis."

Mom snorted. "In other words, he wanted a chance to chew the fat with one of his cronies."

"That's what I said," Phil said placidly. "This particular crony used to teach at Overfeld, so I thought he could give me a better perspective of the applicant's abilities. I called him, and once we'd dispensed with the business part of the conversation, we moved on to discussions of old times. Jean-Luis was at Overfeld for a long time but wasn't entirely happy there, mostly because of Professor Hynes."

"So Jean-Luis is the enemy you were talking about?" Sid asked.

"No, he had no problems with Hynes himself, but he did observe the way Hynes escaped the consequences of his bad behavior. Jean-Luis decided it was only a matter of time before he, too, became a target, so he went to teach elsewhere. Now the event that convinced him it was time to go was when a young man applied at Overfeld whose work was along the same lines as Hynes's, but moving it forward. A true scholar would like nothing better than to see his legacy built upon, but instead Hynes lobbied behind the scenes to keep the man from getting hired. The man went to another school and tried to continue the work, but when Hynes was asked to peer review one of the man's papers, he argued that the paper had too many faults, so the leading journal rejected it. Hynes was so petty that when he was asked to speak at a conference, he would agree to do so only if the other man wasn't invited. Given the choice between someone as famous as Hynes and a newcomer, you can guess who most conferences would invite."

"That's horrible," I said.

"You'll get no arguments from me," Phil said. "Even for academic politics, it was vicious."

"When did this happen?"

"Jean-Luis didn't say precisely, but he's been gone from Overfeld for fifteen years. So assume it was somewhere between fifteen and twenty years ago."

"Then you're probably right about it being irrelevant. If the younger man had been planning to go after Hynes, he'd have done it long ago."

"That was my thought as well. Besides, the fellow was savvy enough to realize what was going on. He abandoned his original line of study and went to work with another scholar, one who truly mentored him. They're still partnered today, down in Tennessee, I believe."

"Tennessee?" That rang a bell. "Did your friend know his name?"

"I don't think—No, wait, yes he did mention his last name because it was so appropriate to what happened. Hynes was the old blood in the field, and this man was the new blood, and it just so happened that his name actually was Youngblood."

I must have gasped or made some noise because Sid gave me a look. "Youngblood?" I said.

"I believe so. Do you know him?"

"No, but I might know his daughter. One of the other adjuncts at Overfeld is Treva Youngblood."

Chapter Twenty-Five

While I thanked my parents for their help, Sid grabbed his computer to see if our Treva Youngblood was related to the Youngblood Phil had been talking about. Without knowing the man's first name or where in Tennessee he was teaching, it was a bit tricky, but it helped that both "Treva" and "Youngblood" were unusual names. Within twenty minutes, Sid had located a picture of a Professor Youngblood at Rhodes College in Memphis. Five minutes later, he found one of him with his daughter, and fellow academic, Treva.

Now all the times Treva had laughed at problems on campus seemed a little sinister.

Sid and I spent much of the night arguing over the best way for me to approach Treva. The big bone of contention was her level of involvement. Had she sent me letters she thought were real, or had she forged them herself? Did she blame Hynes for Neil's murder, or was she the murderer?

"I'm sorry, Sid, maybe she was involved with the letters, but she had no motive for killing Neil."

Sid disagreed. "What if Neil caught her trying to sneak the letters out of the files?"

"She could have come up with some sort of excuse."

"Like what?"

"Like she had heard rumors of Hynes being a predator, or she had a friend he preyed upon. It wouldn't have to be a great story because if Neil thought they were real, don't you think he'd want to investigate just to be sure?"

"Given what I know about Erik Bloodaxe, I'd say so."

"Then Treva would have had no reason to attack him. He'd be doing what she wanted done."

"Okay, say he didn't think they were real. Wouldn't that give her a motive?"

"Not really? What would he have done if he'd decided she forged them? Get her fired? So what? She's an adjunct working a summer position. She'd be gone soon in a few weeks anyway. Sure, nobody wants to miss any paychecks, but I don't think it would be worth killing over."

"He could spread the word about what she was up to. You're always complaining about how fast news travels on the adjunct grapevine."

"Neil wasn't an adjunct. He wasn't even an academic. Maybe he could blackball her in some places, but he probably didn't have that much influence. And he'd have to prove that she was the forger, rather than just a dupe. Not to mention the fact that if he'd fired her, she could still have leaked the fake letters elsewhere. It still wouldn't have been worth killing over."

"So you don't think she's the killer?"

"I really don't, not unless there's something else going on than those letters. Mind you, I still don't intend to go talk to her in a secluded cabin in the middle of the woods."

"What are you going to do?"

"I'm going to go talk to her in as public a place as I can arrange."

As a dorm monitor, Treva was normally in the auditorium for the day's announcements before I arrived, but the next morning, I showed up before she escorted her crew of Andorians to the cafeteria for breakfast and was waiting for her at a table near the door. Therefore I had both an audience and an exit strategy.

She spotted me as she came out of the buffet line with a tray holding a boiled egg, a bowl of fruit, and a roll. I waved the Starbucks I'd picked up for her, so she skipped past the school's coffee urn to sit down by me.

"Why the bribe?" she said, taking it from me.

"I wanted to talk to you about something." I pulled photocopies of the forged letters out of my satchel and slid them over to her. Sid had insisted on using photocopies of our copies to make sure Treva didn't run off with the originals to eat them or light them on fire, and it seemed a reasonable precaution, even if his imagination was running wild.

She took a swallow of coffee, then read the first letter. After a glance at me, she quickly read the other four.

I had a whole list of predicted reactions divided into categories like "Treva as Forger" and "Treva as Murderer/Forger." Somehow, I never anticipated her actual response.

Which was to say, "Huh."

Then she handed the papers back to me. "Are these true? I never thought Hynes was that kind of snake, but you never know, do you?"

"Actually, I think somebody forged these to try to get him in trouble."

"Now, *that* I can believe. He's got to have enemies crawling out of the woodwork. He comes off all touchy-feely-let's-collaborate, but when it comes down to it, he's all about feathering his own nest. One of these days, I ought to tell you about the dirty tricks he pulled on my daddy."

"I heard something about those," I said cautiously. "He really treated him badly."

She shrugged, which also hadn't been on my list of possible reactions. "He sure did, but it turned out for the best. Daddy moved back South, teamed up with the man he's worked with ever since, married my mama, and had me and my brothers. Whereas Professor High-n-Mighty Davidson Hynes is all alone and has nothing better to do than to invite clueless adjuncts to coffee so he can show them what a big shot he is. No offense."

"None taken. I did think he was a big shot."

"Oh he was, back in the day. Nowadays he's nothing but a reputation and a bad dye job."

"So you don't hold a grudge?"

"I wouldn't say that. Like my mama says, I wouldn't bother to pee on him if he was on fire. But inaction is as far as I'm willing to go. The Rule of Three, and all that." When she saw my blank expression, she said, "Did you not know I'm Wiccan? According to our beliefs, whatever energy I put out into the world will be returned to me three times, whether it's positive or negative. So I'm not going to waste any of my energy on a turd like him." She pointed at the letters. "Whoever faked those ought to think about what's coming back at him." She gave me a stern look. "Or her."

I held up both hands as if in surrender. "It wasn't me. These were left in my office."

"Huh."

"What's 'huh' mean this time?"

"Just thinking that I must not be the only one who's heard tales about your playing detective. No offense."

That time I was offended, but I didn't say so because a couple of other instructors had arrived, and I didn't intend to continue the discussion in front of them. I also wanted some time to brood. With Treva in the clear, I was going to have to go home after work and tell Sid I had no idea of what to do next.

CHAPTER TWENTY-SIX

"This is all so complicated," Sid complained after I got back to the cabin and told him what Treva had said. Madison was out by the lake with Byron, which simplified the conversation, if not the situation. "Somebody kills Neil. Then somebody—who may or may not be the killer—forges letters to implicate Hynes. Whether or not the forger is the killer, why not just call in an anonymous tip to the police and say, 'Hynes killed Neil Farmer—go arrest him,' instead of all this sacrum?"

"You're right. The pieces aren't fitting together." We both drummed our fingers on the table for the next few minutes, trying to think it through, but it wasn't until I looked at the clock to see if it was time to make dinner that I had a useful thought. "Sid, when did the forger create these letters?"

"Presumably after Neil's murder."

"Are you sure? Look at the timeline. Tuesday morning, Treva brings up my fascination with murder, which is overheard by most of the other adjuncts and likely spread around to everybody else involved with the Andorians. Wednesday afternoon, the letters appear on my doorstep."

"Right."

"So when did the forger have time for forging? We know he copied the content from that website, but first he had to find the site and decide which posts to use. Then he had to pick out different stationeries, and while three of the letters seem to have been laser printed, the other two look typed."

"Not only that, but I'd bet my sternum that they were typed on two different typewriters," Sid said. "Some of the characters are different."

"That couldn't have happened overnight. Therefore the forger must have already manufactured the forgeries before Neil's death."

"Wasn't the point of the letters to smear Hynes?" Sid asked.

"Yes, but for sexual misconduct, not for murder. Maybe it's not just the order we've got wrong—I think we got the cause-and-effect backward, too."

"I'm confused."

I was, too, but I kept talking in hopes that it would start to make sense. "The letters were the real plan all along. The murder was incidental."

"Excuse me?"

"Sorry, I mean it was unplanned. Neil caught somebody stealing the letters, and the thief panicked." I stopped. "But how did the letters get into the files?"

"The forger planted them."

"Then how did the killer find out the letters were in the files?"

We spent another few minutes drumming fingers and phalanges before Sid sat straight up. "Georgia, we've got that backward, too! Neil didn't catch somebody stealing the letters—he caught somebody putting them into Hynes's personnel file!"

"Yes! The forger must have intended to make sure they were discovered later."

"Right. He could do what you suggested before—plaster the campus with copies, go viral with the accusations, whatever. Hynes would deny it, of course, but his name would still be dragged through the dirt." He held up one bony hand. "High five."

I returned it with enough gusto to make my hand sting, and we shared a quick boogie. Then I pointed out, "We still don't know why the forger hates Hynes enough to do all this."

"We'll figure it out," Sid said. "If what he did to Treva's father is an example of his behavior, there's no telling what other nastiness he's been up to over the years."

"I'm just surprised the forger didn't go further. It's terrible to say, but chances are Hynes would have weathered the storm caused by the accusations. It's not like any of his supposed victims would ever step forward, and with all the identifying information redacted, he couldn't be prosecuted. Maybe the college could have pushed him into retirement, but since the letters were in his file, they couldn't say they didn't know what he'd been up to."

"Overfeld would have been in trouble, too. It's one thing for a single professor to be up to no good—for a college to conceal his activities is even worse. Everybody hates a cover-up."

"As if Overfeld needed more bad press, given the stuff that's been going wrong on campus. All the fuses and bed bugs and. . ." I stopped and looked at Sid.

Sid looked at me. "We're still missing something, aren't we?" he said.

"I think we might be. We'd already decided the killer didn't plan to kill Neil. Maybe he wasn't after Hynes either."

He was right with me. "Or if he was, it wasn't because of him being an egomaniac or dirty trickster, but because he's the college's most famous faculty member."

In unison, we said, "Somebody is trying to destroy Overfeld College!"

CHAPTER TWENTY-SEVEN

Over dinner, which Madison came in to request right after Sid and I reached our latest epiphany, we discovered another advantage of having her as our Padawan. We got to take turns explaining our conclusions to her to see if they made sense to somebody who wasn't us. Fortunately for our peace of mind, they did. Less fortunately, she raised a critical question.

She asked, "Why would anybody want to kill a college?"

"The classic motives for any crime are greed, revenge, and passion," Sid said.

"I think we can leave out passion," I said, "unless somebody loves another school that much and thinks destroying Overfeld would help the other school."

"Some alums are pretty passionate about their alma maters," Sid agreed, "but it seems like a stretch. Especially since the saboteur is likely to be a local, if not somebody on campus."

"Revenge is easy," I said. "Overfeld could have fired somebody, rejected a job candidate or an applicant, or expelled a student."

"Destroying the whole college seems a bit extreme for any of those," Madison said.

Sid shrugged. "Murder is always extreme."

"What about greed?" Madison asked.

"There's the real estate," I said, remembering some nastiness about land ownership when I'd been at McQuaid, "but I don't think the market is that hot around here. There's plenty of undeveloped property between here and Northbury."

"Still, I can do some research," Sid said. "There might be buzz about a resort trying to start up or a big business looking to relocate."

The tourist trade wasn't huge in the area, and given the distance between Overfeld and the nearest airport, it didn't seem likely that the town would be a candidate for a new Amazon branch, but it couldn't hurt for Sid to check.

"What else does a college have?" Madison asked.

"There's the furniture and the equipment, but it's not like Overfeld has anything wildly high-tech like a particle accelerator. Books in the library, and I suppose some might be valuable uncatalogued first editions, but it would be easier to just steal them."

"What about art?" Sid said. "I've seen news stories about schools having nearly forgotten great works on their walls, even murals by famous artists."

"There are some portraits of former presidents, but I haven't seen anything particularly exciting. And again, wouldn't it be easier to do a smash-and-grab?"

"You can't smash and grab sculptures or murals," Sid said. "I'll check the Overfeld website and see if I find anything there. What else?"

Madison said, "Overfeld has an endowment, right? Where does a school's endowment go when it goes bankrupt?"

"Overfeld wouldn't be on the verge of bankruptcy if it had an endowment worth killing for," Sid said.

"That's not necessarily true," I said. "I don't know a lot about college financial wrangling, but the way I understand it, a college's endowment should be twice the annual budget. So if a college has a three million dollar budget, it should have a six million dollar endowment. If you had an endowment of only four million, the college would be in rough shape, but four million dollars would still be a nice chunk of change for an individual."

"But who would get it?" Madison asked.

"It depends, and it can be complicated. I read something about a women's college in Virginia that was closing. First they had to pay their bills. Then they had to return part of the money to donors—some donors specify that if the school shuts down, they either get it back or get to designate another charity to receive it. Anything left after that had to go to the nearest entity whose mission was similar to the closed college's. So if an art school closed down, the money would go to the closest art school. In the case I'm thinking about, the college was going to donate the remainder of their endowment to another women's college."

"So whatever money Overfeld has left over would go to another college that specializes in teaching professors?" Madison said.

"Or to another liberal arts college if the law here is the same as in Virginia."

Sid said, "I'm trying to picture a bunch of ninja saboteurs from another college bringing down Overfeld."

"It doesn't seem likely, does it? They'd have to know Overfeld was in bad shape, that the endowment was worth the risk, and that the money would come to them. Plus they'd need people willing and able to do the dirty work."

As unlikely as it sounded, Sid said that he'd also scout out nearby colleges with missions similar to Overfeld to see if any had sufficiently shady reputations.

He kept at it while Madison and I cleaned up the kitchen, did laundry, and watched TV, and was still going strong when I went to bed. Even though he was working hard, I could tell from his body language, or rather his skeletal language, that he wasn't finding much. So I wasn't surprised that when I got up the next morning, he told me that he'd had no luck. He promised to keep going, but as it turned out, I found a nice juicy motive that afternoon on campus.

Overfeld was being picketed.

Chapter Twenty-Eight

It wasn't a long picket line, only half a dozen people carrying signs that said, "Overfeld: Pay Your Share," but they were shouting out their slogan with great gusto as they marched back and forth on the sidewalk in front of Kumin Hall. The demonstration had been well-timed for maximum effect, during our lunch break. A number of Andorians had taken their meals outside to enjoy the weather, so there was going to be plenty of cell phone footage posted, and a couple of adjuncts were surreptitiously filming, too.

I wasn't surprised when I recognized the woman leading the charge. It was Judy Cater, Jen's mother. Jen was there, too, handing out flyers to the passersby who'd come to see what all the fuss was about, and she very much looked as if she'd rather be someplace else. When she saw me, she looked away, as if embarrassed.

Judy, on the other hand, seemed to be enjoying the spotlight. She had a megaphone to make sure everybody could hear her as she continued to lead her small but vocal group back and forth.

"What in the Sam Hill is this about?" Treva said, coming up beside me.

"I believe they're protesting the fact that the college is exempt from local property taxes," I said.

Ridley trotted out of the building and shouted, "This is college property. You people are trespassing, and if you don't leave, I'm going to call the police."

"You mean the police whose protection you don't pay one penny for?" Judy yelled back, the megaphone making her voice echo nicely. Even more people drifted over from the town green and nearby stores.

"Look, I didn't make the laws," Ridley said. "I don't even live here. If you want to change things, then—"

"Make it fair! Pay your share!" Judy said into the megaphone, and the rest of her crowd joined in.

Ridley looked around in consternation, and when a pair of campus security guards showed up, went into a hand-waving discussion with them. Treva was snickering, Andorians were still filming, and a few more marchers joined the picket line to chant along with Judy.

I don't know how it would have been resolved if President Fernandez hadn't shown up, with Mo beside him. He surveyed the scene, took a deep breath, and walked toward the picket line with his right hand outstretched.

Judy lowered her megaphone long enough to accept the handshake.

"Ms. Cater, I understand you have some concerns. Would you be willing to sit down and talk about them? We could go to my office—"

"I'd rather talk here, if that's all right with you."

"Of course, why not enjoy this weather?" He turned toward Kumin Hall. "Mo, could you have seats brought out for Ms. Cater and myself? And perhaps some refreshments for her companions. They must be thirsty, and it is lunchtime."

Mo put the security guards to work lugging out chairs and distributing a case of bottled water. Then she brought out a platter of sandwiches while Charles carried one of cookies, which they walked around offering like waiters serving hors d'oeuvres at a party. The protestors looked unsure about what they were supposed to do, but most of them accepted both food and drink, which coincidentally left them without free hands to carry their signs.

Meanwhile, Judy and Fernandez were talking, and while Judy started out holding herself stiffly, as time went on, she seemed to be relaxing and listening more. They were still at it when students started to head back inside for the afternoon's classes. The rest of the picket line and the onlookers from town had faded away, leaving Jen sitting on a bench next to a stack of protest signs, eating a cookie.

I walked over to her. "Hey, Jen."

"Thank you for talking to me. I thought you might be embarrassed because of my mother's demonstration. Or that you might be worried about your job."

"If President Fernandez can talk to your mother, I don't see why I can't talk to you."

"He seems very polite. My mother tried to get another man here to talk to her earlier this week, but he wasn't at all polite."

"Would that be the man who threatened to call the police?"

"Yes, that was him."

"Our Mr. Ridley isn't known for his manners, but to be fair, he's been pretty busy. There have been some problems with the summer program, and he's had to manage them." That's when I realized that Judy might have a vested interest in things going wrong. Obviously I couldn't ask Jen if her mother was a saboteur. I felt guilty enough just considering the idea. "Well, I have to get to class." Then, trying for casual, I said, "Are you going to be around town later?"

"I'll be at Wizard Gary's because they moved the Yu-Gi-Oh! tournament to Friday night this week. I wish they were more consistent with their scheduling."

"I think Madison is going, too." Though she hadn't mentioned it, I didn't expect it to be hard to convince her to spend some time gaming. "Maybe we'll see you there."

"That would be nice." She looked bashful for a moment. "I quite enjoyed having ice cream with you two last week."

"Then we should do it again. Why don't you ask your mother to join us this time? Unless she has another meeting."

"I don't think she does, but I'll check with her."

"Great! I'll see you tonight." I headed for my class, trying not to feel guilty about using Jen to get to her mother. I wasn't particularly successful.

CHAPTER TWENTY-NINE

I expected my students to be upset by the midday demonstration, but they settled down to work right away. Of course, given the amount of political unrest in the country, they'd seen and heard about protests involving thousands of people. Some had probably marched themselves. A handful of people complaining about local property taxes just couldn't compete.

Unfortunately, the peace didn't last.

We were just past our midsession break when I noticed that more Andorians were looking out the windows than at their work. I stepped over to see what had caught their attention and saw no fewer than three Overfeld police cars in the nearest parking lot, with their lights flashing. My first thought was that our saboteur had struck again, though I couldn't imagine anything that would require police instead of a repair crew. My next thought was that they'd found another murder victim, and I was fairly sure that's what my students were thinking, too.

"You guys keep writing," I said, "and I'll go check this out." I didn't really think they'd continue working while I was gone, but it was worth a try.

I ran into Charles at the top of the stairs. "What's going on?" I asked.

"That's what I'm hoping to ascertain," he said. "My class is hopelessly distracted by the police presence."

When we got downstairs, we found most of the rest of the adjuncts standing by the building entrance, but from their chatter, they knew no more than we did.

"You think it's another dead body?" Treva asked.

Paul said, "The cops were over by Stevenson, but I didn't see an ambulance or coroner's van." His art class was on the third floor, where they could get natural lighting, so he could see more of the campus than I could from my class.

A group of police appeared from around a building, accompanied by President Fernandez, Ridley, and a man in an Overfeld maintenance coverall.

"They're coming this way," Treva said, and we retreated partway up the stairs. Nobody went back to their classrooms, of course. We wanted to see what happened next.

I heard the door to the admin office open, and Professor Hynes came into the hall with Mo, who was looking put out.

"I'll check on the delivery date again," she said, "but your nibs and ink should show up any day now."

"Perhaps a more reliable vendor is called for," he said in the helpful-suggestion voice I hated. "There must be a local supplier you could use, even if you had to pick up the items personally."

I could tell from her face how much Mo *loved* that idea, but she just said, "I'll see what's available."

The building door opened, and President Fernandez stepped in, the police at his heels. "Professor Hynes, we've been looking for you."

"I did see that you'd called my cell, but I was with Ms. Heedles, and I'm sure you wouldn't have wanted to interrupt us. People are all too willing to ignore the person they're with in favor of a person on the other end of the electronic tether. Don't you agree?"

"This is rather urgent."

"Is it? Then let's go to my office, and I'll make coffee for us while we talk it over."

"I'm afraid your office is temporarily off-limits," a police officer with dark curls and a pug nose said.

"That's Chief Bezzat," Treva whispered.

I nodded, remembering that I'd seen her issuing orders the night Sid found Neil's body.

"Off-limits?" Hynes said. "How can a man's own office be off-limits?"

Fernandez said, "They're searching it, Dave. I gave them permission."

"*You* gave them permission to search *my* office. Valentin, you're not making any sense."

Chief Bezzat pushed forward. "Look, Fernandez is the college president, and he gave us permission to search. It's all legal and aboveboard."

"Legal, but not appropriate," Hynes said. "I'm going to have to speak the board about this." His voice was moving further and further from that we're-all-friends-here tone and toward get-off-my-lawn-right-this-minute.

"You can talk to anybody you want," Chief Bezzat said, "but first you need to talk to us. Now do you want to do it here, or shall we go somewhere a bit more private?" She looked pointedly at those of us perched on the stairs.

"I don't have anything to hide," Hynes said.

"Have it your way." She reached behind her, and a sheet of paper protected by a plastic envelope was slapped into her hand by one of the other cops. I wasn't close enough to read what was on it, but given the size of the dark, red-brown blots on the paper, being closer might not have helped. "Do you recognize this?"

Hynes reached to take it, but when she held it just out of his reach, he wrinkled his brow and said, "I've never seen that before."

"Then could you explain how it came to be in your desk drawer?"

"I have no idea. Perhaps you should ask Valentin, since he's apparently been giving tours of my personal space."

"Your workplace isn't personal, Professor. You should know that." She put her hand out again, and another plastic-wrapped piece of paper was put into it. "Now that first page is hard to read, but this one doesn't have as many stains. See if you can make it out."

His brow wrinkled even more as he tried to read it, and then his lips tightened as he reached into a pocket and pulled out a pair

185

of reading glasses, the old-fashioned kind with half-lenses. "What looks like a date is blocked out. 'Dear President,'" he read out loud. "The name is blocked out, too."

"I'm aware. Go on."

"'As a loyal alumna of Overfeld, I have agonized over this decision, but I've come to realize that I must tell the truth, no matter how much pain and embarrassment it causes me. When I was a student, I was sexually abused by Prof—'" He stopped.

The other adjuncts strained to try to see what the rest of the letter said, but I already knew. I had a photocopy of it at the cabin.

"This is fiction," Hynes said. "Where did you get it?"

"Like I said, it was in your desk."

"That's not possible. I've never seen it, and I assure you, the accusations are not true."

"Yeah? What about the other letters?" Another reach, another hand-off. "You're saying all these people made false accusations."

"One or a hundred, it's all the same."

"The courts might see it a bit differently."

"What court?" He scoffed. "Phony letters planted in my desk don't mean a thing."

"We'll see about that. Now about these stains . . . I know you're a big coffee drinker, but I don't think these are coffee."

"If you say so. I'm hardly an expert on stains."

"That's all right, I am, at least with some stains. We're going to test them, but in my expert opinion, these stains are blood."

"Blood?"

She nodded. "Professor Hynes, can you tell me where you were the night of Friday, July twentieth?"

"Not off the top of my head. Why does that matter? Do you have a letter accusing me of doing something on that day, too?"

"Not a letter, no, but it seems to me that this is an awful lot of blood, and it just so happens that a man named Neil Farmer lost an awful lot of blood here on campus on Friday, July twentieth. The pattern of blood spatter indicated that something was taken from the office after the murder, something like these letters."

Hynes sputtered. "You think that I—That I could have—"

"Right now, I'm only thinking that I'd like to know where you were that night."

"This is insane, and I won't stand for it." He turned around and started heading for the admin office. "I'm going to call my lawyer."

"Tell you what, you can call your lawyer from the station. We'll even give you a ride."

"I'm not going anywhere with you."

President Fernandez put his hand on Hynes's arm. "Dave, please, let's go down to the station together and work this out."

Hynes shrugged him off. "You put them up to this, didn't you? You've always been jealous of my work, my reputation. This college wouldn't exist without me!"

He turned away again, Fernandez moved back, and the police chief stepped forward to touch his shoulder. I was pretty sure Hynes thought it was Fernandez again when he turned around and swung at the hand. Surely the fact that he hit Chief Bezzat in the face was an accident, but it was a loud, solid slap.

Treva gasped, or maybe it was me, but we were all shocked. Hynes was the most shocked of all. His eyes widened, and he opened his mouth, but nothing came out.

Chief Bezzat grinned, but it was more mean than happy. "Professor Hynes, you are under arrest for assaulting a police officer." As she recited his Miranda rights, she turned him around and hand-cuffed him. He didn't resist any further, or speak, or do anything but allow himself to be pushed out the door and down the steps toward the cruiser, surrounded by a phalanx of police officers.

Fernandez rubbed his face wearily. "Mo, could you get in touch with our university counsel, and ask him to recommend a lawyer to represent Professor Hynes?"

"Right away."

Ridley looked at those of us on the stairs. "I'm sure I don't have to tell you that discretion at this point—"

"Never mind, Heath," Fernandez said. "I think we're long past that."

CHAPTER THIRTY

"Hynes can't be the killer," Sid said.

"I know, but they found those bloodstained letters in his office."

"That shouldn't be enough to arrest him. It's circumstantial!"

"They didn't arrest him for murder. Chief Bezzat just wanted him to come to the station to talk. They arrested him for hitting her."

"All that coffee must have gone to his brain!" Sid said.

While my students had withstood the picketing with equanimity, the sight of a professor being led off in handcuffs was more than their powers of concentration could handle, so I let them out of class soon after I got back upstairs. Then I tried to pump the other adjuncts and Mo for an explanation of why Fernandez had gone into Hynes's office, but either they didn't know or didn't want to tell me. So I gave up and headed home early.

"Madison?" Sid asked. "Have you got anything yet?"

"I'm working on it," she said irritably. While Sid and I had been busy being confounded, she'd been at her keyboard, checking her sources in town, and she refused to say anything until she'd found all she was going to find. After a half hour's wait that seemed much longer, she said, "Okay, I think I've got it. According to Bakshi—"

"That's the one whose sister is a cop?" Sid said.

"No, Bakshi is the one whose uncle works maintenance at Overfeld."

"I think I saw the uncle," I said, remembering the man in the coverall.

"According to Bakshi's uncle, President Fernandez called him this afternoon and asked him to come unlock Professor Hynes's office. The uncle really dislikes Hynes, by the way. He says Hynes makes a mess with his little coffee parties and then wants everything cleaned up right away. He's kind of a neat freak."

"Is that important?" I asked.

"You tell me," Madison said. "I'm just the Padawan. Anyway, Fernandez was really anxious to get into Hynes's office, which made the uncle curious, so he stuck around to see if there was another dead body in there. Fernandez looked around like maybe he thought so, too, but there was nobody there, dead or alive. Fernandez got irate and said somebody was playing pranks. Apparently somebody had called his cell from a blocked number and said Hynes had fallen or had a heart attack or something. The uncle looked around, too, wondering if somebody had planted some other kind of prank, and he saw papers sticking out from one of the desk drawers." She stopped. "Huh. I guess Hynes being a neat freak is important because knowing how he complains about cleanliness is what made the uncle open the drawer so he could push the paper back in. Only he realized the papers were bloodstained. Bakshi says his uncle has been in college maintenance enough to recognize bloodstains right away, which is kind of creepy, when you think about it."

"Noted, and we'll think about that later. What did the uncle do?"

"He showed it to Fernandez, who agreed it looked like blood. Then he read the papers."

"Which were copies of the letters we've got," I said. "At least one of them was."

"Right. So Fernandez called 911 and told the police he'd found evidence that might be related to Neil's murder, the police came running, and you know the rest."

"Between the accusations and the blood, he had no choice but to call the cops," I said.

"Not to mention the fact that Bakshi's uncle had seen everything," Sid said cynically.

"I can't believe Hynes slugged a cop," Madison said.

"It was more of a slap than a slug," I said. "I wonder how long the police can hold him for that."

"Long enough for them to test the stains and make sure it's human blood, and maybe to see if it's Neil's blood type," Sid said.

Madison said, "Bakshi says they're trying to track down who wrote the letters, too. Am I wrong, or didn't we decide that the letters are forged?"

"They're as phony as Piltdown Man," Sid said.

"So what do we do now?" Madison asked.

"I don't know, but we've got to do something. I mean, as much as I dislike Hynes, I don't want him convicted of a crime he didn't commit."

Sid said, "Plus those letters! The police think he's a sexual predator as well as a murderer."

"I don't know what to do about the murder part, but we can at least let the cops know the letters are phony. The killer isn't the only one who can use anonymous tips. Let's send them one that includes the link to the site with the real letters. That ought to clear him for that part."

In the past, we'd telephoned in our tips from pay phones, but even small towns like Overfeld had a place on their website for people to report crimes without giving their names. I was a bit leery of how confidential the information would be, but Sid said he'd researched it and was comfortable with the procedure. Besides, I had no idea where we could find a pay phone. I could have searched on my cell or checked to see if there was an app for it, but that just seemed wrong.

Sid wasted no time in sending the tip in on the Overfeld police site. "There," he said, pressing the RETURN key emphatically. "The killer is going to be sorry he played games with us."

"That reminds me," I said. "Sid, check my logic. The only one who could have the blood-spattered letters is the killer, right?"

"Right."

"So the person framing Hynes has to be the killer. And unless we posit that the killer fooled somebody else with the letters, who then sent them to us, the killer is also the one who sent us the letters. So now we can be fairly sure we're dealing with just one person, which is a relief."

"That works for me."

I checked the clock on the wall. "Madison, are you ready to go?" In addition to sharing the news about Hynes, I'd told them about Judy Cater's picket line, and my realization that since she had a demonstrable motive for wanting Overfeld shut down, we should talk to her next. Madison had indeed been intending to go to Wizard Gary's, so our plan was to go into town early and grab pizza for dinner. Then Madison would go play while I waited around in hopes of encountering Judy.

"I guess," she said, sounding unenthused. "Let me get my game stuff."

I looked at Sid, who shrugged with a rattle, and we packed his skull, hand, and phone into the sugar skull bag—the selection he was starting to call his away team—and climbed into the car. If something was bothering Madison, she'd tell me sooner or later.

It turned out to be sooner. We'd barely turned onto the main road when she spoke up. "Mom, I'm not loving the plan for tonight."

"Do you not want to play?"

"No, it's not that. I just don't like suspecting Ms. Cater of being a killer. She's kind of weird about the college and all, but she seems okay. Do you really think she's a murderer?"

"Honestly, no."

"Hey!" Sid said from inside his bag. "She's our best suspect, and the only one we know of with a motive for wanting the school shut down."

Madison said, "Suppose she is the killer—and I don't believe she is—but suppose she is. Suppose we get her arrested. What would happen to Jen? She doesn't get along with her father at all. She says he and her mother got divorced because her mother realized he didn't like Jen being . . . Jen."

I'd never gotten as far as marriage myself. I'd been engaged to Madison's father when I got pregnant, and when he made it plain he didn't want a child then or possibly ever, we parted ways with no regrets, at least not on my side. Knowing Judy had done something similar made me like her more.

"Yeah, but if Ms. Cater goes to jail, Jen will have to live with him, which would be awful for her."

"Georgia, is that right?" Sid asked.

"I don't know. Maybe Judy could make other arrangements. But here's the thing. We may *think* she's innocent, but we *know* Hynes is, even if he is a jerk. I don't want an innocent jerk to be convicted for murder."

"I get that," Madison said, but she still didn't look happy.

"Look, sweetie, if you don't want to go, we'll head back home."

"But you and Sid would still investigate Ms. Cater, wouldn't you?"

"I'm afraid we would, but we can come up with a way that doesn't involve you."

She pondered long enough that I was looking for a place to turn around, when she finally said, "Let's keep going. I don't think Ms. Cater is guilty, but I'd rather we were sure, and if you guys are going to investigate anyway, then you might need your Padawan."

"Okay. It just so happens that it's Padawan's choice day at the pizza parlor."

"Even if the Padawan wants pineapple on her pizza?" she said with a small grin.

"Do your worst."

Overfeld House of Pizza wasn't the best pizza place I'd ever been to, but it was the best in Overfeld, so it was a good thing we'd arrived early. A quintet of Madison's fellow Yu-Gi-Oh! players was at one table, and we sat near enough to them that Madison could socialize while we ate.

Partway through the meal, my phone buzzed with a text.

SID: *Madison has a lot of friends, doesn't she?*

GEORGIA: *My view has always been quality over quantity. Having you as a best friend, for instance, is better than having a whole crowd of other people.*

SID: *You know, you're really good at this friendship stuff.*

GEORGIA: *I learned from the best.*

His response was an emoji of a happy skull.

Since Madison's friends had been dropped off at the restaurant, she opted to walk with them to Wizard Gary's. That left me at loose ends for a few hours, so I picked up a few nonperishables at the grocery store, took Sid to the bookstore and bought him a Dana Cameron thriller, and then got myself a soda so I could sit on the bench nearest to the game store in hopes that Judy would show up early.

Though Sid and I played Words with Friends to pass the time, it was still a long wait, and I was starting to think I'd need to come up with another way to get time with Judy when I saw her coming up the sidewalk.

I waved, and she adjusted her aim to come my way.

"Are they still playing?" she asked.

"As far as I can tell." The windows of Wizard Gary's were so thoroughly decorated with posters advertising games that it wasn't possible to see much. "Would you like to join me?"

"Thank you." She took a seat on the bench. "I noticed you at our demonstration today."

"I certainly noticed you. How did the conversation with President Fernandez go?"

"It was mixed. He did seem sympathetic to the cause, but he didn't commit to anything other than supplying overtime pay for the police doing extra sweeps on campus, and of course that's moot now."

"It is?"

"Haven't you heard? They arrested one of the professors for the murder of Neil Farmer. So the extra security isn't needed anymore."

"I suppose not." It would have made sense if Hynes were actually guilty, but since he wasn't, the saboteur/killer/forger now had an open field. The question of the day was whether or not Judy Cater was that triple threat. "I suppose it's going to be permanently moot, if the rumors I've heard are true."

"What do you mean?"

I pretended to be reluctant. "Maybe I shouldn't say, but . . . Well, I'll be gone before it happens anyway. Word is that Overfeld is in financial trouble."

"You're kidding!" Judy said, looking honestly shocked. "How bad is it?"

"Pretty bad. A lot of the professors are looking for positions elsewhere, which they wouldn't do if there weren't a good chance that the school is about to go bankrupt."

"That's terrible!" Judy said.

"It is? I kind of thought you'd be a lot happier if Overfeld were to shut down."

"Why would you think that?"

"You mean other than the flyers you posted all over campus and today's picket line? Not to mention the Facebook group and that button you're wearing right now." Her pin back badge said *Overfeld College, Pay Your Share* in bright green letters. "You told me yourself you have a knee-jerk reaction against the place."

"That's just because I want them to pay their fair share," she said. "The costs incurred by graduation and homecoming week alone—" She saw my smile and stopped. "Okay, I can see why you'd think I wanted the school gone, but I really don't. Overfeld College is the heart of this town, not to mention one of the largest employers. Their students eat at our restaurants and shop at our stores, and their parents and visiting teams keep our hotels alive. Can you imagine how many bars would shut down without the students? I work in a real estate office, and over half our business involves properties purchased by Overfeld employees or rented by students. Honestly, I'd rather have things continue as they are than to lose the school!"

"I see what you mean." She could have been faking, but I didn't think so, and if Sid and I were right about the killer's ultimate goal of harming the university, then Judy wasn't the killer. I was relieved, and Madison would be, too. Still, just because she wasn't the killer, that didn't mean she didn't have information I could use. "You know, so many things had been going wrong on campus. Fuses burning out for no reason, equipment going missing, microphones suddenly ceasing to work, bed bugs in the dorm. It just goes on and on. I can't decide if it's bad luck or if somebody is doing it on purpose."

"You mean pranks? Or vandalism?"

"I was actually thinking sabotage," I said, "but I can't imagine why. With the school already in bad shape, that kind of thing could tip the balance toward bankruptcy. Who would want to shut down the school?" I looked at her. "I don't suppose you've heard of any big real estate deals in the offing."

"Not lately," she said.

Before I could ask anything else, she drew herself up. "Wait, did you think my committee was behind this sabotage?"

"What? No, of course not." I was even telling the truth—I'd only thought of her, not her committee—but she didn't look convinced. "You're just not the kind of woman who'd do something like that." And she wasn't. Madison's instincts had been spot on.

She was somewhat mollified. "It seems to me that the things you're describing would have to be done by an insider, which I am not. I haven't actually gone into any of the campus buildings in years."

"That's a good point. Maybe a disgruntled ex-employee or—"

"What about the professor who committed the murder? I've heard that he was, if not a rapist, then the next thing to it. Don't you think he must have gone insane?"

It wasn't a theory I could refute without revealing that I knew a lot more than I should have, so we segued into tales we'd heard about crazy people doing crazy things. All we needed was a campfire and s'mores, and it would have been just like a Girl Scout camping trip.

Since I could feel vibrations from Sid-in-the-bag, I knew he was impatient with the discussion, but I couldn't think of a way to get Judy back on track, and I doubted it would have done any good if I had. I just couldn't picture her as a saboteur, forger, or killer. She was, however, great at telling creepy stories. I might have been able to compete if I'd pulled out Sid's skull and got him to make scary noises, but that wouldn't have been fair.

Judy had just finished telling me how her neighbor's cousin's hairstylist had found traces of a stranger living in her attic without her even knowing it when a gaggle of gamers emerged from Wizard Gary's. After fond farewells were exchanged, they scattered in all directions, with Madison and Jen breaking from the pack to join Judy and me.

"Good game?" I asked.

"The best," Madison said. "Jen and I teamed up!"

"Did you win?"

"Yes, we did," Jen said.

"We didn't just win," Madison said. "We annihilated them!" She held up a hand, and when Jen just looked at it, she said, "Don't leave me hanging, Jen. High five!"

Jen gingerly completed the gesture.

"Shall we celebrate with some ice cream?" I said, and we walked to Morricone's. Once we had our treats, the girls talked games while Judy and I talked movies. I felt a little guilty about Sid not having anybody to talk to, but since I kept feeling small vibrations, I was pretty sure he was either playing a game or talking on Facebook, so he wasn't totally bored.

Afterward, we split up into family groups to head toward our cars.

"So Ms. Cater isn't the killer," Madison said.

"How did you figure that?" I asked

"Because you wouldn't have eaten ice cream with her if you thought she was."

From the sugar skull bag, Sid said, "Hey, wait until we get to the car so I can join in!"

"Sorry," I said, but I did mouth *You're right* to Madison.

Once we were driving home, I said, "No, I don't think Judy is the killer. She doesn't have a motive."

"What about her hating the college?"

"It turns out it's more of a love/hate relationship. Sure, she wants them to contribute more to town finances, but she says that indirectly, they already bring in a lot of money." I explained her concerns. "So unless she wants to destroy the town, too, I can't see her going after the college." I tapped the skull in Madison's lap. "What do you think, Sid?"

"I think you're right."

"Then why did you keep bouncing around in the bag while we were talking?"

"If you'd read your texts, you'd know."

"It's not overly polite to read texts in the middle of a conversation."

"Madison and her friends do it."

"It's kind of a generational difference."

"You and I do it."

"It also varies depending on how close a friend you are. When you're BFFs, you can get away with a lot of behavior that would be considered rude with somebody else."

"Friendship is complicated," he grumbled. "Anyway, I was trying to get your attention to tell you I don't think Judy is the killer."

"Two brain cavities with a single thought," I said.

"Right now it's two brain cavities without a single thought," Sid said. "We're out of suspects."

"Maybe we should think about what we know about the killer," I said.

"He's an ossifying piece of sacrum," Sid muttered.

"True, but not overly helpful. I'm going to guess he works at the college in some capacity. Talking to Judy reminded me that most of the sabotage happened inside buildings that would have been hard for an outsider to sneak into. So faculty, admin people, custodial staff, cafeteria staff, even security."

"What about students?" Madison asked.

"I think we can eliminate the Andorians," I said. "They only have run of the campus during certain hours."

"Not to burst your bubble, Mom, but students have been seen all around town long after curfew."

"How do they get away?"

I could tell Madison was making a mighty effort not to roll her eyes. "Seriously? Since some of them are on the first floor, with windows, going out after bed check is easy. And you said yourself that the dorm monitors show movies just about every night—that's a great time to sneak away. Or with some advance planning, they could trade places with other students and confuse the monitors. Plus there's always bribery—some of these kids get generous allowances."

"Should I ask how you know all these methods?" I asked.

"Should I ask why you don't? You must have been a boring teenager, Mom."

"I was not!" I said and pointedly ignored the knowing glances Madison and Sid exchanged. "Okay, Padawan, why would a high school student want to destroy a college?"

"Why would anybody want to destroy a college?" Sid asked.

I sighed. "Okay, fine, we won't eliminate the Andorians. But we are all agreed that it's probably somebody on campus, right?"

Madison nodded, and Sid jiggled his skull as best he could without his neck.

"What else have we got?" I asked.

Sid said, "The sabotage might imply some knowledge of electronics, but I don't think it would require a lot. Ditto the bed bugs. All you'd have to do is go on Yelp and find somebody complaining about an infestation at a hotel, and you could check in long enough to harvest some."

I couldn't hold back my shudder at the thought of carrying around vermin in order to infest another person's bed. "That proves this guy is nasty."

"As if his being a killer hadn't told us that," Madison said.

"Almost anybody could kill, given the right motive and situation," I said.

"You really think so?"

"If somebody tried to hurt you—I mean really hurt you—I would kill in a heartbeat."

She blinked. "Okay, I didn't expect that."

Maybe I wasn't so boring after all. "Since killing Neil was unplanned, that isn't necessarily proof of anything but panic, but painting Hynes as a sexual predator was nasty."

"Does him being a forger help?" Madison asked. "Wouldn't that be hard?"

Sid tried to shake his skull. "All he needed was access to the internet, a printer, and a couple of typewriters."

"Who has a typewriter anymore? Let alone two?"

"There are three in the attic in Pennycross," Sid said.

"And they wouldn't be hard to find in a thrift store," I added. "I bet there are typewriters stuck away at Overfeld, too."

"So we don't know who has a motive, and just about anybody would have means and opportunity." Madison sighed in disgust. "Are all of your cases this impossible?"

"Yes," Sid and I said in unison.

"But there is something else we know," I said. "The killer is getting impatient."

"Why do you say that?" Sid asked.

"Think about it. He sent us the letters Tuesday, and by Friday, he'd already gotten Hynes arrested. You would think he could have waited until after the weekend."

"He must have expected us to break into Hynes's office right away so we'd find whatever so-called evidence he managed to plant," Sid said with a huff. "As if we'd do that."

I raised one eyebrow, something that annoys him because he has no eyebrows to raise. "Please, if we hadn't figured out that the letters were forged—"

"If *who* hadn't figured it out?"

"Fine. If *you* hadn't figured out the letters were forged, you'd be pushing me to break into that office right now."

"I guess we'll never know," he said. "Fernandez got stuck with it, instead." Then he went still. "Fernandez . . ."

"What about him?"

"He works on campus, with access to every building, and he's smart enough to figure out forging and bed bugs. How do we know somebody really called him to get him to break into Hynes's office?"

"We don't, do we?" I said.

"Wait, you guys think the college president wants to kill his own college?" Madison said. "Does he want to be out of work?"

"If the school is already in trouble, he might want it to happen sooner rather than later. Say he's got a job opportunity that won't wait but he can't get out of his contract. Or his contract includes a golden parachute clause in case of shutdown, and he needs the money right away. Or even what Judy said—maybe he's crazy."

"Somebody around here is crazy," Madison said, not quite under her breath.

"Padawans are not allowed to diagnose the mental health of their trainers," Sid said. "Georgia, remember how Fernandez came to see you, supposedly to see if you were doing okay? Obviously he knows about your detective work."

"I just thought he was being nice."

"Maybe, maybe not. When we get back to the cabin, I think I'm going to hit the web and see just what I can find out about him." His hand wriggled around. "Madison, hold your hand up, would you?"

"Okay. Why am I doing this?"

"Because I can't rub my hands together in eager anticipation with only one hand."

This time Madison did roll her eyes as she said, "A Padawan's work is never done."

True to his word, as soon as we got home Sid retrieved the rest of himself and his laptop and went to work in his bedroom. Madison took Byron out, and I'd expected her to either go online or put in a video afterward, but instead she sat on the couch, staring into space as she ruffled Byron's fur.

"Are you still feeling bad about our suspecting Judy?"

"No, I get why we had to. If she'd been guilty, something needed to be done, and I'm glad we know she's not. I was just thinking about Jen."

"What about her?"

"When I asked her to team with me, she looked surprised at first. Then she said, 'I understand. You want to win, and I've got the best chance of beating Nasir.' And I was like, 'Sure, I want to win, but I asked you because I thought it would be fun for us to play together.' And she looked really surprised, which is just sad. She's a little weird, but she's okay."

"I like her, too, but my standards in friends are unusual."

"I heard that," Sid yelled from his bedroom.

Madison and I grinned.

"Anyway," I said, "I'm glad you like her. I think she could use more friends—and you're a good one."

"Yeah? Thanks. Just don't expect us to act out one of those teen movies."

"What teen movies?"

"The ones where a girl who's an a ugly duckling makes friends with a popular girl, gets a makeover and lessons in being cool, and changes into a gorgeous swan."

"Absolutely not," I said. "For one, I don't think Jen is an ugly duckling. She's fine the way she is."

Sid interjected again. "Madison, I hate to break this to you, but I knew your mother when she was a teenager. She doesn't know anything about being popular."

"I'm coming for you, Bone Boy!" I said and started for his bedroom.

He slammed and locked the door before I could get there.

So after everything else that had happened that day, I got Madison to give me my first lesson in picking locks.

CHAPTER THIRTY-ONE

Though I slept in Saturday morning, which should have given Sid plenty of time to dig up any available dirt on President Fernandez, when I got up I could tell by the looseness of his bones that he'd had no luck.

"The guy is like a picture-perfect college administrator," he complained. "The faculty respects him, the board of directors does just about anything he suggests, and even the unions think he's great. On a personal level, he's happily married with two well-adjusted kids. There's no sign of money problems, either. He and his wife are both only children, whose parents were well-off, and they inherited from both sides of the family. If there's anything shady in his background, he is a world-class shade hider."

"I could talk to Mo on Monday, but she seems to love the guy, too. If she didn't, I'd be able to tell. You should have seen her when I asked about the people from—" I stopped.

"The people from where?"

"I told you about the group of people from Hardison Business School touring Overfeld, didn't I?"

"You sure told me how you burned Professor Hynes," he said with glee.

"That was fun," I admitted. "Mo was there, too, and even though she laughed, she said Hynes was a bad enemy to have. Then we talked about him being a predator, and she said she was sure he wasn't and why."

"You told me that already."

"I know, but the point is she was very open about everything until I asked about the tour. That's when she started hemming and hawing and tried to tell me she didn't know what was going on, though she obviously did. She can't lie for beans."

"So you're thinking there might be something important about that tour?"

"Why else would she lie?"

"Can we get the truth out of her another way?"

"Probably not. She likes to gossip, but she's also loyal to Overfeld. Fortunately, I think I know who I can talk to." I dug around in my satchel until I found the card Walker Schild had given me. I figured it was at best a fifty-fifty shot that he'd be available, but when I called, he answered right away and said he'd be happy to meet me for coffee and conversation.

"You want me to come with?" Sid asked.

"I'd rather you stay with Madison."

"Why? Is something wrong?"

"It just occurred to me that since we know Hynes is innocent, then the real killer is still on the loose. We don't know who he is, but he knows I take an interest in murders and . . . It's probably stupid, but I'd rather not leave her alone."

"I will guard her with my lack of life." He waggled a finger bone at me. "You be careful, too! In fact . . ." He popped off one of his fingers. "Put this in your pocket. If you go missing, I'll be able to track it."

"I do have GPS on my phone."

"Phones can go out of range, or run out of power, or be taken away. Nobody is going to want to steal a finger bone."

"Sid, did you just come up with an innovative way to give me the finger?"

"Of course not. It's only on loan." But he was grinning.

The drive to Northbury was about the same distance as it was to Overfeld, but the town itself was more bustling and built up. I drove past the front gates to Hardison School of Business on my way to the strip mall coffee shop where Walker had suggested we meet.

I had stopped along the way to pick up something, so I was carrying a gift bag when I went into the coffee shop. Walker was already at a table in the corner, and as soon as I sat down, I pushed the bag toward him.

"What's this?" He looked inside and started laughing. "You got me Oreos!"

"Note that it's the family-sized package, should you be inclined to share."

"Is that a hint?"

"Oreos do go well with coffee."

"Speaking of which, what can I get you?"

After the ritual negotiation of who would pay and what my coffee specifications were, he treated me to a large cup of the shop's daily special, and we broke out the cookies.

Walker asked about my parents and Deborah, and after I caught him up, I asked about his family in return. Once that topic was thoroughly covered, he said, "Not that I'm not glad to see you again, but I'm guessing you had a particular reason for calling me this morning."

"I do, and I'm not sure how awkward what I'm going to ask you might be. Hence the cookie-based bribe."

He squirmed a little. "Before you start, I should warn you that I have nothing to do with hiring faculty, and we really don't do a lot in your line."

"Oh, I'm not looking for a job. Or rather, I'm always on the lookout for a better job, but that's not why I called."

"Not that I'd have blamed you if you had. I know how tough the academic job market is. Why do you think I switched to the business side of things?"

"I did wonder how you went from Chaucer to checks and balances."

"My own fault. Your mother warned me that I needed to specialize in a less crowded part of the field, but I didn't listen. I was sure that nobody before me had studied Chaucer with my insight."

"He is pretty obscure," I said.

"After a long and fruitless job hunt, I decided academia wasn't for me and went back to school for business. Only to end up working at a college after all."

"It's your job that I'm curious about. Can you tell me why you and your colleagues from Hardison were touring Overfeld the other day?"

Now he squirmed a lot. "That's actually pretty sensitive information."

"Really? Why is that?"

"The fact is, there are some ongoing negotiations and nothing has been signed, and until plans are finalized, I'm hesitant to say anything."

"I'm not going to broadcast anything, Walker. This is for my personal information only." Well, that and Sid's and Madison's. "It's just that the rumor is that Overfeld is in financial straits, and if one were considering taking a position at a college, one would want to know that said college wasn't going to be disappearing overnight."

"Ah, I get what you're saying," he said. "One might offer congratulations."

I smiled and took a sip of coffee while feeling guilty. I knew he thought I was talking about having a job from Overfeld, which was precisely what I'd intended, even though I hadn't actually said I had an offer. I was getting a taste of how Sid had to play with the truth with his online friends, and I didn't like it nearly as much as I did Oreos.

"Since this is purely for your information . . ." He leaned forward and lowered his voice. "Hardison has been wanting to expand for a while. We'd been planning to build a new facility nearby, but then we were approached by President Fernandez to see if we'd be interested in a merger with Overfeld."

"A teaching college and a business school? That doesn't sound like a match made in heaven."

"It's not as big a mismatch as you might think. Our expansion plans are in the area of corporate training and executive education, and you may not realize it, but one of the most revered names in executive education is that of Davidson Hynes."

"Now that you mention it, I think I had heard that. So if this goes through, Overfeld would stay open?"

"It would, though their focus might shift a little. There'd be more corporate communications and less literature for instance—as much as it pains me personally to say that—but no programs would be eliminated, and we'd be able to streamline a lot of their back office functions. As a bonus, Overfeld students would be able to attend Hardison classes and vice versa."

"That's huge. No wonder you want it kept quiet until it's a done deal. Or is it already a done deal other than the paperwork?"

"I won't lie. The situation is a little precarious right now. I'm still in favor of the idea, and came back from vacation to try to move things forward, but it's no secret that the physical plant at Overfeld isn't exactly in optimum condition. Then there was that murder, and now all this bad press about Dr. Hynes."

"I don't think Hynes killed anybody, and I'm sure he didn't prey on any students."

"I hope you're right, but I'm kind of surprised you're willing to defend him. I got the impression that you two aren't exactly friendly."

"We're not. I don't even like the guy personally, and he sure doesn't like me. That doesn't make him a killer or a creeper."

"Fair, but the question from our point of view is whether or not his value to Hardison has been diminished. I don't want to sound callous, but there's something about working at a business school that makes you focus on the bottom line."

"I get that. If Overfeld had been focusing more on their bottom line, maybe they wouldn't be in financial trouble. So what happens if the deal falls through?"

"Hardison reverts to Plan A, which is to buy up some land we've had our eye on and start building a Corporate Education Institute. It'll cost a lot more and take a lot longer to get a program up and running than a successful merger would, which is why I'm against it. Not to mention the fact that it won't be easy to find a marquee-worthy name like Hynes's."

"Then I hope it works out, for everybody involved," I said. "And thank you for telling me."

"Like I said the other day, I owe your mother a lot."

After that, we finished up our coffee, said our goodbyes, and I started back home.

I was nearing the Ashbury/Overfeld town line when a black SUV came up on my bumper and started to pass me illegally. I glanced over, intending to make use of the hand gesture every Massachusetts driver learns to perform even before mastering parallel parking, but I held off when I recognized the driver. It was Director Ridley. He zoomed past and was out of sight in seconds.

It didn't take a detective, even an amateur one, to deduce that something else had gone wrong at Overfeld College, and I wanted to know what. At the next light, I made a quick call to Madison and told her I'd be a little later than expected, and that she and Sid should keep playing the game I could hear in the background. I figured if I got to campus and didn't see any signs of a commotion, I'd turn around and go home.

I did not turn around and go home. As soon as I got to the town green, I spotted a pair of TV broadcast trucks parked in front of campus and a crowd gathered in front of Kumin Hall. A podium had been set up at the top of the steps, and Mo was there arranging papers. If it wasn't a press conference, then every press conference scene in every movie I'd ever seen had it totally wrong.

Since local police had part of the street blocked, I zipped down a side street to get to the faculty parking lot, then jogged over to Kumin, arriving at the edge of the crowd just in time to see President Fernandez come to the podium. Ridley was beside him, looking resolute despite his earlier frantic race from Northbury. Chief Bezzat was there, too, wearing a dress uniform.

Fernandez tapped the microphone, and I thought I saw a brief sigh of relief that it was working as intended. The crowd quieted, and he began. "Good afternoon. I'm here to address the tragic events that have taken place here at Overfeld College. As you know, Neil Farmer, a valued member of the Overfeld family, was recently killed. We've cooperated fully with the police in their investigation, even when evidence was found that seems to implicate one of our own. I assure you that we want nothing more than to get to the truth." In a firmer voice, he said, "There has not been and never will be a cover-up of malfeasance of any kind on this campus."

"What about the letters accusing Professor Hynes of predatory behavior?" a reporter called out.

"Overfeld Police Chief Bezzat will respond to that." Fernandez stepped aside so she could take his place at the podium.

"In regards to the letters found in Professor Hynes's office," she said, "our investigation has established that they were not authentic."

"What do you mean 'not authentic?'"

"I mean that they were fabricated by a person or persons unknown. The events described did occur, but they took place in colleges other than Overfeld, and Professor Davidson Hynes was not involved."

"How do you figure that?"

I'd wondered if she'd claim the credit for the discovery, and I considered it a mark in her favor that she did not. "An anonymous tip alerted us to the real source of the letters," she said. I didn't even mind when she added, "Of course, we had already begun to investigate that possibility, but the tipster did save us valuable time."

"Does that mean Professor Hynes is no longer a suspect in the murder?"

"It does not," she said, and while Fernandez and Ridley kept their faces blank, I suspect it was a strain. "The blood on the letters; their being found in Professor Hynes's possession; and the contents of the letters, no matter how spurious, add up to strong evidence, and we will be keeping Professor Hynes in custody for the time being." The reporter started to ask another question, but Chief

Bezzat held up her hand to stop him. "Our investigation is continuing, and I have no further comment at this time." She nodded at Fernandez before walking briskly down the stairs, ignoring the questions being fired at her as two officers cleared a path to her cruiser.

Apparently Fernandez and Ridley had taken advantage of Chief Bezzat's departure to slip inside the building because they were gone when I turned back around, and a pair of maintenance workers was already wrestling the podium back into Kumin. On a whim, I climbed the steps to hold the door for them and followed them inside.

I'd hoped for an opportunity to eavesdrop, but Fernandez and Ridley were standing just inside the door. Fernandez looked glad to see me while Ridley looked annoyed, which was par for the course with those two.

"Dr. Thackery," Fernandez said, "is there something we can help you with?"

"That was my question for you, actually. With all the . . ." I couldn't think of a word that quite expressed it. "With all that's going on, I thought you might need some extra help with Parents' Day preparations."

"We've got it under control," Ridley said.

"Director Ridley has been doing yeoman labor," Fernandez added, "but we do thank you for asking."

"Good enough. I'll see you Monday."

I felt a little nervous turning my back on Fernandez, but he didn't attack, so Sid shouldn't have had anything to object to.

CHAPTER THIRTY-TWO

My logic did not stop Sid from objecting.

"In what way can going into a building with Fernandez be considered *being careful*?" Sid demanded when I got home, caught him and Madison still up, and gave him back his finger.

"It wasn't exactly deserted, Sid. Ridley was there, the maintenance men were there, and Mo had been around, so she was probably still there."

"All of whom work for Fernandez."

"You're right, he's the Fagin of academia. Or maybe the Godfather."

"Madison, stick your tongue out at your mother on my behalf."

"I'm so not doing that. And before you say anything, that is not part of my Padawan responsibilities." She went back to reading her book.

"And didn't you tell me this morning that there is absolutely nothing suspicious in Fernandez's background," I reminded him.

"I could have missed something!"

"Not you," I said jokingly. Belatedly, I realized his bones were looser than they should have been. "Seriously, Sid, you're good at this."

"Then why can't I find anything that helps? We're no closer to finding out who killed Erik-slash-Neil than the day he died."

"That's it!" Madison said, slapping the book down. "Enough murder talk. If we knew how to get Hynes out of jail, I'd be all for it, but we don't. So we're taking the rest of the weekend off."

"Excuse me?" I said.

"Mom, what do you tell me when I'm pulling my hair out trying to finish a homework assignment?"

"To suck it up, and stop whining."

"No! You tell me to take a break."

"I tell you to take an hour-long break, not a day and a half."

"Well this case has been going on a lot longer than most of my homework assignments, so we need a longer break. Let's go swimming!"

"You two go ahead," Sid said. "There are people in the other cabins, so I'll stay inside."

"Yeah, that's not going to happen," I said. Madison was right. We needed a break, and if we left Sid inside, he'd go back to working, with a side order of moping. "How about a movie?"

"Whose turn is it to pick one out?" Sid said.

"No, I mean let's go to a movie. All of us. Well, not Byron, but the rest of us."

"Um, Georgia," Sid started to say.

"No, we can do this. Madison said the theater in town has reclining seats, right? So I'll recline, put the sugar skull bag on my lap, and you should be able to see just fine."

"You mean I can actually go to a movie? In a theater?"

"Sure as sacrum. See what's playing, and pick whichever one you want to see."

He snapped back together with a loud clack and was typing away at his laptop in seconds. "How about *Ant-Man and the Wasp*?"

"Perfect." There was a show in two hours, which gave Madison and me enough time to grab lunch before heading over to the theater, where a thoroughly good time was had by all. Sid was a perfect movie companion. He kept quiet, turned off his phone, and unlike Madison, didn't steal any of my popcorn.

Afterward, we went back to the cabin to grill burgers, and we spent the rest of the evening playing Mario games on the Wii. Madison even made Sid pinky swear not to work on the case while she and I were asleep, and Sid never breaks a pinky swear.

Sunday wasn't quite so festive because we had chores like cleaning and food shopping to attend to, but we kept music and/or videos playing while we worked and even carried the sugar skull bag to the grocery store so Sid could ride in the shopping cart. Why somebody who didn't eat was so interested in groceries was beyond me, but he enjoyed it, which was the point.

I noticed, however, that Sid did not pinky swear that he wouldn't work on the case Sunday night after bedtime, so I wasn't surprised when I heard him typing away when I had to go to the bathroom in the middle of the night. As for me, I managed to keep my mind elsewhere until Monday at lunchtime, when Professor Hynes walked into the cafeteria in Kumin Hall.

CHAPTER THIRTY-THREE

As usual, we adjuncts and the admin staff were occupying a pair of tables at the end of the cafeteria closest to the entrance. I wasn't facing the door, but Treva was, and she was the first to spot Hynes.

"Well don't that beat all," she said.

"What?" I said.

The people on her side of the table looked up and stared, and when the people on my side turned around, they did the same.

Hynes was still wearing one of his determinedly casual outfits, but for once, the wrinkles looked as if they were the result of being worn too long.

Hynes had to know we were watching him, but he pretended not to as he glanced around the room. Then he approached us. "Hey, guys," he said. "Is Ms. Heedles available?"

"She had a doctor's appointment," one of the admins stammered.

"Could you pass on a message for me?" he said. "I'm not going to be taking any calls today. I'm going to crash in my office." His lips tightened, and his voice sounded strained when he said, "The police are finally finished in there."

"I'll tell her."

"Great. You might ask her to send a janitor, too, when there's one available. There's no telling what kind of mess they made."

"You bet."

"Great. Do you know if my supplies ever showed up? I'm nearly out of ink for my pen."

"I'll check on that right way."

"Hey, no rush. Finish your lunch first." Then he strolled away, ignoring those of us who were watching as attentively as if he was acting out the final episode of *Game of Thrones*.

"That was unexpected," Charles said, demonstrating his mastery of understatement.

That opened the floodgates of speculation, and I listened just long enough to verify that nobody knew anything more than I did before I texted Madison and Sid:

> GEORGIA: *Hynes is out of jail.*
>
> SID: *Released? Or did he break out?*
>
> GEORGIA: *Released. He's here on campus, not running off with Thelma and Louise. Madison, are you there?*
>
> MADISON: *Yes, and I'll consult my sources.*
>
> SID: *I'll check the local news sites.*
>
> GEORGIA: *Ping me if you get anything.*

By then it was time to go back to class. As with the first session, my students were all over the place. Some were still agitated by the murder and arrest; some were working particularly hard because it was the last week of the program; and some were slacking off because it was the last week of the program. The final class sessions would be on Wednesday, though the Andorian dance planned for Tuesday night would probably mean that those final classes would be slept through, and parents would begin arriving Wednesday afternoon to have dinner with the students. Thursday would be Parents' Day, with tours, a release party for the magazine my students had produced, an art show, concerts, two plays, and a ceremony in the evening to recognize special achievements. Friday the kids would be busy packing up their dorm rooms and saying goodbye to one another, though I'd be available in class in case anybody wanted to come by for farewells or to request recommendation letters for college applications.

Madison, Sid, and I would have the cabin for another two weeks, which would be pure relaxation time. At least it would be if we could figure out who'd killed Neil Farmer. If we couldn't, I didn't think any of us would enjoy it very much.

Just before break time, I got a text.

SID: *Local press says Hynes had an alibi for the time of the murder, but he didn't tell the police until Sunday, and it wasn't confirmed until this morning. He's still facing charges for assaulting Bezzat but got bail for that.*

GEORGIA: *Any word on what the alibi was? Or why it took so long for him to mention it?*

SID: *Nope, and probably because he thought they'd let him go because of what a big shot he is.*

MADISON: *I got nothing.*

The only reason I didn't start drumming my fingers is that I knew it would disturb my students. I probably didn't need to know what Hynes's alibi was—if it satisfied the police, it was almost certainly legit—but I just couldn't figure out why he'd taken so long to let the police know. Was it something to do with the way he'd been framed?

I tried to put it aside so I could lead the workshop part of the class but didn't entirely succeed. Fortunately, by that point in the program, the Andorians were well-practiced at giving constructive feedback—even without a talking stick—so I didn't have to do much. That gave me time to come up with somebody to ask about the alibi.

As soon as class was over, I went down to the admin office and found Mo assembling programs for the plays to be performed on Thursday.

"Need a hand?" I asked.

"Hey, no, that's not in your job description."

"I don't mind. The way things have been going lately, we're all doing things outside our job descriptions."

"You've got that right," she said. "If you really don't mind, you can help me fold." As we worked, she said, "If we ever get the budget for a new copier, I want one that folds pages for us."

"Those do save a lot of time." I folded a while. "By the way, did anybody tell you that Professor Hynes was looking for you?"

"Oh, I heard all about it. People around here are crazy, you know. Half the cafeteria staff was afraid to stick around after he showed up. They think he's going to murder them next."

"The cops let him out. He must have an alibi or something."

"Yeah, he's got an alibi," she said with a snort.

"What am I missing?"

"I really shouldn't say."

I shrugged as if it were no big deal. No true gossip can resist that kind of encouragement, and Mo was a true gossip.

"Okay," she said, "I was there when President Fernandez and Ridley saw Hynes, and they asked what had happened, and he said the police were satisfied with his alibi. He acted like that should be enough, but you know Ridley, he wanted the details, and Fernandez thought they should know, too. So he finally told them."

"Should I ask?"

"No, and I shouldn't tell you, either, but I'm going to. It turns out he wasn't in town the night of the murder. He went to Manchester. For a date."

"Really? I guess he's starting to get over the loss of his wife."

"Well, he's trying to. He created an account on Match.com and made a date with a woman he met online. Which is fine, but he was so sure he was going to score that he rented a hotel room and checked in before he went to meet her for dinner. They went to the Hanover Street Chophouse, which is the best place in town, but halfway through dinner, she went to the bathroom and didn't come back."

"She ditched him?"

"She ditched him!"

"Why? I mean, he's not my idea of a hot date, but she must have traded enough messages to know what she was getting into."

"Yes and no. I checked out his profile and noticed something about his picture. It's fifteen years old."

"You're kidding!"

"I mean, he looks good for his age, but he doesn't look like he did when that picture was taken. My guess is that once she realized how old he really is, she bailed as fast as she could."

"I'd feel sorry for him if he hadn't tried to fool her in the first place."

"Anyway, after all that, he was stuck paying for the room anyway, so he went back there and drowned his sorrows at the hotel bar."

"He said that?"

"No, of course not. What he said was that he stayed because he wanted to go shopping and do some other stuff. Maybe he did, maybe he moped in the hotel room all weekend. But the woman verified he was on time for dinner Friday night, the people at the restaurant said he was there until nine trying to act like he didn't care that he'd been ditched, and the bartender at the hotel said he closed the place down. Plus the hotel valet said his car was in the garage through Sunday morning. There's no way he could have killed Neil."

It sounded ironclad to me, too.

While we continued to fold programs, I asked if Mo had heard anything else about the investigation, but if the police had any suspects, word had not made it to her. That probably meant that word had not made it to anybody on campus. Once we'd finished with the stack of programs, I headed back home.

CHAPTER THIRTY-FOUR

I should have felt guilty about how much Sid, Madison, and I laughed over Hynes's short-lived love affair, but it was so like him to think he hadn't aged in fifteen years. And as I pointed out, he should be grateful he had a firm alibi, even if it was an embarrassing one.

"So he's definitely off the hook?" Madison said.

"I imagine the police will poke around to see if they can find a hole in the timeline," I said, "but I think it's a safe bet."

"So what do we do now?"

"Start looking at other people at Overfeld, I guess."

Sid shook his skull. "I tried that. I spent most of the day checking out the rest of the people there. Nothing."

"They're all clean?" I said.

"Mostly. One of the cafeteria workers did time a few years back for auto theft; Director Ridley lost a fight with the Ashbury zoning board over some property he owns; one of the admins has a couple of DUI citations; Matt, the music teacher, was involved in a couple of bar brawls; and Lisa in art shoplifted a sweater, though she swears it was an accident."

"They're not exactly a murderous bunch, are they?"

"Plus I didn't find a single motive for wanting to get the college shut down. As far as I can tell, nobody is independently wealthy, and therefore they all need their jobs."

"I'm almost tempted to give up and leave it to the police," I said, then saw the aggrieved expression that Sid shouldn't have been able to manage with a bare skull. "But of course, we still want to find Neil's murderer."

Sid's skull went back to normal. "I've been thinking about something Judy said, about how the extra police protection had been pulled off of campus."

"Right. Since they thought they had the killer, there was no reason for it."

"Are they going to reinstitute the patrols now that they know the killer is still out there?"

"Maybe not. I mean, nothing went wrong this weekend," I said.

"If I were the killer, I would be sure to lay low if I thought my frame job worked. Now he knows it didn't, and he must be steaming, maybe getting a little desperate. Remember what we decided earlier, that for some reason he's in a hurry to get the school shut down?"

I hated to do it, but I had to point out, "You know, with the session ending this week, most of the adjuncts are going to be leaving town. Particularly the dorm monitors. So if one of them is involved, they'd be looking at a shrinking window of opportunity."

"You're right," Sid said. "The police may not have drawn that conclusion, but they do know the killer is on the loose."

"That doesn't mean they'll add the patrols unless Fernandez helps pay for them."

"Hang on," Madison said, reaching for her phone. "I'll check."

"Bakshi's cousin?" Sid asked.

"No, Yvette's sister the cop. Why is it you can remember every single person who's ever been a member of the Avengers, but you can't remember my sources?"

"Because they don't have cool costumes."

Without missing a beat, Madison reached over and thunked him soundly on the skull, using just the right amount of force to keep from hurting her finger. I was so proud—our Padawan was growing up.

A few minutes later she was shaking her head. "Nope, no extra patrols. The cop sister is half-glad because she's got a hot date but half-mad because she was making overtime pay."

"Coccyx!" I said. "The killer could go after Hynes again, he could commit more sabotage, he could—He could do anything! I hate the idea of just waiting for him to act again."

"We don't have to," Sid said. "Somebody other than the police could patrol the campus."

"Like who?" Madison asked.

I didn't have to ask—I knew what Sid was thinking. "You want to guard Overfeld yourself, don't you?" Even before he nodded, I said, "Coccyx."

CHAPTER THIRTY-FIVE

I absolutely hated the idea. There were just too many ways that stationing Sid alone on campus could go wrong. But leaving the campus unwatched except for the regular security guards—the ones the saboteur had easily avoided before—didn't seem like a great idea, either. So I couldn't argue with his intentions, and I knew he was a grown-up skeleton and needed to make his own choices. That didn't stop me from trying to talk him out of it, of course, but since I didn't expect it to work, I wasn't surprised when it didn't. The best I could manage was to make suggestions about how he went about it.

To start with, I wanted him in disguise. It wasn't going to hide the fact that he was a skeleton—nothing but a full body-covering garment would do that, and the only ones we had available were a Deadpool costume I hadn't known he had and his long, black Death robe. For Sid to wear either of those would rouse as many suspicions as they soothed.

Instead, he put on my navy blue hoodie and a pair of Madison's black leggings over black sneakers stuffed with socks so his feet wouldn't rattle around in them. We rubbed down everything that showed around that with charcoal from the grill, which would make him difficult to see in the dark.

Once that was settled, I wanted Sid to familiarize himself with the layout of Overfeld. My suggestion was for him to study campus maps and maybe use Google Earth to take a virtual tour, but Madison had a better idea. It would still be light for a couple of hours, so she suggested we head back to campus and that she and I walk all around campus carrying Sid's skull in the sugar skull bag. If anybody asked what we were doing, we'd show them Pokémon Go! on our phones and say we'd heard there was a Mewtwo in the area. We only had to use the excuse twice, and by the time it got fully dark, I was pretty sure that all three of us knew the grounds better than most faculty members did.

We went back to the car, and I drove to the worst lit corner of the most remote parking lot on campus. Then Madison pulled Sid's skull and hand from the sugar skull bag while I unzipped his suitcase for the rest of him to emerge. Once Sid reassembled himself, Madison and I rubbed another coating of charcoal on his exposed bones.

"What do you think? Ninja material?" he asked when we were done.

"Absolutely," I lied. He really was hard to see in the shadows, and I was reasonably sure he'd make it through the night without scaring anybody into a heart attack. After making sure he had his phone tucked into a black pouch hung around his neck, he slipped away into the shadows.

I really hated leaving Sid behind when Madison and I headed back to the cabin. Not that I didn't trust him to be careful, but I was still worried and restless for the rest of the night. The only thing that made it bearable was Sid's texts reassuring me that everything was peaceful.

Despite sleeping badly, I got to campus extra early the next morning and bypassed the scrum at the coffee urn to head to my classroom. I closed and locked the door behind me and blocked it with a desk, just to be sure. Then I went to the storage closet at the back of the room and knocked.

"Who's there?" said a high-pitched voice.

"Who do you think?" Though Sid had continued to send texts through the wee hours of the morning, at some point he'd said his battery was dying, so he wouldn't be able send any more. The plan had been for him to pick the necessary locks to sneak into my classroom, but those few hours of not hearing from him meant I hadn't been sure he made it until I heard his silly voice. "You okay?"

"Of course." He opened the door. It was a good-sized closet, which I'd been using to store resource materials for my classes. Now it was being used to store a different kind of resource. "Did you bring my phone charger?"

"I did." I rolled over his suitcase. "Also a couple of charger bars, some books, and your laptop." Since the drive to and from the cabin was so long, Sid was going to have to spend the day in the closet, and I thought he could use some diversions.

"You're the best!" he said, grabbing for the bag. "I've already read all your class materials twice. Boy was I wishing I could sleep—it's boring around here at night."

"Boring is what we were hoping for," I reminded him. "I take it there was no trouble."

"Not a bit. I had no problem avoiding the security guards, when they ambled by, which they should be doing a lot more often than three times a night, in my opinion. Those guys wouldn't last a day in Runes of Legend with that attitude. They totally missed the two Andorians who snuck out of the dorm. Madison was right about that."

"Where did they go?"

"Right back into the dorm. Quickly."

"Can I safely assume you had something to do with that?"

"All I did was yell, 'Hey, you kids, what are you doing?' They didn't even look to see who was yelling." He grinned. "I enjoyed that."

"I'll bet. Anything else?"

"Nope. No saboteurs, infiltrators, or riots. Nothing but squirrels. I had no idea how many squirrels there were around here."

"Squirrels we can handle." I checked my watch. "I've got to get downstairs for morning announcements, and students are going to start showing up right after that. Text me if you need me, and remember to keep it quiet in there."

"They won't even know I'm here."

"That's kind of the point." I shut the door and locked it. If need be, Sid could open it from inside, but this way, no curious Andorians would happen upon him.

Morning announcements were even less interesting than usual. There were no disasters to report, and while the details about that night's Andorian dance were of vital interest to the Andorians, they were of less importance to me.

The rest of the day was uneventful. I did text Sid to see if he wanted me to visit with him during my lunch period, but he said he was in the middle of a good book and that I should go eat and scout around for useful gossip from the adjuncts.

When I got to the cafeteria, I was afraid a feud was brewing. Treva was sitting at a table all by herself, a box of tissues close at hand. I saw Charles stop by and leave a tray with soup and crackers, but he left her and came to join the rest of us.

"Is something wrong with Treva?" I asked.

"The dreaded summer cold, I'm afraid. She's isolating herself as much as possible to keep it from spreading."

"Poor thing. And of all weeks to get sick!"

"I'm afraid she's not looking forward to the program's ending festivities, especially the dance tonight. We dorm monitors are required to act as chaperones."

"That's going to be rough," I said, but my tone may have been more speculative than sympathetic. Last night I'd come up with every excuse I could find to stay in town, and now a honking big one had just been handed to me. In between bites of my chicken Caesar salad, I started texting.

GEORGIA: *Are you doing okay?*

Treva looked at her phone, then over at me.

TREVA: *No, I'm miserable. You know, you could come talk to me. Or are you afraid of catching the plague?*

GEORGIA: *Do you blame me if I am?*

TREVA: *Not really.*

GEORGIA: *Are you still on the hook for the dance tonight?*

TREVA: *You really think Ridley is going to cut me any slack?*

GEORGIA: *What if you got a substitute?*

TREVA: *Like who? Unless you're volunteering.*

GEORGIA: *I am.*

TREVA: *You mean it?*

GEORGIA: *Sure, why not? I can bring my daughter along. It'll be fun.*

TREVA: *Lady, you've got a different definition of fun than I do, but if you're willing, I won't say no.*

GEORGIA: *I'm willing. You go ahead and eat your soup. I'll get the details from Charles.*

Even at a distance, I could tell Treva was a lot happier. She even flashed me a grin in between sneezes.

"Charles," I said, "I'm going to substitute for Treva tonight, and since I was dozing off during the last meeting with Ridley, I need to know when to show up and what I'm supposed to do."

"Georgia, you are a paragon of virtue."

"It's no big deal. I've chaperoned high school dances for Madison before." It wasn't my favorite way to spend an evening, but I had survived. I jotted down the times and other information, then texted Madison.

GEORGIA: *How about a dance tonight?*

MADISON: *???*

GEORGIA: *Treva is sick, so I volunteered to take her post as chaperone at the Andorian dance. Thought you might want to come along.*

MADISON: *No, thanks.*

GEORGIA: *Why not? You love dancing.*

MADISON: *Not with a room full of people I don't know.*

GEORGIA: *Isn't dancing a good way to get to know people?*

MADISON: *Only in Pride and Prejudice. Can you make polite conversation at a high school dance?*

GEORGIA: *Good point. Are you okay with staying home alone?*

MADISON: *Actually, Jen invited me to go to a movie tonight. If you'll give us a ride there, Ms. Cater will pick us up after and take me home. Or bring me to meet you on campus, if you want.*

We conferred about times and dinner plans, and once that was dealt with, it was time to go back upstairs. Though class went fine, I admit I was impatient for it to be over so I could let Sid in on our plans. I was a little afraid that he'd think I was horning in on his patrol mission, which I was, but not because I didn't trust him. It's just that I'd spent most of my life helping to hide him, and to have him risk exposure made me increasingly nervous.

Fortunately, he didn't seem to mind. In fact, I realized that he was also feeling a little unsettled when he said, "I'm glad you'll be around. Being on campus without you or Madison nearby is unsettling."

After that, we modified the plans a bit, and I took Sid home with me. For one, he needed more charcoal for his ninja-inspired look. For another, it would be easier for him to get into position without being noticed if he was in the car, instead of in my classroom closet. And most important, it meant he wasn't left alone for several more hours. Though the circumstances of his not-quite-life had meant he'd had to spend a lot of time in isolation, that didn't mean he liked it.

By seven-thirty, I was back at Kumin Hall working so hard I almost regretted taking Treva's place. The Andorians were enjoying a cookout on the quad while we chaperones transformed the cafeteria into a festive dance venue. In other words, we pushed tables out of the way, strung fairy lights, twisted Mylar streamers around posts, left bouquets of helium balloons at every third table, and hung a disco ball. The DJ was set up, kitchen workers had put out munchies and drinks, and Paul was arranging a photo booth with backdrops and props. It didn't look like much, but I knew from past experience that once the music was turned up and the lights turned down, the kids would be more than satisfied.

At eight on the dot, the music started thumping and the lights dimmed, drawing the Andorians inside for their fun. Had Sid and Madison been there, I might have joined in on the dancing, especially when they played "Uptown Funk," but since I was on duty, I cleared abandoned drinks and paper plates off of tables, helped a young woman in need of sanitary supplies, distributed light sticks for Andorians to wave in time to the music, and kept an eye out for trouble.

My phone was on silent, not that anybody would have noticed it over the sounds of "Despacito," "Herp de Derp," or "Shut Up and Dance," and it vibrated with Sid's status reports every half an hour or so. I didn't hear from Madison as much, but she did let me know when the movie was over, and that she and Jen decided to go for ice cream.

We were in the last half hour of the dance when my phone vibrated again, but this time it was a phone call, which alarmed me. Sid's a texting fiend, but he never calls. I waved at Charles, held up my phone, then pointed to the door to let him know I was going somewhere I could actually hear. I went across the hall and stepped into the auditorium, which was empty except for an Andorian couple holding hands and quiet enough that I could answer the phone.

"Sid? What's—"

"Dobson is on fire. Madison and Jen are in there!"

Chapter Thirty-Six

I must have stuck the phone into my pocket after that, but I don't really recall doing so. I just remember running out the door as fast as I could, and though I heard Charles calling my name, I didn't slow down until I was at the steps of Dobson, where I could see a thin stream of smoke rising from the roof.

Sid trotted up to meet me, and it's a measure of my panic that I didn't even consider the fact that he was out in the open, where even his clothes and blackened bones wouldn't hide the fact of what he was.

"You're sure she's in there?" I asked.

"I saw her and Jen go in, and a minute later I saw smoke and texted her a warning, but she didn't answer. So I called you. Come on!"

The door wasn't locked, though it should have been, and as soon as we opened the main door, we smelled it. It wasn't decomposition this time, but burning building. The way was still clear, but smoke was curling down from the stairs. There was a fire alarm on the wall right inside the door, but there was no sound when I pulled it.

"Madison! Jen!" I screamed. There was no answer. "Where are they?"

"I don't know!"

"Start trying doors." When the first one was locked, I was ready to move on, figuring Madison wouldn't have been able to get in, either, but Sid was taking no chances.

Sid's strength, like the rest of his existence, is based entirely on what he believes it to be, and that night, he believed he could break down doors. The first one flew open, and I rushed into Mo's former domain. Neither girl was there.

We made our way down the corridor, breaking and entering as we went. When we reached the next-to-the-last door before the stairs, we saw nobody at first and were about to keep going when I spotted movement from behind the desk.

"Madison!" But it was neither Madison nor Jen. It was Jen's mother Judy who was lying on the floor, mumbling fitfully. She didn't respond to my touch, or to my gentle shake, or even to the more vigorous jostling that came next.

"What the sacrum is she doing here?" Sid asked.

"I don't know, but we can't leave her. Can you carry her?"

Sid picked her up and put her down in an office chair. "This has wheels. Get her out! I'll keep looking for the girls."

I wanted to argue, but Sid is stronger, better able to deal with smoke, and less flammable than I am. So I pushed Judy to the front door, shoved it open, and rolled the chair out to the top of the stairs. I could hear sirens and see people running toward me, so I left her there, knowing somebody would retrieve her. Then I turned and ran back the way I'd come.

There was more smoke now. It was getting hard to breathe and even harder to see. On television, fires look so well-lit, as if the flames worked like a million candles. But inside Dobson it was so dark that I could barely recognize anything.

Sid reached out from the shadows. "They're not on this floor. Upstairs or down?"

I knew where the stairs to the basement were, but Madison wouldn't have, so I said, "Up."

Sid went ahead of me and as soon as he opened the door at the head of the stairs, I could feel the heat.

"Madison! Jen!" Sid yelled.

It was bad enough that the air was filled with smoke, but the hallway was cluttered with paint ladders, and when I stumbled over a tarp spread out on the floor, I remembered Fernandez saying the building was being fixed up.

"MADISON!" Sid and I both bellowed. "JEN!"

I heard coughing from the right and turned to see somebody stumbling toward us, clinging to the wall to keep herself upright. When I grabbed her, I realized it was Madison.

"Where's Jen?" I asked as I pulled my daughter toward the stairs.

"She went that way," she answered hoarsely, pointing toward the Human Resources offices. "Her mom is in the building!"

"We found Judy. She's okay." I didn't really know that she was okay, but since she was out of the building, she was better off than we were.

Sid put his hands on our shoulders. "Georgia, take Madison out of here. I'm going after Jen."

"You can't!" Madison said between coughs.

"At 1400 to 1800 degrees, it would take two hours to destroy my bones. It's not that hot in here, and I'll have her out long before that."

"What?"

"Get out of here! I'm not losing you two, and I'm not leaving my friend."

When I saw the expression on his skull, I didn't argue. Instead I hooked Madison's arm over my shoulders and started back down the stairs. She stumbled, and I was afraid she'd fall, taking me with her, but we managed to stay upright. It seemed to take forever to get the rest of the way down, and the walk down the corridor to the entrance was endless.

When we finally got outside, I kept dragging Madison along until we were well clear of the building, and suddenly Charles was there next to us.

"Are you injured?" he demanded as he took Madison's other arm to help hold her up.

"I'm fine." Then I made myself into a liar by breaking into a coughing fit.

"Is there anyone else inside?"

"My friend Jen is! And—" Madison started sobbing, and I knew how much it hurt her to not say that Sid was in there, too.

Charles looked at the building, but in just those few moments, the door we'd come out of had become impassable.

"You can't, Charles," I said. "Maybe she got out another way."

I think he muttered a prayer under his breath as he helped me get Madison to a nearby bench. More people were coming to stare at the conflagration, and Charles made us sit while calling out, "I need water!"

One of the Andorians, still carrying one of the light sticks from the dance, shoved a plastic bottle into his hand, but Charles held it out of my reach long enough to warn, "Don't drink until you rinse out your mouth. There's no telling what you've inhaled, and you won't want to swallow any more of it."

I pushed the bottle toward Madison, but a moment later, another bottle appeared and we both followed instructions before finally allowing ourselves cautious sips.

"Did you find Judy?" I asked.

"The woman who was out front? I should have known that was your work. Lisa and Matt took her to the hospital."

That was a relief. I hadn't wanted to leave her that way but hadn't had a better option. I just hoped she wasn't going to wake up and find out that her daughter was injured. Or worse.

An array of emergency personnel arrived moments later. The firefighters went to work trying to douse the flames, police started herding people away, and the ambulance attendants shined lights in Madison's and my eyes and took our vital signs. Everything looked okay, they said, but they thought it would be a good idea for us to be checked out at the hospital. I thought it was a good idea, too, and over Madison's objections, I let them put her on a stretcher while I followed along.

"But Mom, what about—?" Madison asked.

"There's nothing else we can do here," I said, trying not to let my voice break. Either Sid would get Jen out, or he wouldn't, but no matter what, he was on his own.

CHAPTER THIRTY-SEVEN

The fact that it was my second ambulance trip to an emergency room that year gave me reasons to think about my life choices as we sped to the hospital.

Fortunately, Charles had retrieved my satchel from the dance and gave it to me before the ambulance took off, so I had all the insurance information needed to satisfy the admitting nurse.

They wanted to put Madison and me in different rooms for examination, but I stared them down until they put us together to check our vitals, rinse our eyes, and give us oxygen. The upshot of it was that we were fine, but they suggested we stay overnight for observation to make sure we didn't have any lasting effects from smoke inhalation. Considering how far the cabin was from help if something should go wrong, I agreed. Madison kept giving me meaningful looks, and I knew she was worried about Sid, but I had to focus on her health.

We'd been given hospital gowns to replace our smoky clothes but hadn't yet been moved to our room when we heard a commotion in the hallway. I wobbled over to the privacy curtain to peer out and saw Jen rolling by on a gurney, with Charles following along behind. Jen was awake, which was a relief, though her eyes were red and irritated looking.

"Please stop," she said to the nurse when she saw me. "Georgia, do you know where my mother is?"

"I haven't seen her." I looked at Madison, and she was waving at me to go on, so I said, "Do you want me to come with you?"

"I'd prefer my mother. I would appreciate it if you could locate her." To the nurse, she said, "We can continue."

Charles let them go on ahead. "I did tell her that you got her mother out safely, but she is naturally concerned."

"She's young—of course she wants her mother." I wouldn't have minded having my own mother nearby right then, and I was considerably older than Jen was. "How did she get out?"

"Truthfully, I'm not certain. While I was with you, I sent teams of Andorians to circle the building in case she was at a window, waiting for assistance, and they found Jen at the back of Dobson. She had wrapped one of the workman's tarps around herself before jumping out a window and had made it a safe distance from the building before collapsing. Quite remarkable, really. There's not a scratch on her from either the window or the jump."

"That's amazing," I said mildly, though I wanted to cheer. Charles might believe Jen had rescued herself, but I knew it had to have been Sid, which meant he'd made it out of the building, too.

"I apologize, Georgia," Charles, said, "I haven't asked after Madison's and your welfare."

"Madison has some bruises, and they're going to keep us overnight just in case, but otherwise, we're fine."

"I am relieved. Is there any service I can do for you?"

"I shouldn't ask because you've already done so much, Charles, but there are two things I need."

"Name them."

"Can you locate Jen's mother and find out what her condition is? They did bring her here, didn't they?"

"Absolutely. I saw Lisa and Matt in the waiting room. I shall make inquiries immediately. What else?"

"Since Madison and I will be here overnight, would it be possible to ride out to our cabin to tend to our dog?" We'd fed Byron before we left, and he had plenty of water, so I wasn't overly worried about his welfare, but I was less sure about the well-being of the cabin's floor and the furniture.

"It would be my pleasure." I gave him my car keys and directions to the cabin that I hoped were coherent. He started to leave, but before he bustled away, he kissed me on the cheek. "I am so glad you're unharmed, Georgia."

"Okay, I didn't see that coming," I said after I closed the curtain again.

"Mom, Sid may be your BFF, but I think you're Charles's."

"I never thought of it that way." I went back to my bed. "Now that we know everybody is all right, I would like to know just what you were doing in a burning building."

"We didn't know it was on fire when we went in," she said indignantly.

"That's something anyway. But why were you in there in the first place?"

"We were looking for Ms. Cater. She wasn't there when Jen and I came out after the movie, and Jen figured she'd been hung up at her meeting, so we decided to get some ice cream. Jen texted her to let her know where we'd be, and I did the same for you."

"You're not in trouble for getting ice cream."

"Okay, so we walked to Morricone's, and we got our ice cream and waited a while, but it was getting late, and Ms. Cater hadn't responded to any of the texts. So Jen used a find-your-friends app and saw that her mother was at Overfeld. We knew the dance was going on, and Jen was worried her mom and some of her demonstrator friends were going to make trouble or get into trouble or . . . She wasn't sure what, exactly, but she was pretty clear on the trouble part. But when we followed the app to that building—"

"The Dobson Building."

"Isn't that the one you found Neil's body in?"

I nodded.

"If I'd known that I might not have gone inside. Anyway, we couldn't see any lights on, but the app said Ms. Cater was in there, and Jen says it has like a ninety-seven point three percent accuracy rating. So we went to find her."

"Wasn't the door locked?"

"Um, it might have been."

"You picked it, didn't you?"

"Jen was getting worried, Mom, and if it had been you in that building and I had a friend who could have helped me get in, I'd have wanted them to do it."

"Fair enough."

"Once we got inside, the office doors were all locked, but we looked through the windows and didn't see anybody. I offered to pick those locks, too, but Jen said we should look upstairs first. When we got to those doors at the top of the stairs and opened them, we smelled smoke and . . . Okay, that's when we freaked out. I know we should have called 911, but we panicked. I went one way, and Jen went the other, both of us calling for Ms. Cater. I thought we had time to find her, but the smoke got bad really fast, and it was so hard to see."

I went to sit next to her and put my arm around her. "I know. It was awful."

"I got turned around and couldn't find Ms. Cater or Jen or even the stairs to get out, but then I heard you calling. You know the rest."

"If it makes you feel any better, the only reason I didn't panic myself is because Sid was with me."

"Given that you ran into a building knowing it was on fire, I'm thinking you did panic, at least a little."

"I'm a mother. We mothers spend so much of our time in a panic about one thing or another that it's hard to tell the difference." Losing someone to fire had never been one of my phobias, but I had a hunch it would be from that point on.

"I'm sorry to have scared you," she said, hugging me tightly. "Thank you for coming to rescue me."

"It's all part of the job. But next time text me before you break into a building."

"I will, pinky swear. So what about you? Where did you find Ms. Cater?"

"She was in one of the offices on the first floor."

"How did we miss her?"

"She was unconscious, lying behind a desk. The only reason I saw her is because she rolled over just as Sid and I were leaving the room."

"How did you get in there? Did Sid pick the lock?"

"In a manner of speaking. He busted the door down."

"Seriously?"

"Sid busted down all the doors on that hall."

"Wow. I wish I'd seen that."

"It was impressive, but not as impressive as jumping out of a second-story window carrying a teenaged girl. Because I'm pretty sure that's how Jen got out safe and sound."

"Do you think he's okay?"

"Don't worry, sweetie. If I know Sid, he's either making his way home, or he's found a good place to hide until we can retrieve him." As it happened, I was wrong, but I didn't find that out until much later.

CHAPTER THIRTY-EIGHT

Eventually we were moved to a room upstairs. Madison fell asleep almost immediately, so I closed the curtain around her bed to keep my lights from disturbing her. I would've liked to have gone to sleep myself, but I kept waiting for word from Sid or Charles. It must have been a couple of hours later that Charles tapped softly on the door.

"Come on in," I said. "Don't worry about Madison—once she goes out, it takes a lot to wake her up."

"I'm delighted she's resting."

I waited a minute for him to say more, but he just stood there, looking uncomfortable. "Did you find Judy? Is she okay?" I asked, fearing the worst.

"She's in tiptop condition—you should have no fear for her health."

"That's good news. Then what aren't you telling me?"

He clasped his hands together. "I'm afraid that other news is not as good."

"Is Jen—"

"No, Jen is also perfectly all right physically and is holding up emotionally remarkably well under the circumstances."

"What circumstances? Spit it out, Charles."

"When the firefighters extinguished the blaze at Dobson, they discovered signs that an incendiary device was used."

"Like a bomb?"

"More akin to an accelerant teamed with an igniter on a timer. The fire alarms were disabled as well."

"Oh my spine and sternum." In the midst of all the tumult, I hadn't given any thought to what caused the fire. "Do they have any idea who did it?"

He took a deep breath. "Apparently materials like those used were found in the trunk of Ms. Cater's car."

"No. No! Judy did not set that fire! She almost died in it herself."

"The police found evidence of two devices. There was one on the second floor—that one ignited successfully. Another one was found in a downstairs office, but apparently it leaked, and the police suspect that Ms. Cater slipped on the spilled accelerant, hit her head, and was then overcome by fumes."

"I don't believe it," I said. "Where is Judy now? What does *she* say?"

"When I went in search of her, I found her with Chief Bezzat and another officer. They were questioning her quite forcefully, so I suggested that she might want to wait until she had legal counsel before she said anything further."

"Good for you."

He made a wry face. "It's just as well that I'll be leaving Overfeld soon. From Chief Bezzat's reaction, I suspect I would be getting more than my share of speeding and parking tickets if I were to stay much longer. At any rate, Ms. Cater took my advice and said nothing more. Unfortunately, that did not stop the police from taking her into custody."

"She's in jail?"

"No, she's still here in the hospital, but she's being kept under close supervision."

"What about Jen?"

"She took the news better than I expected."

"Did she?" I said skeptically. "Do you know what room she's in?"

"She's on this floor, as a matter of fact, three doors down."

"Will you stay with Madison for a minute?"

"But—"

"Please?"

"Of course."

I was still a little wobbly, but not so bad that I couldn't put on the flimsy hospital slippers and trudge down the hall until I found Jen's room.

The door was open, and she was sitting in a chair next to her bed, just staring.

"Jen?"

"Hello, Georgia. Your friend Mr. Peyton found my mother for me. She's well."

"I heard. I also heard what the police said, and you and I both know it's not true."

"No, it's not." She started to speak again but just swallowed.

With anybody else, I'd have been hugging her by that point, but with Jen—What the patella was I thinking? I stomped over and put my arms around her. She stiffened and didn't move for a long time, but she didn't push me away, either. Slowly, softly, she began to cry.

"It's going to be all right, sweetie," I repeated over and over again.

Sid had been right—that ossifying piece of sacrum trying to destroy Overfeld hadn't given up when his framing of Hynes fell apart. He'd just picked a new target.

What he didn't know was that by going after Judy, he'd made himself our target.

CHAPTER THIRTY-NINE

I couldn't leave Jen alone after that, and I didn't want to leave Madison alone either. So I called the nurse and explained the situation, and she came up with the right solution. I took Jen to Madison's and my room, and tucked her into my bed while Charles retrieved her belongings. Since the chair in our room folded out into a narrow but moderately comfortable bed, I slept there. And as late as it was, Charles still insisted on driving out to the cabin to take care of Byron.

I slept with my phone in my hand, hoping to hear from Sid, but I never did.

Breakfast came all too early the next morning. Madison was too polite to ask why Jen was in my bed, and I was trying to decide how I could delicately describe the situation when Jen took care of it for me.

"Good morning, Madison. Your mother brought me in here last night because I was distraught."

"Is your mother all right?"

"She's fine, but she's under arrest for setting that building on fire. She didn't, of course, and I have every confidence that she'll be exonerated soon."

"So where are you going to stay?" Madison said, giving me a significant look.

I was about to invite her to our place, knowing Sid wouldn't mind the temporary inconvenience, but Jen said, "I've been thinking about that. My mother's cousin lives next door to us. With her supervision, I should be able to stay in my own home, at least during the day. Of course, if the police don't find the real arsonist soon, it may cause problems, but I think it best to deal with this one day at a time."

"Makes sense to me," Madison said.

An assortment of doctors and nurses came to examine all three of us, but even after we were pronounced fit to go home, there was still a delay. Charles had called to let me know he still had my car and would be delighted to pick us up whenever we so desired, but the hospital wouldn't release Jen other than in a parent's or guardian's care. It took the neighbor, Judy's newly hired lawyer, and various pieces of paperwork to get around that.

Then, after Charles arrived, Chief Bezzat showed up to question us about the fire. She really wanted to speak to the three of us separately, but I wouldn't allow her to talk to Madison alone, and the lawyer insisted that Jen could only be questioned with her present, so in exasperation, Bezzat took us all into the doctor's lounge for the interviews.

Jen went first and explained every step in clinical detail, as only she could. As far as I could tell, the only thing she hedged was saying that the door was unlocked when she went it. That was technically true, but the reason it was unlocked was because Madison picked it. Jen was definitely starting to loosen up when it came to rules. As to her escape from the burning building, she said only that she didn't remember it clearly.

Next up was Madison, who corroborated everything Jen had said. Fortunately, Chief Bezzat didn't ask her about the front door. While owning lock picks was legal in New Hampshire—I'd checked before allowing Madison to bring them with her—using them to break into a building was not. Given the circumstances, I didn't think anyone at Overfeld would have prosecuted her, but I was just as glad it didn't come up.

The tricky part about my piece was explaining how I'd known to go after Madison and Jen, but unlike the girls, I have no compunctions about lying when I've got a compelling reason. In this case, I was protecting Sid, which I considered an extremely compelling reason. So I told Bezzat that Madison hadn't shown up when expected, I checked on her with my find-your-friends app, saw that she was at Dobson, and thought that there'd been a miscommunication. When I went to get her and saw the smoke, I'd gone after her and found Judy along the way.

I had no idea if Bezzat could check to see if I'd really tracked Madison with that app, but she wasn't all that interested in that piece of the story anyway. What she wanted was my description of how I found Judy surrounded by arson supplies, and she wasn't happy when I insisted that I'd seen nothing of the kind. I did have to admit that since I'd been more focused on rescuing her and the girls, I hadn't really looked around enough to notice anything.

Bezzat wasn't entirely satisfied with our answers, but I couldn't tell if it was because she thought we were lying to protect Judy or if we were telling the truth and Judy was innocent. Finally, after Judy's lawyer pushed back, Bezzat let us all go. There were local reporters waiting for us out front, but the lawyer ushered Jen into her car without missing a beat, and Charles did the same for me and Madison.

With Charles right there, and the press trying to get quotes, I couldn't stop to open Sid's bag to see if he'd managed to make his way to the car, but Madison reached in back to push at it, checking to see if it was heavy enough to be carrying the requisite amount of charcoal-covered bone. She caught my eye and shook her head.

I was driving to the college to drop off Charles when it occurred to me that I hadn't done anything about my classes. I said as much, adding, "Ridley is not going to be happy with me."

"You had more urgent matters to attend to," Charles said, "and as it happens, today's classes were cancelled. The welcome dinner will take place as scheduled, but we've moved the awards ceremony to immediately after dinner because a number of students will be going home with their parents tonight."

"What about tomorrow?"

"Director Ridley insists that we carry on, though the schedule will be truncated to reflect the lessened number of attendees. There will only be one play, the art show is being combined with the debut event for your literary magazine, and the concert will be the final event."

"Final is right. I don't think they're ever going to want to run a program like this again."

"I fear you're right, which is a pity. I think the students enjoyed it a great deal, and I found the work and living arrangements quite congenial."

It all made me so angry. Neil murdered, Hynes humiliated publicly, Judy falsely accused, Overfeld in danger of closing . . . Plus my students, who should have had a great time, had been affected by it all. I just didn't know what to do about it, not without Sid to help.

Sid, who I still hadn't heard from.

After thanking Charles profusely, I left him at the college and headed home.

"Where can Sid be, Mom?" Madison asked as we drove. "You don't think he was trapped in the fire, do you?"

"Absolutely not. You know sure as sacrum Jen didn't jump out of that building on her own. Sid had to have been carrying her."

"Then why hasn't he texted us?"

"I don't know, sweetie. Maybe he found a way to get home." I was hoping, but I can't say I was surprised when we got to the cabin and there was no sign of him. It was a long drive from Overfeld to the cabin—for Sid to have done it on foot would have taken hours. "There's a lot of undeveloped woods between us and town. He could still be in transit," I said to comfort her.

"That's probably it," she said, trying to comfort me in return.

We'd had to put our smoky clothes back on because I hadn't thought to ask Charles to bring fresh ones. So our first order of business was to throw them all in the wash and take showers before getting dressed again. Then Madison gave the much neglected

Byron some extra attention while I fixed lunch and fretted over where Sid could be. I hated that I'd encouraged him to go out in the world more, and now he was lost, and I had no way of reaching him and no idea where to find him.

All I could think of was to go back to campus to search for him, or maybe figure out where he'd gone.

As soon as we finished eating, I said. "I don't care about the dinner tonight, but I do want to say goodbye to my students, and I've got some awards to hand out. So I think I'll head back to Overfeld."

"Nice try, but the dinner isn't until six. You're going to look for Sid, and I'm coming, too."

"Are you sure? After last night, I thought you might rather stay here."

"Sid came into a burning building for me. I think I can manage a college campus in broad daylight for him."

"Truly, you are a worthy Padawan."

I had to change clothes again because shorts and a T-shirt wouldn't give the right impression to parents looking to meet their kids' gifted and/or talented instructors, but that didn't take long, and we were back on the road to town.

"I'm surprised nobody's ever developed all this land," I said as we drove.

"Jen said somebody tried. They wanted to do a resort or something, but the group Ms. Cater is a part of stopped it. They like it quiet around here."

"I wonder how they would have felt about the expansion of the business school."

"Wouldn't that have been in Ashbury?"

"I don't know, actually. The towns are right next to each other, so it might have been here instead."

She shrugged, not all that interested. I wasn't either. I was just trying to distract myself from repeatedly checking my phone for a message from Sid.

The faculty lot was more crowded than I'd ever seen it. The parents had begun to arrive, and I had to dodge a couple of family groups lugging suitcases and bedding to their SUVs before I found a place to park.

The plan was to start our search in my classroom, in case Sid had decided to hide out there. Along the way, Madison and I were stopped twice by Andorians who wanted to introduce me to their parents, and though it was more of a strain than usual, I managed to say the right things: their child was a very talented writer and had been a pleasure to work with. I even meant it, which made it easier to sell. I asked if they'd be coming for the debut party for the magazine, but both families claimed they had previous engagements, so I promised to locate copies of *Andorians Ad Astra* to hand out at dinner.

"Are there are going to be any parents around for Parents' Day?" Madison asked me.

"Who knows? I can't really blame them. If you were in a program that had a murder and a nearly fatal fire, I'd be taking you home, too."

"Oh please. You'd be doing just what you're doing now: working the case."

I started to argue with her, but since she was probably right, I decided against it.

Once again, as soon as I got into my classroom, I closed, locked, and barricaded the door before knocking at the closet, but this time, there was no answering voice. I opened it anyway, and Sid wasn't there. There wasn't even a note or any sign that he'd been there. "Coccyx!"

"Make that double from me," Madison said. "Where now?"

"Let's start with the Dobson Building. Maybe he couldn't get far because of the firefighters and Andorians running around, and he ducked into a storage building or climbed up a tree."

As soon as we got in sight of Dobson, we stopped to stare. What remained of the second floor was burned black, or covered with ash and soot, and chunks of wall had collapsed onto the grass, leaving gaps that revealed parts of rooms that looked almost normal. Water was puddled in spots, and the only bits of color were the yellow stripes from the DO NOT CROSS tape strung around the gutted building.

"Oh my spine and sternum," I said.

"Will they be able to rebuild it?" Madison asked.

"I think they may as well tear it down and start over. Assuming the college still exists, that is."

"Do you think the merger deal is dead?"

"I'll call Walker later to find out. Right now, let's concentrate on finding Sid."

Unfortunately, concentrating didn't do the job. We checked every outbuilding, every tree, every good-sized bush, but there was no trace of him. After two hours of searching, Madison was close to tears. In fact, we were both close to tears. I was just trying to hide it so as not to upset her further.

"Look," I said, "it's time for the welcome dinner. Let's go get something to eat and see if there's any news. If anybody saw Sid last night, it will have been mentioned by now."

"Is it okay for you to bring a plus-one?"

"I doubt they'll even notice in the crowd."

As it turned out, they may have noticed, but they didn't mind because the crowd was so much smaller than expected that there was far too much food available. A lot of Andorians had already left.

Madison and I sat with the adjuncts to eat our share of chicken parmesan and salad. Though there was plenty of discussion about the fire, nobody shared any rumors about a mysterious skeletal figure seen exiting the blaze. Over dessert, Madison whispered to me, "I bet there were a lot of people taking cell phone pictures last night, which means hashtags on Instagram. Maybe Sid showed up on one of the pictures."

"Good thought. You want to take this one, Padawan?"

"I am on it."

"You stay here. I need to check on something."

She started tapping away on her phone, which might have been considered rude, but after a summer spent with high school students, my fellow adjuncts weren't going to mind.

I excused myself to find Mo and ask about early copies of the literary magazine. As usual, she was several steps ahead of me. There was a stack of copies waiting.

"Are you okay?" she asked. "Shouldn't you be at home resting?"

"I'm fine, thank you, and I didn't want to leave the Andorians hanging for the last couple of days."

"That's considerate of you, but there aren't a lot of Andorians left to worry about." She looked around the cafeteria sadly. "President Fernandez must be regretting he ever came up with this program."

"It was a great idea. The kids learned a tremendous amount—I'm amazed by how much better my writers got in just a few weeks. If Overfeld tries again, it could be even better."

"Given the bad press we've gotten, I'm pretty sure this is a one-time deal. Even Ridley accepts that, and you know how much he enjoyed being in charge for a change."

"Where is he anyway? I haven't seen him, and I thought he'd be front and center. Or is he still trying to rearrange the schedule?"

"More like trying to rearrange his resume. I caught him trying to sneak out a box of his personal effects today. Like a rat deserting a sinking ship! Well, he'll be sorry if—" She stopped suddenly and looked away. "If things start looking up."

"You mean if the merger with Hardison goes through?"

"Wow, you really are good at this detective stuff. But you didn't hear it from me!"

"No, you kept that cat in the bag." Other than being such a terrible liar, but I didn't think she needed to hear that. "Is it going to happen?"

"President Fernandez hasn't said anything to me, but he doesn't act like he's given up. Every minute he wasn't dealing with the fallout from the fire, he was on the phone or in meetings with the board of directors, the lawyers, and people at Hardison. So, fingers crossed."

I looked around and spotted Fernandez chatting with a set of parents. Their daughter had that expression of mixed pride and embarrassment that results from having one's virtues praised publicly.

If Fernandez was discouraged about the future of Overfeld, he was hiding it well.

Mo said, "I've got to go to the auditorium and make sure everything is set up for the awards. Professor Hynes announced that he'd be making an appearance and wants to be on stage, even if he didn't do a single solitary thing to help with the program."

"I thought he'd be too embarrassed to be seen in public after his arrest."

"Not him! He thinks he's fighting the establishment! And you know people are going to be taking pictures, so of course he's going to show up."

She left, and after a minute's thought, I went over to where Fernandez had just finished his conversation.

"Dr. Thackery! I'm so pleased you were able to make it. Dr. Peyton has kept me up to date on your condition, and rest assured that Overfeld will be paying for your hospital stay."

"Thank you. I've got insurance, but I haven't even had time to think about the money part."

"Nor should you have. You're a courageous woman, to rescue your daughter, as well as Ms. Cater. Even if—"

"Even if." It wasn't the time to debate Judy's innocence and wouldn't be until I knew more. "I have a question that's not really any of my business."

"All right," he said warily.

"It's about the proposed merger with Hardison Business School."

"How did you—?" He waved it away. "Never mind, I'm aware of your reputation. What did you want to know?"

"I was told Overfeld approached Hardison with the merger idea."

"Yes, we did. It hadn't occurred to them before then."

"What put the idea into your head?"

"It was actually Professor Hynes's idea. He'd learned Hardison was looking to expand in the area of executive education and thought this would be a viable alternative for both schools. I imagine you're aware of the financial difficulties we've found ourselves in at Overfeld, so you can see why we were eager to explore the possibility."

"How did Hynes find out? I was told the expansion plans were hush-hush."

"He alluded to hearing rumors, but nothing specific. And now that you bring it up, the people at Hardison did seem surprised when we first made contact with them."

"One other question. What's the status of the merger now?"

He gave a brief, but sincere, smile. "I think we're going to be able to pull it off. The terms of the agreement won't be exactly what I'd hoped for, given the fire and the possibility of further community disputes, but I can live with them. More importantly, Overfeld can survive with them. By tomorrow or perhaps Monday, we should know for sure."

"That's great news. Thank you for your candor."

"Can I ask why you wanted to know?"

I hesitated. "You said you know my reputation, right?"

"Then I think I understand. Good luck, and please be careful."

He turned to an approaching family group, and I went to get a cup of coffee and ponder. Though the fact that the merger might go through despite everything was good news for the school, the killer might see it differently, and he didn't have much more time to act.

How had Hynes known about Hardison's plans to expand when Walker had said they hadn't even bought the land for the project? There was still an hour before the awards ceremony. Maybe I could catch Hynes before it started and ask him.

I pulled out my cell phone and dialed his office number, but the call went to the main Overfeld number, and I remembered that he'd asked for his phone calls to be rerouted. I wasn't thrilled by the idea of a face-to-face meeting. Sacrum, I wasn't even sure that he'd talk to me—but if nothing else, I could look around for Sid along the way.

I stopped by the table and told Madison, "I'm going to go talk to Professor Hynes. It turns out he was the one who suggested the merger, and I want to know why."

"Is that important?"

"You keep asking me things like that as if I had a good answer."

"Got it."

"Any luck on photographs?"

"Maybe. I thought I spotted Sid in one taken an hour after we got to the hospital, but it's hard to say."

"Why don't you keep at it? I should be back before the ceremony starts, but if not, save me a spot near an aisle so I can go up to give out the writing awards."

"You bet."

I kissed the top of her head because I was still feeling shaky about last night's close call and took off for Stevenson Hall.

I saw a few people out and about. Some Andorians were showing the campus to their parents while Andorian couples indulged in farewell make-out sessions. And of course, a group was playing one last game of hacky sack. There weren't as many people on the side of the quad near Stevenson, but the building's entrance was unlocked, and the lights were still on.

Hynes's door was open, too. He was sitting on the sofa, intently regarding the cup of coffee he was holding in front of him with both hands.

I knocked on the open door. "Professor Hynes?"

He looked up at me as if his eyes couldn't quite focus. "Georgia Thackery," he said. "I don't like you."

I blinked. "I'm sorry to hear that." I wasn't, actually, but I didn't know what the proper reaction should be in that situation. "Can I speak to you for a moment?"

"Are you sure I'm not too old to talk to?"

I didn't have an answer for that, either, and decided this wasn't the time to dance around. "How did you find out about Hardison's plans to expand?"

"He told me," he said, nodding past the open door.

Only then did I notice that there was another cup of coffee on the table. An arm emerged from behind the door, grabbed my sleeve, and pulled me into the room.

As the door slammed behind me, I spun around to see Director Ridley glaring at me.

"He has a gun," Hynes said, sounding more befuddled than frightened.

It didn't matter. I was scared enough for the both of us.

CHAPTER FORTY

"I used a gun in an experiment once to see if fear made one more aware of details in the surroundings or less." Hynes wrinkled his brow. "That's odd, I can't remember the result."

"Just drink your overpriced coffee, Professor, and then you can take a nice long nap," Ridley said.

"You drugged him?" That explained why he was acting so loopy. "He's going to remember that when he wakes up."

"He's not going to wake up, and I hate to break it to you, but you're not going to be telling anybody anything either."

"The police will find the drugs in his system, and they'll know something was wrong," I said. "Or are you planning to frame him for killing me? But then how will you explain where he got the gun, or what his motive was?"

"I'm not going to explain anything! What's the point? I tried laying out neat scenarios. 'Look, these letters prove Hynes messed around with students and the school covered it up.' Only Neil shows up when I'm trying to slip the letters into the files, and he's too suspicious to let live. It's not what I planned, but I could work with it. I moved his car, and I thought if I stalled with the air conditioner, nobody would know exactly when he died. Only the cops had no trouble working out the timing, and to top it off, the person who found the body is a freaking amateur sleuth, and everybody says you're sure to go sniffing around."

I hadn't found the body. Sid had. But I didn't interrupt.

Ridley went on. "But hey, I've still got the letters, so I send them to you anonymously to create a new story. Now it's, 'Poor

Neil found these awful letters or caught Hynes trying to steal them, and Hynes must have killed him.' But you didn't take the bait!"

"Because I knew they were forged!"

"How did—? You know what, I don't care. Good for you—you figured it out. But since you were no help, I planted the letters in here." He nodded at Hynes. "Professor Big Shot almost never remembers to lock his door, but if he had, I have a passkey. Once the letters were in place, I got Fernandez to come find them. I wondered whether or not he'd try to bury them, but he's too much of a straight arrow for that. He called the cops, and I lucked out when the professor took a swing at the chief of police. It was perfect."

"Until his alibi came out."

"I know, *right*! The guy hasn't even looked at a woman since his wife died, and he picked that night to go out looking to get laid. What are the odds?"

He almost seemed to want me to commiserate with his exasperation.

"But I can think on my feet. The town kook has been fussing about the college not paying taxes for years, and now she's leading protest marches. She was just what the doctor ordered. I called her from a pay phone and told her I'd found papers that said the school promised to pay regular taxes years ago, and that once they're revealed, the school will have to honor them. Then I whined that I was afraid to go public myself because I didn't want to lose my job. I got her into Dobson, knocked her over the head, and set the timers on my little inventions." He made a face. "If the one downstairs had worked like it was supposed to, it would have been perfect, but even the one upstairs should have been enough to burn down the building. When they found what was left of her body, they would have blamed her for everything. Then you showed up and screwed it all up. Sorry about your kid, by the way, but you know, she shouldn't have gone into that building."

"Maybe I should ground her."

THE SKELETON MAKES A FRIEND

"Whatever. The point is that my carefully thought-out plans haven't done the job, so screw it! I'm going to tie up the both of you, set off more of my toys, and the cops can make up whatever story they want. I'll be clean, and the merger will be done for."

"Why do you hate Overfeld so much?"

"I don't give a crap about Overfeld."

"Then why are you—" Finally the pieces came together. "You're not trying to stop the merger to destroy Overfeld. You're destroying Overfeld to stop the merger!"

"That's right. Now tell me why I want to stop the merger."

"Land." When I'd asked Judy if she knew of any big real estate deals, she'd said, "Not lately." And hadn't Sid said that Ridley lost a zoning dispute, meaning he was stuck with land he couldn't develop? I'd assumed it had been in Overfeld, but Ridley lived in Ashbury. "You own the land Hardison was going to buy for their expansion project."

"Now she gets it! I spent my savings buying that land, and every time I tried to do anything with it, the zoning board shut me down. So then the guy from Hardison calls to feel me out about selling, and I think I'm finally going to get a nice, fat payout. He said they couldn't make a definite offer yet, but that they'd be in touch. I didn't mind—I could wait. My property is the only available acreage in this part of the state that's big enough for their plan, and the location is just what they need.

"Then the guy asked if I could arrange for him to meet the Great Man here. I wanted to know if it was something to do with the project, but no, he just wanted to meet him. It turns out that they worship him in the corporate training world." He looked over at Hynes, who had finished his coffee and was starting to doze off. "Go figure.

"I fixed it up, and the guy was pathetically grateful to drink coffee and listen to Hynes bloviate for an hour. When he left, I started thinking about how happy Hardison would be to have Hynes on their faculty full time. If I helped set it up, maybe when it came time to hire administrators for the new school, they'd remember me. With Overfeld on its way out, I'd already been looking around. Do you know how tight the job market is?"

"Intimately," I said.

"I guess you do. So I went to Hynes in confidence to tell him about the expansion plan. I told him that he'd be a great fit for the new school, and if he talks to them right away, he'll get a much better offer than if Overfeld shuts down and leaves him high and dry. I was doing him a favor! And he knew that I've got money on the line. Did he care? No, all he cared about is keeping his cushy position here. So he told Fernandez about the expansion and said they could merge with Hardison and 'Save Overfeld.'" He used one hand to make air quotes in case I didn't pick up on the sarcasm. "Fernandez loved the idea, the Overfeld board loved the idea, Hardison loved the idea. And my contact stopped returning my calls.

"So I set out to show Hardison just what they'd be getting into with Overfeld. It's not like it was hard to make the place look bad. The buildings are falling apart, the equipment is outdated, our enrollment has been dropping for years, and our star scholar is a has-been."

Fortunately for the star scholar's ego, he couldn't hear the insult over his snoring.

"Now the merger can die along with Hynes. Hardison will buy my land, and with luck, I'll still be able to wrangle that new job. Even if I don't, I'll have a fat nest egg to keep me happy." He looked smug. "I might not have a doctorate, but I'm no dummy."

"And you might have gotten away with it if it weren't for that meddling skeleton," I said.

Sid had finally shown up.

CHAPTER FORTY-ONE

While Ridley had been patting himself on the back, Sid had been slowly lifting the lid to Hynes's antique coffee chest, holding one finger to his lipless mouth to tell me to stay quiet as he carefully climbed out, keeping his bones from rattling in the unfathomable way he did most things. He was clothes-free again, and though he was still smeared with charcoal, he was by far the most beautiful skeleton I had ever seen.

Ridley looked at me in confusion, but before he could ask what I was talking about, Sid slammed the lid on the coffee chest.

Ridley whirled around, and Sid popped off his left arm with his right and wielded it like a sword to slap the gun out of Ridley's hand.

"What the—?" Ridley tried to say, but Sid grabbed him in a one-armed bear hug and put his skull right to Ridley's face. "WHERE IS THE BOMB?"

Ridley fainted.

"Coccyx," Sid said and let him slide down onto the floor. "We've got to get out of here."

"I'll help you with Hynes. We can come back for Ridley."

"I can carry them both." He popped his bones back into place and tucked one man under each arm. "Come on."

I ran for the exit with Sid right behind me. It wasn't easy for him to fit through the doorways while carrying two full-grown men, but he managed without banging Ridley's head too badly.

We got outside and didn't stop until we were at what I thought was a safe distance from Stevenson Hall.

Sid put Hynes down carefully and dropped Ridley. "Did you leave the gun?"

"Why would I need a gun when I've got you?"

He grinned widely, and I really wanted to hug him, but first I needed to call 911, and for once, I gave them my name. They wanted to know where Ridley had put the bomb or device or whatever category the ossifying thing fit into, but I had no idea.

Once that was done, it was time for hugs. "Where have you been?"

"I was going to try to get into the car, but there were too many people around. Then I heard the cops talking, and I realized that the killer had framed Judy. Since that wasn't going to work with you on the job, I was afraid he'd go after Hynes again, so I hid in his office to keep watch. The only things in that chest were blankets, so I stashed the blankets under the couch, climbed in, and I've been there ever since. Fortunately Hynes has been so rattled that he hasn't been going far."

"Why didn't you text me?"

He looked abashed. "When I was getting Jen out of Dobson, I broke my phone. I'm really sorry."

"You think I care about a phone? Seriously?" I thumped him on the skull and then hugged him again. "You could have borrowed a phone. Hynes even has an office line."

"Georgia, I don't know your cell phone number."

"You're kidding."

"I never needed to know. I just select your name on the menu. How many numbers do you have memorized versus being in your phone's memory?"

"One. Maybe two."

"See? I'd have written a note, but the car was gone, and I was afraid to leave anything in your classroom or to use interoffice mail because I didn't know who the killer was until just now."

"Okay, then. The cops are going to be here any minute, and I better let campus security know what's going on. Can you find a place to hide until things settle down? If Madison and I have to leave campus, we'll park on the other side of the town green and wait for you."

"Right." He turned to go, then stopped. "He said toys."

"What?"

"Ridley said he was going to set off more of his toys! Plural!"

"He had two in Dobson. Maybe he set two in Stevenson."

"And maybe he set them in more than one building."

"Coccyx!" If Ridley really wanted to destroy Overfeld and didn't care who he hurt in the process, there was one obvious target. I started running, and then suddenly I was flying. Sid had picked me up and was moving far faster than I ever could have.

Somehow I managed to pull my phone out of my pocket as we went and dialed it. "Answer, answer, answer!"

Finally, she did. "Mom?"

"Get out of the building! Get everybody out of the building! NOW!"

I hung up without waiting for a reply and texted Charles, knowing he was too well-bred to answer a phone in the middle of the ceremony which would just be starting.

GEORGIA: *BOMB IN KUMIN GET EVERYBODY OUT*

I did the same for Mo and Fernandez, adding that they should also evacuate the dorm, in case Ridley had gone for that as well. I was about to call Treva when we got in sight of Kumin and saw people streaming down the stairs.

Sid put me down. "I've got to go."

"Across the town green!"

"I'll be there."

He disappeared almost immediately, and I saw Madison in the crowd, holding the hand of a toddler who I later learned had gotten separated from her family in the confusion. Charles and President Fernandez were ushering people to get them away from Kumin Hall, and the building was totally empty by the time the police arrived and flames flared up from the top of the building.

CHAPTER FORTY-TWO

Firefighters put out the fire before there was much damage to Kumin, and the bomb squad found the device in the dorm before it could go off. Ridley had set it for later that night, when the Andorians still in residence would be in bed. As for the one in Stevenson, apparently he hadn't set the timer yet because he was waiting to make sure that Hynes was down for the count.

Chief Bezzat kept me cooling my heels for hours—first waiting for her to make sure everything and everybody was safe or in custody, as appropriate, and then to ask me what had happened in a variety of different ways to try to shake my story. She couldn't because I was telling the truth. I just left out the parts involving Sid and, to a lesser extent, Madison. And of course I didn't mention anything about Odina or Skalle or Erik Bloodaxe. Maybe it wasn't the whole truth, but it was my story, and I stuck to it.

I think she was particularly offended by the fact that I'd put the pieces together and she hadn't. If I could have, I'd have told her that I was sure she'd have solved it herself if she'd known all I had, but that would have involved telling her that I was holding something back, which she already strongly suspected.

She was about to start up again when President Fernandez, prompted by Charles, interrupted to tell her any investigating I might have done was at his behest, on behalf of Overfeld. And since my efforts had meant nobody had died or been injured, he thought the least she could do was to let me and my daughter go home. After all, he reminded her, we'd only been released from the hospital that morning.

She reluctantly relented. Charles and Fernandez walked Madison and me to our car, but fortunately didn't notice when we went no further than the other side of the town green. I parked near where a streetlight was out, unlocked the doors, and waited. A couple of minutes later, Sid slipped in and dove under the blanket we always carry for such occasions.

Finally, we were all going home, and we all cheered when as we were driving, Madison got a text from Jen. With her characteristic style, it said only:

JEN: *My mother has been released. I would like to treat you both to ice cream whenever it is convenient.*

Sid was so glad to be back at the cabin that he even petted Byron. Once.

Thursday's activities were cancelled, of course. The Andorians had all gone, and the adjuncts had been given hotel rooms in town to stay in through the weekend, so I said my goodbyes to most of them via text. The adjunct world being what it is, I'd probably meet up with them again sooner or later, and Charles and I always kept in touch.

I only went back on campus once, on Friday afternoon, to pick up the stuff I'd left in my classroom. The police had had to go through everything, of course, but afterward Mo had boxed it up and had it waiting for me in Mather Hall. I'd never been in there, but it was one of the last buildings on campus that wasn't a crime scene.

Mo was somehow taking it all in stride. When I got there, she was packing up copies of *Andorians Ad Astra* and the various award certificates we'd intended to hand out in person.

"Your box is on top of the stack," she said. "I put a bunch of the magazines in there, too."

"Thanks." I saw an envelope on top of the box. "What's this?"

"How would I know?" she asked, not meeting my eyes.

I opened it up and read the enclosed note out loud.

I really appreciate your help last night. I don't know all the details, but I guess you really made things happen. Maybe we could get together for dinner before you head out of town.

It was signed with the familiar *DH*. "Tell me he's not asking me out on a date."

"You're both consenting adults—I don't judge."

"I'm afraid my father wouldn't approve." I opened the box enough to slide the note inside. "So you get stuck with the cleanup?"

"Hey, it's job security, which I would not have if it weren't for you."

"Does that mean that the merger is on?"

Again, she wouldn't meet my eyes. "Hmm . . . I don't know what you're talking about." But she did look right at me when she said, "I will tell you this. I want you to put me on speed dial because if you ever need a favor, I'm your gal."

"Thanks, Mo."

"One other thing. President Fernandez is across the hall, and he said he'd like to talk to you before you go."

"Sure thing."

Fernandez's temporary office was a particularly worn-out looking classroom, and he'd already spread papers all over several desks.

"Mo said you wanted to see me?" I said.

"I do, and I appreciate your stopping by." He rose to escort me to a desk that looked as old as I was. "Dr. Thackery—"

"You know, you can call me Georgia."

He smiled. "Georgia, I wanted to thank you personally for . . ." He hesitated, which I wasn't sure I'd ever seen him do before. "For everything you've done. If I were to go in more detail than that, you'd be here all afternoon, and I'm sure you've got more pleasant things waiting for you."

"You're welcome. I did have help."

He raised an eyebrow, but when I didn't volunteer any more information, he continued. "In addition to what you've done outside the classroom, I've heard nothing but praise for your work with the students. The magazine you helped them produce is excellent, and every student I've spoken to has sung your praises. Overfeld would be proud to add you to its permanent faculty."

In any other circumstance, hearing those words from a college president would have made my heart soar. The reason I skipped the soaring was because I could hear the *but* in his voice.

"The problem is, I have no position to offer you."

"Then the school is going to close?"

"No, thanks to you, the merger is going to go through. We signed the papers this morning."

"That's great," I said, but I felt let down that even after that, he still wouldn't hire me.

"The problem is that, as I told you before, the terms upon which Overfeld will be operating have changed. We will have to shift over to a more business-centered curriculum. Not that we'll completely abandon our core courses, but we will have to trim our schedule, and the only reason we won't have to lay off professors is that some of them have already found other jobs. Unfortunately, there is no way to justify a new hire. I hope you understand. Mr. Schild at Hardison sent his personal regrets as well. He also says he owes you some Oreos. I assume you know what that refers to."

"It's an old joke," I said. "And I do understand."

"Thank you." He glanced out the window, and since that particular view didn't include a burned-out building or crime scene tape, it looked just like people expect a New England college to look. "You know, Overfeld has trained countless devoted academics over the years. Our alumni are scattered all over the country." He turned back to me. "I intend to let each and every one of them know that Overfeld owes you an enormous debt. If you don't have a job lined up for the fall yet, I guarantee you will before the week is out."

Now that was worth a soar. "Thank you. It's been an honor being even a small part of Overfeld's history."

"The honor has been ours."

CHAPTER FORTY-THREE

After all that had gone on, I wasn't sure if Madison would want to go to Wizard Gary's that night or not, but she said she wanted to do something normal, and that was what passed for normal in our household. I think she was eager to see Jen, too.

Sid wanted to come along, of course, so I packed him in the sugar skull bag, and the two of us took our time in the bookstore before heading for our favorite bench near Wizard Gary's. I was expecting Judy to come by, but instead, Jen left the store early and came to join me.

"Are you not playing tonight?"

"I already beat Nasir once. It seemed rude to do it again."

"That's thoughtful of you."

"I also wanted to tell you something about the night you came to rescue Madison and me, and saved my mother. I know it was mostly for Madison, of course."

"It was for both of you," I said firmly, and "I'm so sorry I left you in there, but—"

"You shouldn't be sorry. If you'd stayed, all three of us would have died. Besides, I had help from somebody else."

"You did?" I'd been worried about what she remembered from that night.

"You won't believe me. My mother didn't."

"Try me."

She gave me a long look before speaking. "How much did Madison explain to you?"

"Your mother was late, ice cream, GPS app, picking locks, going upstairs, splitting up."

"Those are the main points. In retrospect, we should have stayed together, but I thought we could cover more ground separately. The doors on the second floor weren't locked, but it was hard to search for my mother because it was so difficult to see and breathe. I'd read that one should stay close to the floor in a fire, so I got down on my hands and knees, but apparently I wasn't low enough because I passed out. The next thing I knew, someone was pulling me to my feet. At first I thought it was my mother, but when he said my name and asked if I was all right, I knew it wasn't because it was a man's voice."

She hesitated, as if making sure I was still listening. I nodded to show her I was.

"The truly strange part was that he called me Odina, my name in Runes of Legend. My mother would never have called me that. Then the man picked me up in his arms as if I were a baby and carried me. The air was quite smoky, but I never heard him cough or even breathe hard. We went a little way, and he started . . . Well, it sounded like cursing, by the tone of his voice, but it wasn't the curse words I'm used to." She shrugged. "He carried me a little further, but then put me down and said, 'You need to stand up for a minute.' Then I felt him wrapping me up in something. I found out later it was a painter's tarp. He picked me up again and said, 'Don't worry, I've got you.' Then he started running, and we crashed into something. I heard glass breaking and realized it must have been a window. We fell for what seemed like a long way. I'm afraid I screamed."

"I think most people would have screamed."

"He didn't, and somehow he landed on his feet. Isn't that unusual?"

"He must have been very strong."

"He carried me a bit farther, sat me down on the grass, and uncovered my face, but I still couldn't see much because it was dark and my eyes were so irritated. Then he said, 'I've got to go. You'll be okay now.' But right before he left, I felt something on my forehead. I think he kissed me."

"He did?" I said, but I wasn't surprised. Even without lips, Sid manages the occasional smooch. "And nobody else saw him?"

She shook her head. "My mother thinks I must have found the tarp and jumped out the window on my own. She says that if somebody had done something like that, he'd have come forward by now. But I think I know who saved me."

"You do?"

"This is the part you won't believe. When the man was carrying me, I couldn't see or really touch him, but I know it didn't feel like a normal person's body. It felt hard."

"What do you mean?" I said, trying not to panic.

"Hard, like armor."

"Armor?" I definitely hadn't expected her to go there. "That's—Um—Wow."

"Erik Bloodaxe wore armor."

"You think Erik Bloodaxe saved you?"

She gave me a look. "Of course not. Erik Bloodaxe was a game character created by Neil Farmer. I think Neil saved me. Wherever he is now, I think he's got the armor he wore in the game, and he came back to be the hero he always wanted to be. And maybe he came to reassure me about death."

I realized Jen had tears in her eyes, and I found a tissue in my satchel to hand to her.

"Thank you," she said, and carefully wiped her eyes. "I don't blame you for not believing me."

"I do believe you."

"You do?"

"Let me tell you a story. When I was a little girl, I got lost at a carnival, and there was a fire, and a hero appeared from nowhere to save me. Nobody believed me when I told them about him, but he was real, and so was your hero."

I patted the sugar skull bag to make sure Sid knew what hero I was talking about, and a minute later, he texted his happy skull emoji.

CHAPTER FORTY-FOUR

Madison showed up a little while later, triumphant from finally having defeated Nasir on her own. When Judy showed up a few minutes after that, we went to Morricone's as planned.

Judy was oddly shy, and I suspected she wanted to thank me, both for rescuing her from the fire and for helping Jen, but she couldn't come up with the right words. After we'd eaten our ice cream, she disappeared for a minute and came back with a gallon each of dark chocolate and cake batter ice cream, the flavors Madison and I had chosen that night. She shoved them at me and gave me a brief hug before nearly running out. For once, I could see the resemblance to Jen.

Saturday night, Sid logged on as Skalle Beinagrind for the in-game memorial service to Erik Bloodaxe. Since it was the closest to a funeral he'd be able to attend, he'd asked Madison and me to sit with him and read over his shoulder.

All four surviving members of the party were there, right on time. They started by speaking out-of-character so Sid could explain how and why Neil had been killed. He managed to give all the important details without saying exactly how he knew them or what his role in the investigation had been, but he implied a lot, and that seemed to convince them that he really was a detective. Even Gudron seemed satisfied.

Then they assumed their game personas to share stories about their fallen companion Erik Bloodaxe. Jen, speaking as Odina, even told a revised version of how she'd been rescued, though Kiersten and Gudron thought it was just good roleplay. Sid, in character as Skalle, shared the poem he'd composed in Erik's honor.

As the conversation was winding down, they went back out of character to address the elephant in the game room:

GUDRON: *I hate to be a downer, but you guys know we can't keep the party going without a fighter. It's been a great ride, but . . .*

SKALLE: *Can't we look for somebody else?*

GUDRON: *We can try, but I don't think we'll ever get the right balance again.*

KIERSTEN: *You're probably right.*

ODINA: *I know somebody. She doesn't have a Runes of Legend account, but she is an experienced gamer, and I think we could help her level up fairly quickly.*

GUDRON: *Are you sure she'll fit in?*

ODINA: *Yes. Shall I ask if she's willing?*

SKALLE: *Why not? It couldn't hurt to try.*

GUDRON: *I guess.*

KIERSTEN: *Yay!*

ODINA: *I'll text her immediately.*

A second later, Madison's phone buzzed.

"I knew it," Sid said. "I thought about inviting you myself but didn't know how to explain the connection. Are you interested?"

"It sounds like fun! Mom?"

"Go for it!" At least I wouldn't have to worry about some scuzzy guy harassing her in that game.

She texted Jen back, and I got a little confused watching the texting along with the stuff in the chat room while they worked it out. The upshot was that Madison would create an account right away, and then the whole party would meet up the next night to try a simple quest and see how well they meshed.

Sid logged out while Madison headed for her room to log in. "Any ideas for a character name?" she yelled a minute later.

Sid grinned and searched for something on his computer. "How about Laerling?"

"What does that mean?"

"It's Norwegian for Padawan."

Madison burst out laughing. "Laerling it is."

I could see Sid was looking very pleased with himself but had to ask, "Don't you mind Neil getting the credit for rescuing Jen?"

"Not really. I mean, he was a hero, wasn't he? If he hadn't caught Ridley and tried to stop him, he'd still be alive. Plus it was his sacrifice that led us to the killer. He deserves the credit."

"But you were the one who saved her life."

"That's what friends do."

"That's what heroes do," I said, patting him on the scapula. "I think you deserve a parade and a medal."

"Heroes don't worry about credit," he said loftily. "The heroism is its own reward."

"Uh huh."

"Besides, you and Madison know the truth. That's good enough for me."

"Since we can't do the parade, would you settle for a couple weeks of movies, swimming, and dance parties?"

"Sounds perfect! Do I get to pick the movie for tonight?

"Go for it!"

He headed for the television while I made a mental note. I didn't think I could manage a ticker tape parade, but I was sure going to get Sid a medal.

ACKNOWLEDGMENTS

With thanks to:

- My daughters Maggie and Valerie for explaining the mysterious world of MMORPGs.

- The real Judy Cater and the real Mo Heedles, for their enthusiasm and generosity in bidding for character naming rights.

- The Facebook hive mind for continuing to answer my most random questions with accuracy and speed.

- The team at JABberwocky Literary Agency for keeping me on track.

- My BFFs Charlaine Harris and Dana Cameron, for unswerving support.

- My husband Steve for just about everything else.

LEIGH PERRY takes the old adage "Write what you know" to its illogical extreme. Having been born with a skeleton, and with most of her bones still intact, she was inspired to create Sid and write the Family Skeleton Mysteries. *The Skeleton Makes a Friend* is the fifth in the series. As Toni L.P. Kelner, she's published eleven novels and a number of short stories and has coedited seven anthologies with *New York Times* bestselling author Charlaine Harris. She's won an Agatha Award and an RT Booklovers Career Achievement Award and has been nominated for the Anthony, the Macavity, and the Derringer awards. Leigh lives north of Boston with her husband, fellow author Stephen P. Kelner. They have two daughters, a guinea pig, and an ever-increasing number of books. You can visit Leigh online at LeighPerryAuthor.com.